GIL
ANTE

-

Jessica Gadziala

Cover image credit: istock.com/ stevanovicigor

DEDICATION

To the righters of wrongs.
And everyone in need of a vigilante.
Also to everyone who needed the lye info.
It's true, btw.
Just sayin'
;)

ONE

Luce

The body was half-melted in the tub. The lye was doing its job beautifully. It was heated to over three-hundred degrees. In case you were wondering, in case you have a douchebag who beats you or know of a pedophile who isn't 'reformed,' you have to heat the lye to dissolve a human body. Three hundred degrees and two or three hours, and you will have a tub full of post-human fluid the consistency of mineral oil. Then you can just pour it down the drain like nothing happened, using a catch to get any possible bone shadows, crush those up, dissolve them again, then drain that as well.

If you have the time and want to make sure there is no chance of anything ever leftover, sulfuric acid does the job in about two days, but can cause third-degree burns, and the fumes are enough to send you running from the room.

After that, you just need some running water and a couple bottles of bleach. Then it was like that person never existed.

I obviously have a lot of experience with removing bodies. This is mostly due to the fact that I take a lot of lives. I do this killing without shame, without regret, and with a clear mother fucking conscience.

Some bastards don't deserve to walk the earth.

I make sure their footprints aren't lasting.

"What can I say, Harold," I started, flipping open his wallet as I leaned against the sink vanity. "Actually, can I call you Harry? I think we're intimately acquainted enough to use nicknames, wouldn't you say?" We had spent some time together before the messy dying and melting part happened.

I always gave them a chance to fess up, to take the easy route and go to jail. But as I took the photos out of the wallet, explicit sexual images of small boys, and tossed them in the tub with him, I knew the reason he didn't want to go that route. The twenty some-odd years he would do if the feds started digging like I had been digging, wouldn't be easy time. He'd spend a lot of that time with a dick up his ass for raping little boys. A fitting end, I believe. Eye for an eye and all that. So that was why he got the chance to choose that option.

He didn't.

So that was when the killing started.

The killing was fast. It was the clean-up that took the longest.

I didn't just have to get rid of his body. I had to go on and wipe all that nasty shit he plastered all over the dark web. That was no easy feat either. But it was just part of the job.

For my troubles, the five grand he had in his Bitcoin wallet would be transferred, washed, and put into my own.

Most jobs left me out of money, not gaining any. And while I did shit because it was right, because the system failed the population, because sickos like Harold could walk free, I was still human. I had to eat. I had black hoodies to buy. I had lye and bleach to stock up on. Normal shit.

So Harold's contribution to the cause, albeit unwilling and unwitting, was going to do some good.

"At least something came out of your sorry ass existence."

There was a telltale, all-too-familiar vibrating at my hip. Not a cellphone, of course. It was old tech, most thought the stuff of museums, but in case you were curious, yes, they do still manufacture pagers. And I had one. They were reliable due to low traffic, anonymous thanks to the code you had to reach me with, and easy to smash if you needed to clean shop and delete traces of it.

The 8.0 was the code for who was calling.

The 422 was the reason why.

Yes, if you were interested, there were 500 codes you could possibly call me with. And I remembered each and every one of them off-hand.

Let's just say I got a lot of pages a day from one of over two-hundred contacts across the country. After a while, that shit becomes as ingrained as the mother fucking alphabet. There was no forgetting it.

A 422 was pretty pressing, but that being said, I was a careful SOB, and I never made calls from my bunker. That just wasn't worth the risk.

I only had another twenty or so before I could pull the drain and get to work on the bleach. I could be heading into town in a bit to call back and, likely, get the lead on what would be my next case.

An hour and a half later, Harold Grains was officially no longer even a speck of human; his dark web presence was gone, replaced with a warning page from me, like I always did; my clothes were embers in a firepit, and I was five grand richer as I stopped into She's Bean Around for my usual fix.

"Hood off. We want to check out that pretty face of yours," Jazzy, one of the smartass, hot-as-sin owners called as I stepped in. Jazzy was all sass, unsettling honey brown eyes, and her medium-dark skin that I still couldn't tell if it was because she was half-black or half-Latina. Whatever it was, it was working for her with her curvy, just shy of chubby body with great hips, ass, tits, and thighs.

"You can eye-fuck me once I've had my coffee, Jazz," I demanded, dropping the money on the counter. "One for Barrett too," I added. At her blank look, I shook my head, remembering that while he was a huge caffeine addict, he usually made it in-house. "Large black, dollface," I said, tossing a ten into one of the tip jars. They changed daily, requesting you put your money into the one you liked more.

That day, it was *Dexter* and *Hannibal.*

"This isn't even a fucking contest," I scoffed, almost annoyed that anyone would have put money into just about any other fake serial killer above Hannibal Lecter. I mean, with his origin story? Come the fuck on.

What could I say, I was passionate about my flicks.

"Last week we had Hunnam and Momoa," Jazzy said as she reached for the pot of coffee with a smile. "It practically caused a gang fight. Those Hunnam chicks are, ah, passionate."

"Did he win?" I asked as I took the coffee.

"A lot of women aren't into blondes," she said with a shrug. "All I know is, I took home almost a hundred in tips thanks to that one. We're thinking of doing a *Harry Potter* versus *50 Shades* one. We're a little worried there might be blood spilled."

"And vote tampering," I agreed with a smile. "Keep it sexy, Jazz," I called as I turned to leave.

"As if it was possible for me not to," she agreed, and I walked back out onto the streets of my town with a smile.

Navesink Bank.

It was simply where you went if you were a criminal on the east coast. Why, you might ask? Because with all the other criminals around, it was easy to get away with shit. Plus, the police force was corrupt as fuck and you could, quite literally, get away with murder in broad daylight with witnesses if you knew what palms to grease. Evidence just so happened to go missing a lot. And witnesses rescinded their testimony. Or fell off the face of the earth.

It had been my home for the better part of a decade.

It had been my place of business for almost as long.

As such, I knew where I needed to make my calls. Hence the extra coffee.

Barrett Anderson was a computer whiz, private investigating, code-breaking, verifiable genius. Literally, he had papers. He was also careful to the point of paranoia, so he did sweeps for bugs every morning when he opened. That and, well, he had bomb-ass wifi.

He also didn't give a shit if I came in twenty times a day to deal with work stuff.

"Got you a coffee," I announced as I walked into the shoebox he conducted business in. It was small and dark and a disaster. There was a desk to the middle and back, covered in files, books, and about five coffee mugs. "Only five today?" I asked as I put the to-go cup down.

"It's only nine, Luce," he reminded me distractedly.

"You have a computer out? Must be serious." Barrett, while better at computers than most so-called hackers, was careful about when he used them. He did most of his work on paper. In Polish. And, just to make sure even a Poland-native couldn't read it, also in code. He used computers when necessary, then destroyed them. He literally had a desk drawer full of cheap ones he bought in bulk.

"Collings," he agreed, barely paying me any attention, which was just how he was, so I wasn't offended.

"*Detective* Collings?" I clarified, moving away. Didn't matter that he was retired and was a pretty chill guy, I wasn't getting anywhere near that shit. "Just making a call," I declared, moving back into his bathroom. There was nothing but a robotic message on the other end, proving to me again how good some of my contacts were. They could be, and often were, every bit as careful and paranoid as I was. They were, after all, handing me information that could lead to the death of another person. No one wanted that tracing back.

"Busy week," I murmured to myself after I ended the call, pulling apart my burner, pulling out the sim card, and walking back out. "You mind?" I asked, pointing to the microwave he kept in a corner. Barrett wasn't a man who heated up leftovers or cooked ramen in the office. He was a man who knew that microwaves were the best way to fry electronics.

"Help yourself," he invited, and I threw the shit inside and turned it on. I stood there for a second, watching the pieces inside start to warp and catch fire, then turned to look at Barrett again. It wasn't my business. He and I were both loners. We handled our own shit. But there was something too tense about him right then, something that made me feel like I needed to say something. "If you need another set of eyes on this," I offered, nodding toward his laptop, "let me know."

He didn't answer.

The microwave beeped.

The flames died.

I waited a minute, then grabbed the destroyed pieces and headed outside.

"Catch you next time," I called, not expecting an answer as I yanked up my hoodie and walked down the street.

I didn't have friends.

Men like me, who did what I did, who came from where I came from, we didn't get to have something as clean, as normal, as friends. I had contacts. I had fans of my work. I had people I interacted with on a daily basis who knew nothing about me.

That was as good as I could hope for.

In a way, it was enough.

It *had* to be enough.

Because it was all I could have.

I parked at the bottom of the hill, knowing from experience that nothing, save for maybe a heavy-duty truck or an off-roading vehicle could make the trip all the way up. By the time I reached it myself, my legs were screaming, as they always did, and my lungs were burning. My home, or bunker as I generally called it seeing as there wasn't one damn thing homey about it, was set back another twenty minutes inside the woods, built there by some crazy survivalist doomsday fuck a couple generations back. Must have cost him a fortune to not only build an above-the-ground structure, but also sink a whole other one.

Waste too, seeing as he obviously croaked before his version of apocalypse came.

But, hey, it worked for me.

Especially since, if you looked into the structure, all that was on the official city plans was the legal blueprints for the small cottage. There was no evidence of the bunker below. Hell, I hadn't even known when I got the place. I just wanted the seclusion of the woods and the so-called 'castle defense' of being on a high hill looking down at possible threats coming up.

I likely never would have found it if I didn't hate mirrors. There was an enormous one in the basement of the cabin, all gilded and full-grown man-sized, taunting me, mocking me, making me face up the person I had been made into.

When I went to pull it off the wall, though, it wouldn't budge.

Because it was built into it.

Which sent me on a two-day hunt to try to find the switch which was also concealed, this time behind a clever fake-front of DVD spines with a trip switch.

Then there was the massive underground bunker complete with plumbing, well water, lighting that was provided by the solar like the rest of the house, air filters, beds, food stores, and since it was buried, it kept cool year-round, and was completely airtight.

If I were someone who believed in signs, that would have been one.

As it was, it was just a golden opportunity that I used to my full advantage.

I reached into my pocket for my key, half-dreading another full night of research. No rest for the wicked, as the saying goes.

I didn't hear anyone.

I didn't see anyone.

I didn't smell anyone.

But one moment I was about to head into my very secluded home.

The next, I was taking a baseball bat to the back of the head.

And everything went instantly dark.

TWO

Luce

"Fuck," I growled, coming slowly toward consciousness. That slowness was proof of the fact that I hadn't just been bashed in the back of the head. No, the fog over my brain, the dryness in my mouth, the weird atrophied feeling to my muscles, yeah, that could only mean one thing.

Once I was out, someone drugged me too.

I let out a sigh, my eyes drifting open to find the source of the cold hardness beneath my cheek. A basement floor.

Yeah, that was about right I guess.

While I had never been taken down before, men like me didn't get the luxury of being surprised by it. It was only a matter of time. Someone was going to get me someday, want to pull me apart, want to melt me in a tub, want to bleach me down the drain.

Maybe a part of me was hoping for another couple weeks, let me take down that newest scumbag I had heard about, but I couldn't say I was exactly broken up about it either.

This was my fate.

I was never going to live to ninety and sit on a front porch bitching about how good things used to be when people knew their neighbors and electronics didn't take over the world. First, because fuck neighbors. Second, because electronics were the shit.

But I knew I would be lucky if I made it to forty without ending up in a cell or a grave, no matter how careful I was.

Why now? Yeah, that was more what was on my mind. It wasn't like it was when I first started out, when I was willing to just... take somebody out on the street or in their own car, no doubt leaving a shitton of evidence behind. It wasn't like I had gotten careless. My methods were even more strict than ever before. I also hadn't taken anyone out who I had considered a risky target. No crime bosses or any shit like that. The last risky move was taking on some shits running a pill mill. But I took out the whole operation. There was no one left to want vengeance.

I took a breath, feeling my lungs burn, as I forced a swallow, rubbing my tongue against the roof of my mouth to get rid of a film I felt coating it.

Fucking poison.

I rarely worked with it. It was too unstable, too unpredictable, too hard to fucking come by.

Poison to kill? Yeah, that shit was easy.

Poison to keep someone out, to keep them down, to keep them weak? Yeah, that spoke of a professional. That spoke of years of studying poisons, of experimenting with them.

"Great," I hissed at myself as I forced my weighted arms to move to press into the floor, willing the strength back to push my weight up so I could look around. All I could see was darkness and a cinderblock wall not too far off.

Poison people were like knife people.

They lived to play with their toys.

I had the distinct impression that I was about to be a very large, very trapped, lab rat.

You know, I might have been a real shit, I decided as I managed to plant one hand on the cold, dirty floor, and find enough strength to propel me onto my back, but I didn't fucking play with my victims like a cat with a mouse.

Sure, they woke up tied up and scared to shit. Usually literally. They literally pissed and shit themselves almost without fail. But our chat was always amicable. For all intents and purposes. I laid out their crimes, showed them my evidence, then gave them a choice between fessing up to the cops or dying by my hand. I didn't poke and prod at them to get any desired result. I guess because there *was* no desired result. I was just as happy to drop them at a specific location and have a cop ally of mine pick them up and book them.

Surprisingly, very few went that route.

In my tenure doing my job, I think there were maybe three who did. One serial rapist, one serial killer who preyed on prostitutes, and one trafficker.

See, Jersey didn't have the death penalty. And juries were notoriously stupid.

They stood a better shot with our fucked up criminal justice system.

But, hey, who am I to judge?

I was just as happy to get to the killing part.

Of course, that part could never be fully painless. And I was a firm believer in fairness. So I untied them for the big finale. They wanted to get some punches in, in some last ditch effort to think they had some control, so be it.

They didn't realize I had a flawless record.

I always won.

The bad guy always went down.

Then down the drain.

"Fuck," I growled as I landed on my back, able to look around, my eyes adjusting to the dark.

Not only was I in a basement with cement floors and cinderblock walls and, from what I could tell, no windows. No. I was in a mother fucking cage.

It was a good one too.

I forced a leg out, kicking with my admittedly crippled strength into one of the beams, nodding when it didn't so much as budge, sending a slow shot of pain up my leg. Yep, that shit was cemented in deep and bolted into the ceiling. It wasn't going to budge. There was no way out.

I should have been freaking out. My heart should have been frantic, trying to break free of my ribcage. But it was a sluggish, heavy thing sitting inside my chest.

Granted, I wasn't as freaked as a normal person would be, but my heart should have been getting a mild workout right about then; I could only assume it wasn't because it was another side-effect of the poison.

It was likely the reason my stomach felt torn the fuck up too. Luckily, there was nothing in it to throw up.

"Deslanoside. Digitoxin. Digitalis glyoside."

Oh, man.

Fuuuuck me.

That was a fucking woman's voice.

See, there wasn't one fucking sexist bone in my body, not even in regard to female criminals.

Why, you might ask?

Because violence didn't come as easily to them.

Studies have shown that little girls are inherently more gentle than little boys. Now, whether that is nature or nurture is up to the professionals to decide.

But what I did know was that whichever of those they were overcoming - something in their DNA, or a lifetime of programming - whatever trigger was bad enough to send them over the edge, to send them to the dark side, when they got there, Jesus fucking Christ, they were different creatures entirely.

I'd never seen something as ruthless, level-headed, and unforgiving as a woman in power over a criminal empire.

And I had never seen someone as brutal as a female killer.

Maybe it was as simple as whatever sent their lives in that direction had stolen an important part of their humanity from them. But I was inclined to think it had less to do with brokenness and more to do with them realizing their potential. Not being held back by things like fragile egos their male counterparts were afflicted with gave them a lot more time and brain-space to focus on more important parts of their missions.

So being in the hands of a woman who was a fan of poison? Oh yeah, I was in for a world of shit.

Sure, maybe I even deserved it.

But that wasn't an easy reality to resign yourself to.

"Foxglove," she explained when I made no response to her comment.

I had no idea where she was.

Even with eyes adjusted, the space seemed huge. There were plenty of dark corners to hide in. She could be anywhere.

Of course I was poisoned with some pretty goddamn flower.

Couldn't be some badass shit from South America that I could feel like warranted the shitty feeling through my whole system.

Nope.

Pretty pink backyard flowers.

"How quaint," I ground out, focusing on trying to force life into all the seemingly useless parts of my body. "What's next? A little oleander tea?"

"Don't be ridiculous," her voice called back, calm, but if I wasn't mistaken, there was the smallest spark of amusement there. "Oleander doesn't grow in New Jersey. Besides, it would tear up your stomach. And I might want you in pain, but I don't want to be dealing with your bodily fluids."

"Unless you're planning on killing me in the next hour or so, doll, I'm afraid you're going to have to regardless."

There was the distinct click of heels on hard floor, thicker heels, not stilettos, but heels nonetheless.

Then there was nothing for a long second.

Followed by a click.

And light.

My eyes squinted instinctively against the harshness, but also because the brightness caused an almost immediate headache which was, no doubt, thanks to the stupid flower poison too.

I blinked hard several times, looking over to find the heels I had heard. Combat boots, but with heels. Sexy, actually. I liked them. Wasn't exactly opposed to the long, shapely legs that extended from them, clad in tight, dark pants that must have been leather. She had somewhat wide-set hips and a simple black tee showing that while she had a banging curvy lower body, she hadn't been quite as lucky in the chest department. You can't have it all, as they say. She had plenty... and I hadn't even gotten to the face yet.

And what a damn face too.

As evidenced by my interaction earlier with Jazzy, I always had a bit of a thing for women from different ethnic backgrounds.

This woman, well, she was Latina. That was about as good of a description as I could give seeing as there were dozens of Latin countries and I didn't know shit about what region looked like what. She was sexy with her deep-set, sultry, dark eyes, her flawless skin, her full lips, and her black lashes, brows, and long hair.

Fucking gorgeous.

And young for a poison expert.

Young for any kind of criminal really.

I'd put her in her mid-twenties, though there was no way to know but asking.

I watched as her chin angled up during my inspection, not calling me on it, not demanding I look away, but making it clear she knew she was the one with all the power. Then she jerked her head to the far side behind me, making me hold in a grumble as I forced my head to turn.

And find a toilet.

"Don't go getting hopeful," she said, tone empty. "It's a prison toilet."

It was too. All stainless steel and one giant piece, none of the inner workings accessible, no parts that could be pulled off and used for a weapon, but with a small sink area on the top.

"Set you back, bare minimum, fourteen-hundred. You want me enough to shell out that kind of money?"

"Who says you're the only person I've had down here?"

"Fair enough," I agreed, finally feeling some of the brain fog lifting.

"Get comfortable," she said, waving a hand.

"What? No introductions? No 'hey, I'm the poison-wielding hell bitch, nice to meet you?'"

"Careful," she said, coming closer to the bars, putting her hands on them, and leaning in slightly. "Or I will give you just enough sodium thiopental to make you feel like your veins have turned into liquid fire. Without the blissful release of death."

With that, she was gone, leaving me with what was most assuredly a psychotic-looking smile. What can I say? Women in charge were sexy. Women who threatened you without blinking were sexy.

Christ.

Where the hell would she even get her hands on lethal injection drugs?

The foxglove made sense. Natural poisons were easy enough to come by. But that shit they used for capital punishment, that was highly controlled. Our good ol' government likely didn't want it getting out that they paralyzed their inmates then set their insides on fire as way of 'humane execution.'

And people thought firing squads were barbaric.

Who was she?

Why did she have me?

Was she just a middle man?

Did someone hire her to bring me in and keep me just alive enough for them to retrieve me and play with me?

That made more sense.

I couldn't think of anything I could have done recently to piss off a poisons expert.

I sighed as I forced my body to curl up, finding the weighted numbness slowly moving away, leaving me with at least a little control over my limbs. I pushed to a sitting position, and dragged my ass over toward the toilet. Reaching up, I used the edges of the sink part to pull myself up, cursing savagely as my legs screamed and almost gave out.

I needed water.

I needed to flush that shit out of my system so I could think, and react, appropriately.

Was I especially keen on the idea of having to fight my way out of that basement? Nah. Was I enthused about the fact that, to do that, I needed to put my hands on a woman? Again, no. But survival was survival. I needed out. And if I had to put my hands on her, hopefully, it was just to restrain her long enough to slip away.

Once I got away, I could figure out who the hell she was. I knew a lot of the players in the underbelly, many of the experts in different fields. I didn't know nearly as much about poisons as I did about guns, drugs, bombs, and trafficking. I needed to remedy that. Starting with one sexy as fuck dark-haired woman with lethal injections at the ready.

You know, if I made it out.

There was no guarantee of that.

And it wasn't me being pessimistic, just honest.

The chances were truly unknown at this point. There were too many variables.

Was she going to open the cage to feed me, if she planned to feed me at all? Unlike the ingenious jailhouse toilet and sink combo, the cage I was fenced in by did not have a slot to slip trays through. But maybe if she was planning to feed me, whatever it was would be small enough to fit through the bars.

Was she going to come in the cage at some point to try to get more poison in me so she could tie me up and do whatever she wanted with me?

Or could she maybe just shoot that shit into me from her side of the bars?

The better a criminal she was, the less a chance I had at getting out.

If she came alone and she opened that cage, I was getting out.

If she didn't open the cage at all, fuck if I knew what my fate would be.

Likely a lot of torture and a messy fucking death.

Truly, in the realm of fairness in the world, that would be rather fitting.

I didn't want to die per se, but it wasn't like I was some great loss to the world. Hell, the only people who would likely even notice were people like Jazzy and Barrett, people just used to seeing my face. Because I didn't have anything even close to resembling a friendship, relationship, or family. A part of that was being a genuine loner. But perhaps a bigger part was knowing that anyone who associated with me was by default in danger.

I wasn't bringing anyone down with me.

And, to be honest, I had done a lot of good with my life. Maybe I had done it in a dark and dirty way, but the end result was the same. I took predators off the streets.

It wouldn't be a tragedy if this was how I went down.

But, that being said, I was going to fight.

As soon as my lovely captor made another appearance.

THREE

Evan

I slammed the door to the basement, taking the narrow, time-worn stairs up two at a time, my heels a frantic clicking sound, needing to get above-ground, needing air that wasn't stagnant, needing a couple minutes to pull it back together.

It wasn't that I had lost it in there.

Actually, I was pretty proud of how well I kept it together.

Kidnappings weren't exactly my forte.

The poisons? Well, I learned that at my daddy's knee. Twenty some-odd years of studying which ones did what. I was a walking encyclopedia of poisons. That being said, I hadn't been in the poisoning *people* field like my father was; I was just all about the facts.

I knew what I was doing, of course, but there were always factors that could screw up the outcomes. Like preexisting conditions, the level of panic, and therefore adrenaline the person might feel, sometimes it was even as simple as the type of food they did (or didn't) eat that day. The variables were what had my heart thundering in my chest from the moment of injection to seeing the effects finally starting wearing off in the basement.

Hitting the landing, I stormed right outside the side door, collapsing back onto the side of the building and taking a long, slow breath, deep enough for my chest to feel like it was burning.

I tried to tell myself that the hard part was over.

I mean, I had been watching him for weeks, hiding out in those godforsaken, bear-filled woods trying to figure out his moves, what might be the best time to take him down. Then I had had to do the bashing-of-the-head thing and the drugging thing. And then, as proven by the screaming ache in my arm muscles, the dragging of him into the woods where I had a vehicle parked. Then dragging him again out of the car and down the basement stairs.

But there was no convincing myself it was all downhill from here.

Because from here, I had to question him.

And then kill him.

So, yeah.

That was where I was at.

That was why my heart was as frantic as hummingbird's wings in my chest. That was why I had a cold sweat all over my body. That was why I needed to get away from the notorious Luce for a while.

I don't know what I had been expecting when I finally got a close look at him.

See, while I had been following him, he had this hardcore dedication to his black hoodies, with the hood almost always pulled up. I had only gotten small glimpses of his features. Not even enough to pick him up out of a lineup.

I had expected a face as ugly as his soul.

I guess it often never worked that way.

Most serial killers were good looking.

Luce was no exception.

He had dark hair, dark eyes, and this amazingly chiseled, sharp jawline, dark brows, a ton of lashes, and the slightest cleft in his chin.

What freaked me out most were those eyes, though. They were set deep and heavy-lidded, giving him an almost sleepy look, completely hiding the evil that lay underneath.

Body-wise, he wasn't a big guy. Tall? Sure. But he wasn't overly wide or muscular. In fact, he might have been called thin by some.

If he were anyone else, he would have been attractive.

Just my type, actually.

But that was obviously completely beyond the point.

The point was, things were finally in the works.

The plan had been in place for almost a year. I had worked out every possible little kink. I had plotted it to the most minute detail. I had made sure there was no chance of me getting caught, or him escaping. Both were equally important in my opinion. First, I was not the kind of woman who would do well in prison. I liked long showers, private bathroom visits, and very specific skincare products. Second, if he got free, I was pretty sure I was dead. There was nothing about Luce that said he was the kind of man to let people go.

If he set his sights on you, you no longer existed.

Case closed.

That was why I spent three months in a plumbing class, learning how to drop my own bathroom into a basement, so I didn't have to hire anyone who might think it was odd that I was putting in a prison-style toilet and sink combo in my basement. Then I spent a couple long, exhausting, sweat and blood-soaked weeks painstakingly installing the prison bars. I had actually broken a finger trying to get the cement dug up enough to sink in the bars, then re-cement it.

It had all been worth it when I grabbed a sledgehammer and went to town trying to make the bars budge... to no avail.

I had a steady prison just waiting for an inmate.

I pushed off the wall, and made my way back inside, walking through the garage which led to the basement, through the small, very stark white laundry room, then in through a door that led into the dining/ kitchen/ living space I had been calling home for the past ten months.

It didn't feel like home. I was maybe half-convinced it never *would* feel like home. But it was nothing to do with the house. I really liked it. It was small and secluded. There were warm, pale yellow walls, charmingly scuffed and worn hardwood floors, cabin-style cabinets in the kitchen, a clawfoot tub in the bathroom, and three bedrooms. Two of which were all but useless to me and, in fact, I hadn't actually stepped foot inside of either since I officially moved in.

I had spent hours looking for furniture that I thought would fit the space. There was a spacious off-white tufted headboard queen-sized bed in the master, along with white dressers, and a very pale robin's egg blue on the walls and my comforter. There was a small dark brown sectional in the living room with a wide glass-top display coffee table before it on top of a multi-color rug, facing the brick fireplace. There were three floor-to-ceiling bookshelves where I stored some books, but mostly just keepsakes from my travels.

It was the homiest home I had ever been in.

Therein, I guess, lay the problem.

I had never actually *had* a home before. Home, for me, had always been RVs or the backs of vans or tents in the woods. Home was dozens of countries I had visited, had immersed myself in all my life.

Hell, I had never actually slept in a real, stationary bed until I was seven years old when we stopped into the States for a brief visit, and stayed in a hotel since the RV was in the shop, and you generally weren't permitted to just pitch a tent anywhere you wanted in the US.

I hadn't been able to sleep.

I had taken my blanket and curled up on the floor instead.

For twenty-six of my twenty-seven years on the earth, I had been a nomad, a gypsy, a traveler. I had taken tokens when the vehicle we were in was getting too full, and shipped them to a friend of my father's in the States for safekeeping.

When I had shown up just shy of a year before, I had found a sprawling ranch in the south with its own food taking up almost three acres, and animals from horses, goats, and cows, to pigs, chickens, and rabbits taking up the rest of his twenty acres.

"Can't be trusting the government to be feeding us real food anymore," he had explained to my questioning look.

Having not spent more than a couple weeks of my life in the US all my life, I had no idea what he had meant, but had nodded as he led me to a huge barn where he stored all my mementos.

"Saved it all," he told me as he led me into a stall piled high with boxes. Not one had been opened. The first one I reached for was in handwriting from when I couldn't have been older than eight or nine.

He had saved it all too. Not one single item was missing. Items I had completely forgotten about, a tribal figurine of an owl from New Guinea, an intricate beadwork collar from Saraguro, a Dia de los Muertos skull from Mexico.

My entire life in boxes.

Taking them back to my new house and opening them had been a painful experience. Not because the memories were bad. Far from. But because they represented a part of my life that I could never have again. They represented a loss that cut so deeply that I was sure there would always be a hollow feeling inside.

But I had taken them, and the pain associated with them, and displayed them proudly on my shelves. They were a part of me. They were the endless memories that I thought about at night before the misery would set back in. They were pieces of the life I wanted again but knew I could never have.

The places I had walked before, the life I had led, it wasn't safe for me to try it alone. That reality was a bitter and metallic taste on my tongue. No matter how much scrubbing, it wouldn't go away. I had led such a carefree life, had enjoyed such freedom, that the prison that was living inside a female body that was weaker, that could be invaded, was absolutely bone-deep infuriating. I wouldn't trek the rainforest again. I wouldn't walk into tribal land without fear. I wouldn't be able to move through the most dangerous areas of Colombia or Mexico with the carefree ease of a woman flanked by a man so feared that no one would even think twice about staring at his daughter.

Until that man was taken away from her.

From *me.*

And for that, I would do whatever was necessary to exact vengeance.

On the man one floor below me who was, if he had even a single working brain cell in his head, drinking his body weight in water to try to get the last dregs of poison out of his body.

Yes, Luce No-last-name was going to pay.

Dearly.

An eye for an eye.

Or, a life for a life as it were.

"Diego, shush," I demanded half-heartedly, knowing it was a useless battle. Diego was all I had left of my father. He had outlived his owner. Hell, he could possibly even outlive me.

Diego was a thirty-inch-long blue-and-gold macaw who my father had owned since before I was born. He was messy, oftentimes aggressive, and his calls could be heard for miles in the wild. Which would tell you how loud he was *inside* the house. But he was family. He might give me splitting migraines several times a month, and maybe he chewed the edges of my coffee table, and used positively everywhere for a bathroom seeing as he had always been kept fully flighted, but I was, for all intents and purposes, used to it.

It had cost me a small fortune to smuggle him into the country. The laws regarding moving around exotic birds were absurd and unfounded, but wholly unavoidable. So, I had needed to employ and trust five different people with his wellbeing. I had spent two weeks with my heart in my throat waiting for him to finally cross into the US so I could look him over and settle him in.

"*Yummy*," he demanded back, about ten decibels higher than he had been when I shushed him in the first place.

Oh, the joys of bird ownership.

"Alright, alright," I said, reaching into the fridge for a bowl of fruit and veggies I had cut up for him, pouring it into a dish heavy enough for him to not be able to flip, and set it on the table. "Here's your food. Now, I need to feed the prisoner," I said, moving back to the fridge to throw together dinner.

I wanted him to suffer, sure.

I wanted him dead, eventually.

But until then, I needed to keep him well enough to get the information I wanted out of him.

Namely... *why*.

Why my father? Was he a good man? By general standards, maybe not. He had killed people. He had offered up information about dangerous poison to people who would use it to inflict pain on their enemies.

But he had standards.

He only killed men who had it coming, men who threatened him or me, men who he caught abusing animals in public forums, men who had tried to steal something of ours.

And he never operated on US soil.

So why would Luce have been after him?

Why had Luce sought him out when there were more deserving candidates much closer to home?

Questions that needed answers.

I would get them.

And to do that, I had to keep him fed, mostly-conscious, and relatively healthy.

I piled the beans, corn, rice, meat, and salsa onto the counter and set to cooking them up and rolling the burritos for both myself and the so-called vigilante in my basement. Maybe a part of me wanted to be petty and force-feed him something truly disgusting and borderline inedible. But the fact of the matter was, I was too lazy to cook twice. Plus, burritos would fit through the bars without me having to get too close to him and risk him yanking me against them and knocking me out.

It wasn't like that would do him any good. I wasn't an idiot; I didn't carry the keys on me. But still, I would prefer to avoid the massive headache it would cause.

I sat down beside Diego and ate my food, taking my time, trying not to rush the process. I would have plenty of time to spend with him. He wasn't going anywhere.

I got up, rolling his food in foil, then taking a deep breath before going back down the stairs.

"You know, you never did give me your name," he greeted me as soon as my foot hit the bottom landing.

"You can call me God," I offered as I walked toward the bars, finding him standing back from them several feet, head ducked to the side, watching me.

"Because you decide when I live or die," he assumed, looking down at the foil-wrapped cylinder as it rolled into his cell.

"Something like that," I agreed, lifting my chin.

Cool, collected, and detached.

That was how I wanted to present myself to him.

Let him believe I was some hired expert, just a cog in a wheel, that it was business.

If he knew how personal it was, he could use that against me. I didn't know how capable he was at things like emotional manipulation. In fact, I didn't really know much about him at all.

This was likely because *no one* seemed to know much about him.

There was a huge online fan club dedicated to him. Some insane chick wrote crazy, twisted, violent, and explicitly sexual erotica starring Luce.

Luce, the vigilante, was a shining star.

Luce, the man, was a complete enigma.

In fact, I could not find a trace of a man named Luce anywhere in New Jersey. Granted, cyber sleuthing was not my forte. In fact, very little was in the way of the internet. I had basic knowledge, but I spent most of my life off-the-grid in places that didn't even *have* wireless towers. So I wasn't even at the 'jealous ex-girlfriend notices her ex has a new girlfriend" stalker level. Social media as a whole was a complete enigma to me. Why does anyone care that you 'checked-in' at a local coffeeshop, or that you are going to such-and-such concert next month?

Banal drivel.

If people wanted to connect with other people, why didn't they *go out* and do it?

I digress.

Anyway, yeah, maybe Luce wasn't a complete ghost to a trained professional. But I was no trained professional. So, to me, he was a wild card. Maybe he was a master manipulator. Maybe he was just a violent asshole.

Who knew.

"I'm Luce," he offered after a long silence. "But you already know that," he said as he walked closer toward me, those dark eyes unreadable, but I got the distinct feeling that they were somehow reading me. He leaned down, picking up the food, then standing. "Poisons expert. That bone structure. Your skin tone. This food. The slightest hint of an accent. South American, right? But removed. You're US born, but traveled. Sizable scar on your left wrist, raised, though it's long healed. Burn, most likely. At least five years old. And your hands are covered in scratches. Cat, maybe. But no," he said, squinting. "Not with those crescent shapes. Bird, probably. Given the other hints and the size of that beak impression, I'm guessing a macaw. Not the most likely pet for a woman your age. So, willed to you?"

Jesus.

I literally didn't know his last name or where he was born, but he got a huge chunk of information about me just by being in my presence for a couple of minutes.

"Your middle finger didn't set right and, judging by the blood marks I see on the floor, it was broken when you were putting in the bars. That implies that you don't have a whole crew of men one floor above waiting to come down here and take me out if something happens to you. No, you're working all by yourself. You're either that good... or that stupid."

I wanted to believe I was that good. The longer I listened to him, though, the more I was starting to believe I was perhaps a lot more stupid than I had realized.

I had underestimated his intelligence at least. It went to follow that I maybe underestimated his strength as well. Especially because he was on the thin side. There were plenty of martial artists that appeared skinny but were just as lethal as their more sizable counterparts.

"Are you about through trying to read me, because none of that is going to get you out of here."

"But I'm right, aren't I?" he asked, smiling. Which was, well, completely inappropriate. And maybe a bit telling as well.

He cared more about the facts than his freedom.

"I mean, if you're keeping a macaw here, it's only a matter of time before I hear it and it confirms my suspicions. We have to be closing in on sundown, right?" he asked, unraveling the foil, and taking a healthy bite without even looking at what I made him. "He will be doing his evening calls soon."

God, he was good.

What person who didn't own a parrot knew things like that?

He was a dangerous kind of smart.

And knowing his body count, there was an emphasis on *dangerous.*

I had no idea how he killed. There was a signature online for all his kills, but there were no details about it. Was he a gun man? Knives? Bare hands?

There were some fresh cuts and bruises on his hands.

"Trying to imagine if I would use them around your throat if given the chance?" he asked, making my gaze shoot up to his face, watching as he brought the food up to take another bite. "To save you the trouble, I don't hurt women. But to save my own ass, I would choke you out to get free. No permanent damage. I wouldn't even need to bruise that pretty neck, doll face."

Whoa.

Okay.

There was not, was absolutely *not* a weird fluttering feeling between my thighs at that.

Because that would be insane. Certifiable.

And if maybe there was that sensation, it was likely because I hadn't gotten laid in well over a year and a half, when this whole charade started. Hell, this was probably the closest I had been to a man near my own age in that amount of time.

Just hormones.

Stupid animal instinct.

"You should be more worried about your own neck than mine," I offered as he finished up the burrito, and rolled the foil.

"I'm assuming you are going to want me to toss this back," he said, holding up the foil. "You know, because filed down for long enough, it makes a pretty decent weapon."

And I did not know that.

Damnit.

"Of course," I agreed. "Just go ahead and toss it out."

"What? You don't want to come in and... take it from me?" he asked. It was maybe meant to be threatening, but the smirk on his face completely undermined that.

And that move was, well, stupid. If I didn't demand the foil back, he could have done what he said he could; he could make a weapon. Or, he could have threatened to make a weapon which would, rightly, make me go in there and get it from him, giving him a chance to try to take me down.

Why turn that down?

I thought the more time with him I spent, the more answers I would get.

That was proving entirely untrue.

"What's the matter, God, I'm not what you thought I would be, huh?"

That was an understatement.

"I don't particularly care who you are as a person."

"Ah, but that was a lie," he said, looking delighted at the idea. "You're just disappointed because you can't peg me. Tell you what, sweets, I'm in a giving mood. Ask me anything you want," he said, holding his arms out. "I'm all yours."

I wanted to ease into it.

That was the plan.

I wanted to get, and keep, the upper hand.

I wanted to feel him out.

But there was no stopping it.

It burst out of me.

"Why did you kill my father?"

FOUR

Luce

So, not some hired chick on a mission.

This was a personal vendetta.

That made her wholly unpredictable.

Did I kill her dad?

Who knew.

It was definitely a possibility.

Fact of the matter was, the rumors on the web about me were, well, a bit *inflated*. Did I do a number of the jobs? Of course I did. Did so-called fans perhaps claim I did a shitton of jobs I didn't do? Yep.

Until I asked, there was no way to know if she was working on flawed data or not. And even if she was, and I told her such, there was no guarantee that she would let me go. I mean, of course she would expect me to lie. My life was in her hands.

"Well, that depends," I said as her eyes went huge, like maybe she hadn't meant to ask me that. At least not yet. She likely had some long, drawn-out plan on extracting information from me. That was why she was feeding me so soon when I obviously could have gone days without eating before I even got lightheaded.

Good shit too.

She knew her way around the kitchen.

I had never been in a position to admire that about a woman.

"On?" she asked, jaw tight, chin lifted again.

"On who your father is," I said, shrugging, reaching up to straighten my hood pulls so they were even.

There was a long pause, something working behind her eyes.

"Alejandro Cruz."

Guess she was deciding on whether to tell me or not, because she knew it would give away her hand.

In the end, though, the need for truth often outweighed the need for self-preservation.

"So that makes you Evangeline," I said, smile pulling at my lips a little. That actually made everything make a fuckuva lot of sense.

Alejandro Cruz was something like, well, me, in a lot of ways. He was someone people whispered of; most believed he was an urban legend. And while, like me, maybe many of the tales were false or embellished so much that the truth was barely even discernible anymore, he was a real person. He did have real skills. Namely, the most lethal, the most respected, the most sought after man of his kind in the world. A poisons expert. A contract killer who could take down an enemy and leave no traces of what caused the death in the first place. Or, just as often, use his poisons for torture for his employers, extracting information before the final, blissful end.

Alejandro Cruz was something else, though, too.

See, I had no problem as a whole with criminals. So long as they stayed in their own lanes and only killed people who were just as dirty as they were, I minded my own business.

That wasn't the case with Alejandro though.

I certainly didn't bring him in because he drugged some Colombian cocaine smuggler to get information for a rival cartel.

No, his crimes were a fuckuva lot worse than that.

"You haven't answered my question."

Because it was a little more complicated than she wanted to believe.

"Alejandro Cruz absolutely did die in my bunker."

I wasn't much for lying.

Or sugar-coating anything.

She wanted facts; I was giving her facts.

"You son of a bitch!" she shrieked, moving closer toward the cage bars, eyes wild, body rigid, everything about her suggesting that if there weren't bars between us, she would be clawing my face to shreds right about then. "You evil, selfish, piece of shit!" she went on, slamming her hands into the bars before turning and running back up the stairs.

I didn't have a chance to explain.

Sure, Alejandro Cruz definitely died in my bunker.

But I hadn't killed him.

I had barely gotten a chance to lay his offenses before him actually.

See, the thing about poisons experts is, you never actually know if they have some on them or not. It wasn't like the fucks carried around a suitcase full of carefully labeled vials, though I was sure they had some of those stashed somewhere. They did their best to hide them so they couldn't be found.

Alejandro Cruz, with a lifetime in the trade, knew exactly how to conceal emergency drugs to use in a critical situation. You would think it was for the use on others. At least, that was what I had assumed.

It shocked the shit out of me to walk back down there to find him still tied to the chair where I left him, clutching his rosary in his hand because I wasn't some animal who would deny someone the (to me) empty comforts of religion in their final hours, but stone dead.

At first I figured maybe the son of a bitch had a heart attack. While not common, it certainly was plausible. He wasn't a young man. He was facing his own inevitable death.

But when I got closer and looked him over, I'd be damned if that white rosary set in his hand wasn't missing a fucking bead.

Cyanide.

I wasn't disappointed that he was dead. That was always the plan anyway. But I wanted to hear them fess up first, to admit to their wrongdoings. I don't know why. I didn't need them to. I always had more than enough evidence before I even thought of bringing them in. But I liked to hear it. It validated that I was doing the right thing.

He took that away from me.

I was in a pissy ass mood the entire time I had to get his body dissolved.

I mean, I guess him killing himself was all the proof I needed that he had committed the crimes I laid before him. But still, he ruined the whole thing for me.

There was the frantic slam of heels on steps as she came thundering back down, her hair flying all around her face.

"What do you mean he 'died in your bunker'?"

"That it was the place he took his last breath," I said, inwardly grinning that she was smart enough to pick up on that small nuance.

"Where you killed him, you mean."

"I didn't say that."

"Would you? If you killed someone, would you own up to it?"

"Well, when you picked me up, I was fresh off of taking Harold Grains off the surface of the earth." Literally. He was below it in a sewage pipe. Where pieces of shit like him belonged.

"Harold Grains," she repeated, trying not to sound surprised with how forthcoming I was being.

"Yeah. Disgusting pedo with a penchant for young boys. He had to go. He was nothing but a waste of perfectly good oxygen on a planet that, quite frankly, could use about five billion fewer people than it currently has."

"So you killed him because he was a child molester."

"Didn't you hear? That's what I do. I'm the vigilante, baby," I declared, smirking.

"Did you kill my father?"

"Unfortunately, no."

Shit.

That was harsh.

I didn't interact enough with people to remember to watch the way I phrased things sometimes.

In fact, the only reason I realized it was the wrong thing to say was that she shocked back from my words like I had struck her.

"Why should I even believe you?"

"I'm a lot of things, Evangeline, but a liar isn't one of them. I didn't kill your father."

"Then... what? He had a sudden heart attack while in your *custody*?" she spat, disbelief clear not only in her tone, but her face.

"He bit into an emergency cyanide pill he kept in his rosary when I left him alone for a couple minutes."

Everything about her changed in that moment.

Her lips parted; her eyes went hollow; her shoulders dropped.

Because she knew it was the truth.

Maybe she didn't trust my words fully per se, but there must have been a recognition of the truth in them, in the reality of him having a pill of cyanide. In his willingness to use it.

"Why would he do that?" she hissed, her voice barely audible despite being just a few feet from me.

"Guess he didn't want to face up the punishment for his crimes."

That was, apparently, enough reality for her.

Her chin jerked upward, she spun on her heel, and she flew back up the stairs again.

I wish I could say that I felt sympathy right then, but that would be a lie.

First, because what I did, I had no guilt about. Scumbags like Alejandro Cruz deserved the end I planned to give him. Second, because if she knew his crimes and she still supported him, that made her a real shitty person as well. Third, well, I just wasn't good with all those squishy emotions.

I learned to lock that shit down from the cradle.

I wasn't raised in an environment that would allow me to show weakness. And sympathy, as noble as it might have been, was a weakness. It exposed an Achilles heel. It showed where someone could cut you.

Of course there were innocents affected by my actions. Most scumbags weren't lone wolfs, weren't freaks doing dirty deeds all alone in their basements. No. Most of them were your next-door neighbors. Most of them had wives, mothers, sisters, brothers, friends, co-workers. Most of them were surrounded by people who loved them and were completely oblivious to their often heinous crimes.

Harold Grains for example.

He wasn't some freak trolling the dark web in his basement.

Harold Grains was a successful businessman with ten people in his office who thought he was a great co-worker. He had a wife of twenty years at home. He had an almost-grown daughter who wasn't his biggest fan, but judging by the full-on goth look to her, it was more teenage rebellion than actual dislike of the man who had raised her. He had a brother and parents he saw at every holiday. He had friends he saw in church every third Sunday.

If you looked at the man from the outside, he was just your average guy.

The sad thing was, most child molesters and rapists came off that way.

Everyone was always shocked.

What? No! Not my son! Not my Charlie-boy! He'd never lock women up in his basement for a decade and rape them. That's not possible.

Meanwhile, the sick fuck did.

And they had visited his house with women suffering one floor below.

It was only a matter of days before Harold's friends and family figured out he was truly missing. A few months before they likely decided he was dead. And they would grieve. And they even had the right. Because they didn't know the depth of his depravity.

I often wondered if I should compile up all the evidence and ship it out to them. I debated whether that was a kindness or the ultimate cruelty. A part of me wanted them to know that the man they were hurting over was nothing like the man they thought he was, that he had caused misery to countless others, that he wasn't worthy of it.

But then I remembered how I watched a couple of girlfriends inside She's Bean Around one afternoon. One, a pretty strawberry blonde, obviously more shy, more timid, was trying to clearly, calmly, and emotionlessly explain to her brunette best friend that the latter's boyfriend had been coming on to her for months. It didn't matter that the strawberry blonde had explicit texts from said boyfriend, had proof that all she had ever done was tell him to stop texting her. The friend stood up, shrieking about minding her own goddamn business and leading him on and all kinds of bullshit.

People were many things in many different situations.

But, a great percentage of them the vast majority of the time were irrational and reactionary.

Harold's family would likely scramble to discredit the evidence, claim it was some cruel joke, defend the man they knew. Because to not, they would have to admit that they were so fully, so completely deaf, dumb, and blind to the truth.

So I just kept that shit to myself.

It was fine.

I was used to shouldering the knowledge of peoples' evilness.

I had been doing it since I was a child.

What was a few more years?

If I lived that long.

The longer she kept me alive, the better chance I had for getting away. Not because she would necessarily slack. It was more likely that she would lose her nerve to kill me. Now that I knew she wasn't a professional, that this was a personal mission, I knew a lot more about Evangeline Cruz than she would think I did.

Once she got over the shock of my honesty, she would likely lose whatever nerve, whatever righteous anger had fueled her enough to follow through with her kidnapping plan.

What then?

Well, that was the question, wasn't it?

She knew I was a merciless killer. She knew I had done it before and would do it again if left to my own devices. Would she risk opening that door and letting me go? Thinking, wrongly, that I might kill her. Maybe she would dose me, unlock the door, and run. Or, possibly, dose me, load me up back in her car again, and drive me back to my place so I was never any the wiser about her place. In case I got any ideas to come after her.

I wouldn't, of course.

But I would have to respect that level of prudence.

As I heard the distinct clicking of heels one floor above me, my head angled up to look at the ceiling, listening to the long stride, then a pause, then the stride again.

She was pacing.

I wasn't sure I had ever met an actual, real-life person who paced when they were stressed. I was mostly convinced it was a dramatic device used in film and TV.

It went on for almost a half an hour too, only muffled occasionally by what I assumed was carpet, and the scream of a macaw that was all the proof I needed to show me that I wasn't losing my touch.

Not having a lot of friends, or really any at all, I had a lot of free time. So I studied shit. At first, things useful to my lifestyle- how to navigate the dark web, basic coding, advanced hacking, disposal of remains, best killing methods, how to interrogate. You name it, I studied it. I was a motherfucking crime encyclopedia.

But when that got stale, I just read random shit.

I learned more tapping and scrolling away in front of my laptop than I did in all the years of school put together.

Anything could be click-bait to me.

How to write a horror film? Sure, why not.

Migration patterns of North American birds? Eh, could be useful.

How to dismantle a car fully and put it back together? I rarely drove, but why not learn that vital life skill anyway, right?

And because they generally weren't topics of normal discussion on the rare occasion that I engaged in such a thing, it was good to know my brain hadn't done an Etch-a-Sketch and deleted all that old, less-than-useful information.

I called that macaw, damnit.

That was good if I do say so myself.

Considering I had absolutely nothing to occupy myself with in the bare walls of my cell, I had to turn my attention to the one and only Evangeline Cruz to keep myself from going insane.

I had heard of her, of course, when I had researched her father. Though, I didn't think she truly even knew the whole story of her life. If she did, I didn't think she'd be so broken up about her old man.

It was possible she did know, but was too programmed to see how warped he was. It happened a fuckuva lot more often than people realized. It was becoming harder and harder in modern times for parents to get away with forcing children to believe antiquated or downright awful beliefs with public schools, the internet, and the fact that most people weren't ignorant assholes.

But Alejandro Cruz had a unique opportunity with Evangeline that most parents no longer have. He raised her away from most outside influences. Judging by how little an online footprint I could find of him, and absolutely none of Evangeline, it was safe to say he just... kept that part of the world away from her. Which wouldn't be too hard given the remote parts of the world he generally traveled through with her in tow. There wasn't wifi or cell towers.

She only knew what he wanted her to know.

Because all it would take is ten minutes into a basic Google search to find out what I found out. You didn't even need the dark web.

So she obviously never got the chance to do that.

And when a beloved parent died, it wasn't exactly a common thought to go online and dig up their dirt.

Had she not come after me, she likely would have been able to live a long life and go to her grave never knowing the true nature of the man who had obviously only shown her his good side.

Even the vilest pieces of pond scum human beings often had a good side.

They'd never be able to get away with what they got away with otherwise.

I was starting to wonder if she was going to let things lie as her pacing got slower above me. But then there was a pause before the clicks moved in the telltale direction across the house over my head. A door. Then another. Then the click right above the stairs. Another pause. It was so quiet I could swear I could hear her taking, then letting out, a deep breath before she started moving downward, her pace slow and deliberate.

"It's ironic," she said, moving toward me, hatred a burning thing in her eyes, "that you would bring him in for crimes you yourself are guilty of."

I shook my head at that. "No, doll, his crimes are sure as fuck not my crimes."

"He killed people. You kill people."

"I don't give a fuck about criminals killing other criminals."

"Then I don't know what his crimes were," she said, eyes squinting, head shaking.

Right then, I felt it.

It was so unfamiliar I almost didn't recognize it.

Dread.

I was dreading telling her the truth.

Of all the asinine things to be feeling.

And, at the end of the day, I believed in honesty when asked for it.

So, even if my stomach was clenched up oddly at the idea, I gave it to her.

"Across three continents and spanning three decades, Alejandro Cruz was known as a notorious, and viciously brutal, serial rapist."

FIVE

Evan

It was like everything inside me shut down at once.

My brain just blanketed, blocking out every thought except one.

No.

Just... no.

He was lying. He had to be lying.

There was no way my father, my good, giving, gentle, loving father was some piece of shit serial rapist. No freaking way. That wasn't possible.

This was a man I had been beside daily my entire life. I had never seen him even catcall a woman before. He didn't leer. He didn't threaten. He didn't grab-ass, or make unwanted advances. In fact, I had only seen him dance or share a drink with a woman before. Everything was always friendly.

Was my father a 'good' man in the traditional sense? Well, he killed people. So no.

But I absolutely refused to believe he was some evil monster like Luce was suggesting. He had to have the name wrong. He had to have been mistaken.

"Can't help you accept the truth if you are going to slip right into ignorant denial."

"I'm not ignorant," I spat immediately, feeling my pulse start to pound in my throat and temples, making me immediately feel overheated even in the cool basement. "You're mistaken."

"If you did any research at all into me, Evangeline, you would know what a ridiculous thing that is to say. I am never mistaken. I don't ever pull somebody in unless I know with one-hundred-and-ten percent certainty that they did what was accused of them."

"Your math was off this time."

"Get me a phone or laptop, and I can prove otherwise."

The crazy thing was, even through the layer of denial, I heard nothing but a confident sincerity in his tone.

But that being said, he thought he was fighting for his life. He would say anything to save his skin. And being that he was a lifelong criminal, it went to follow that he knew how to lie well. It wasn't like he could just walk around his life answering the typical 'hey, whatcha up to today' with the truth. *Oh, hey Bill. Just dismembering some bodies with a hacksaw. Then maybe some Chinese takeout. You know, the usual.*

He was playing me.

Case closed.

And, hell, I couldn't even blame him for that.

He probably lied about the cyanide too.

True, my father did always carry it. And, yes, it was hidden in his rosary. But that was for situations where he was caught by a cartel and tortured or whatnot. Luce probably found out about it after he killed him, when he was going through his personal effects. He was almost scarily observant; he would have noticed that the one bead wasn't shiny and smooth like the others. He likely just cataloged that information and spewed it back at me to try to make me think twice about keeping him captive and, eventually, getting my vengeance.

"Right. Like I would trust you with a laptop. The man who could make a weapon out of tinfoil."

"While true, any laptop connected to the internet can be turned into an incendiary device, you need another device to activate that. So, what am I gonna do with it? Knock you over the head? Get real."

Being a prisoner, he was supposed to be begging for my mercy, kissing my ass, trying to get on my good side.

But was he doing that?

No, of course not. Because I had to have the cocky, condescending, know-it-all, jackass prisoner.

"No?" he asked, watching me with those deep, fathomless eyes in a way that I swear seemed to see right through me somehow, see into all my dark, cobwebbed corners, see all the things I wanted to keep hidden. And why that thought made a shiver of not discomfort, but anticipation, course through me was wildly beyond my comprehension. "Well, do yourself a favor, and power up a laptop, and do a quick search. It really won't take long to send you back down here to me. For some real answers. There are a lot of blanks I can fill in."

"Because I should trust *anything* you have to say. You would do anything to try to save your own ass right now."

"Would I?" he asked, lips quirking up ever-so-slightly. "You know, you ran out of here in such a hissy fit the last time that you forgot to make sure I threw out the tinfoil. But as you can see," he said, waving a hand toward the floor outside his cell where the foil could clearly be seen, "I tossed it out anyway."

"Probably part of your grand plan," I grumbled. I was losing my argument and I knew it.

"Right, because I could have anticipated exactly how this conversation would go. I must be a fucking genius."

Honestly, I was starting to think he just might be.

And that was a bit terrifying.

Some two-bit brute, some mindless muscle, I could handle that. I had been around that a lot in my life. It was easy to outsmart someone who thought more with his dick than his brain.

But Luce, this elusive, lethal, intimidatingly observant so-called vigilante was not a mindless brute. In fact, he wasn't brutish at all. A little abrasive? Sure. Maybe kinda cool? Yeah, that too. But in the brain department, I was pretty sure I was out of my league.

I didn't like that at all.

"Hardly," I said with a dramatic eye-roll. "Well, why don't you go ahead and get nice and cozy," I offered sarcastically, waving a hand to the cold, unyielding cement floor. "We can talk some more when you decide to stop being such a smartass."

I stooped and collected the tinfoil in case he had some elaborate plan to use his hood pulls and shoelaces to retrieve it, believing he was entirely capable of that, turned, and walked calmly up the stairs.

Where I promptly began to freak the hell out.

I mean, what else could be expected of me?

That whole interaction was just... surreal.

Surreal.

*Un*real.

That was what I kept telling myself as I poured some more birdie kibble into Diego's food dish on his play stand where he was happily preening his feathers, getting ready for sleep after his calls to wake up the neighborhood. I also told myself that as I stripped and showered, feeling like the entire day was a layer of filth and slime over every inch of skin that I needed to scrub at until it was red and just shy of raw.

I was even still trying to tell myself that as I dressed in a tee and PJ pants, sat down on my bed, and reached for it.

My laptop.

I wasn't going to do what he said.

No freaking way.

Because I knew who my father was.

I was totally just going to check the weather, my email, new stories. I had missed out on a lot internet-wise being off the grid like I had been. I had used it before, of course. My father didn't want me to be a complete Luddite. But my usage was just a couple minutes here and there every month or two.

I had no idea how useful it could be in all kinds of ways. I could *order groceries* online. I could have my home insured without ever speaking to another human being.

It was no wonder Americans were so damn unhappy. They never interacted with one another.

I mean not once, in my entire life, did I have a dinner alone until I moved back to the States. Often, it wasn't even just my father and me either. Meals were a communal thing. They were for sharing of riches, for sharing of stories, of wisdom, of mutual enjoyment. It was always my favorite time of day, dinner. It never mattered that these people often didn't have a clue who we were, they welcomed us with open arms and hearts.

Hell, I went to a bar a few months back, and the people sitting almost shoulder-to-shoulder with each other were steadily looking ahead at the TVs.

No one interacted anymore.

It was all digital.

And while it was good that it was a way to bring people together who would never be able to know one another any other way, it was still lacking.

Nothing compared to sharing actual face-to-face interactions.

Just yet another thing I missed from my old life.

But I would adjust.

If there was one thing being a nomad your whole life taught you, it was how to seamlessly go from one extreme to another, to accept things as they came to you.

I exhaled hard at that, shaking my head.

If I believed that, if I believed things came to you, that you must accept them at face-value, why then was I being so reluctant to open a new window and do the search Luce challenged me to?

Was it because there was a part of me - albeit a minuscule part of me - that wondered if maybe there was even a slight chance of him being correct?

I wasn't sure, but with oddly numb fingers, I started typing.

Just his name.

Just Alejandro Cruz.

Not rapist.

Just a man. One of many.

There was nothing even relating to him for a long time, just other men by the same name who had done more public things with their lives.

Ten pages of the search in, my shoulders relaxed, my chest loosened enough to allow me to draw in a proper breath, my jaw unclenched, making me realize for the first time how much it hurt.

And it was right then, right that second, as I was wiggling my lower jaw around to loosen it up, that my eyes caught it.

The Rapist of Papua New Guinea.

That was the headline, making my heart plummet, and my belly twist painfully as I forced my eyes down below to read the blurb under it.

And that was the first shred of proof that Luce wasn't lying.

Because there was his name.

Alejandro Cruz was the rapist of Papua New Guinea.

I scanned the article even as my mind wandered back to our first trip there. I remembered the serious talk we had as we landed, before he would even let me get in the car. We were standing in the suffocating heat, the sun beating down relentlessly. At seventeen, I had been annoyed from the long travel and anxious to get somewhere to bathe and eat and get some sleep that wasn't interrupted by turbulence or someone else's too-loud speaking. But something in his eyes stopped me mid-grumble.

My father wasn't often serious with me.

So I knew it was time to listen.

"This is a very diverse land," he started with.

I had rolled my eyes at that. I knew that. I had learned that from the book he threw at me while we were still in Chile, telling me it was our next stop, and that I needed to brush up on the country. That was very much my father's homeschooling technique.

Papua New Guinea was one of the most diverse places in the world with over eight-hundred known languages, large amounts of 'un-contacted peoples,' and because it was one of the world's least explored territories, it was thought to be home of many undiscovered animals and plant life.

"Don't give me that look, mija," he scolded, tisk-tisking me for being a pain in the ass. "This is serious."

"What is so serious? They can't be worse than those cartels in Colombia, Papi."

"You didn't finish the book, did you?" Again, there was the tisk-tisk in his voice. He didn't often need to tell me how disappointed he was; it was in his very tone.

"I read most of it. I glazed over in the law chapter."

"And that law chapter is what has me standing here warning you, Evan." And then he went ahead and said something that, as time would prove it seems, was completely ironic. "Papua New Guinea is ranked the number one country for human rights violations against women. Fifty-percent of women in this country will be raped. Sixty-percent of that fifty-percent happens before the age of eighteen."

I felt my stomach twist at those facts.

Even at seventeen, even as white as a lily sexually, that word had a painful effect through my system. And it no longer felt like it was a hundred degrees in the shade. Because I was cold all over.

"Do you understand what I am telling you?"

I had to swallow before speaking, choking back the bile that seemed to work itself up my throat. Because this was never a topic I needed brought to my attention before. Not because it was not an issue. There were perverts, child molesters in every culture. Human trafficking was a very real and growing problem. But it had never really been on my radar. My father protected me. My father was feared by most. He had never needed to put fear in me because it had never been necessary.

So, if he was telling me, then the issue was serious.

And that was terrifying.

"Yes."

"You have me most of the time," he comforted me, touching my shoulder.

I always had him *most* of the time. Work always took him away from me, often leaving me in the company of some local group of women who promised to keep me company and, it went without saying, safe.

But this was a country where half of the women weren't safe themselves. They wouldn't be able to protect me.

"And this," he said, reaching into his bag and pulling out a small rectangle of thick leather material, tied around the center loosely. "Is what you have when I am not here," he told me, flipping the top flap open to reveal eight pointed, slightly shiny, thin as matchstick pieces of wood. "One scratch and they will be dying within seconds. So you keep this on you at all times," he said, reaching back into his bag to get a long leather strap which he threaded through two holes in the satchel, then moved to tie it around my waist. "And you use it even if there is a hint of unwanted advances. Yes?"

My stomach turned over at the idea.

It was one thing to learn about poisons, to know their effects in a detached sort of way. It was a whole other thing to be willing to inflict them upon a living being.

Even if said human being deserved it.

But I nodded with certainty, even though I felt anything but.

It was four days later, in some remote village where women went bare-breasted, something that wasn't unusual to me since I had seen it in countless places and had recently grown a pair of my very own, and was kinda happy with them, and the men wore nothing more than loincloths. It was a practice I used to find almost charmingly wild, but in this new place, in this women's rights violation capital of the world, all my brain could seem to wonder was if they wore them so they had easy access to their offending cocks when they wanted to take a woman by force.

My hand had gone down and stayed on the pouch as I watched my father disappear.

I had no idea at the time that he wasn't off to do business.

No, according to this article, this very in-depth, very well-researched article by a known and respected investigative reporter, he had been out committing a chain of gang rapes with other men like him- foreigners, looking to cause terror on a different continent and get away with it.

What better place than a country where the women were so subjugated, so accustomed to the abuses of men?

I scrolled a little further, my stomach tightening into knots.

And that was when I saw the worst thing I could imagine seeing.

I saw my father, clothes only half-fastened, standing beside a group of other men similarly dressed, all from different regions by the looks of them, smiling.

That wasn't the bad part.

Oh no.

The bad part was what they were apparently smiling at.

A group of naked native women laying on the ground several feet away, clutching one another, and crying.

I flew off the bed, running so fast out of the room that my hip collided full-force into the doorway, sending a shooting pain up my body. But there was no time to think about that.

Because the bile wasn't just bile anymore.

I dropped down onto the cold tile floor and let it all purge out.

The vomit, sure.

That was first. Violent. Seemingly never-ending.

Then after there was nothing left in my stomach, as I blew my nose, and rinsed my mouth, the tears started. The *pain* started. It was a clawing, a ripping sensation, like something was trying to burrow its way out of my chest.

And, I realized with a loud whimper, I knew exactly what was trying to free itself from my body- my heart.

The love of my father.

Because you couldn't or, more accurately, *I* couldn't love a man that vile. I couldn't be that piece of shit, spineless family member standing there saying 'but he was good to me' meanwhile the bastard brutalized other women.

Fuck that.

Evil is as evil does.

And evil was something that lived inside my father, was a big enough part of him to have him traveling the world, not to expand my horizons, not to give me a childhood that many would envy, but to get away with serial rape while wearing the mask of a doting father.

I refused to be his beard.

Because there was no hiding anymore.

I refused to be his defense attorney too.

Because his actions were indefensible.

I lowered myself back down on the floor, pulling my knees up into my chest, wrapping my arms around them, and pulling tight.

There was this strong, almost overpowering sensation of falling apart, that if I didn't physically hold myself together, I might genuinely just break into little pieces. There would just be splinters of myself that would be too small and jagged to glue back together.

I couldn't tell you what the drive was that pulled me up onto my feet, moving silently through my house, then, oddly, into the garage, and down the stairs, the cement floor frigid on my bare soles, making goosebumps work up my legs, and my nipples tweak.

"You alright?" Luce's voice reached me from his position sitting against the back wall, wide awake still. His deep-set, heavy-lidded eyes looked even more set back with tiredness.

He was supposed to be the enemy.

I had no idea why the words tripped from my tongue, but they did.

"The Rapist of Papua New Guinea?" I croaked, eyes stinging again, hinting at a fresh stream of tears, and I knew the sound was heavy in my voice.

He watched me for a long second seeming to show no reaction at all to the mess I knew I must have been in that moment. Which was weird to me. Usually, there was some reaction- namely discomfort, a strange fear, a helplessness, something. Not in Luce. He was just as blank as ever.

"Is that as far as you got?"

"Before my dinner decided to come back up, yeah," I admitted as he slowly rose from his seated position, and moved across the floor to reach up and grab the bars only a foot or so from me. He could have reached out, grabbed me, and slammed my head against the bars in a heartbeat.

But he didn't.

"I was with him on that trip," I admitted, unsure why I was saying it. Maybe I just needed to purge it, and he was the only one who would understand. "He warned me about how chronic assault against women was, and gave me a satchel of poison to keep on me. You know, while he went off and attacked women himself."

"What's this for?" he asked oddly, but then his hand moved between the bars, his finger gently swiping the tears off of one of my cheeks.

"Because my father is a disgusting rapist."

"Well, you're both right and wrong," he said, making my brows draw together.

"What do you mean I'm wrong? You're the one who told me he was a rapist in the first place."

"True. And he is that. Worse than you realize too, unfortunately."

Ugh.

That hurt.

I didn't think there could be a worse feeling in my chest than there had been half an hour before, but I was obviously wrong. There was always more pain, new pain, deeper pain. Always.

"Then what was I wrong about?"

"Ever look at your father, doll face?"

"I looked at him every day of my life," I said, eyes squinting.

"Ever look in a mirror?"

"What are you trying to say here?" I asked, feeling my stomach tighten.

"I'm not convinced that fuck was your father."

Okay. So we didn't exactly look alike. That was definitely true. My features were more delicate, my eyes very dark, almost black. My father's features were very wide, almost burly. He was tall, wide-shouldered, broad-chested. And his eyes, well, they were hazel.

But it took two to tango, as they say.

I always figured I must have just looked like my mother.

"Didn't notice it right at first, but the longer I look at you, the less likely I think it is you two share any DNA. I mean, your skin is a completely different shade than his. He had olive undertones. You're warm."

"I had a mother at some point," I reasoned.

"Hazel eyes versus almost black. You're long and lean, but hold your weight in your hips. He held it in his chest and belly. His hair was at least five shades lighter."

"That's all circumstantial."

"He had that giant fucking cleft in his chin too. You don't have a hint of it."

"The only way that would prove anything was if my mother had a cleft too, and I don't. Again, I don't know anything about her."

"It's a lot," he said, shaking his head. "I like when things add up, and something is off with the math here."

"So I should just... bring you a laptop and let you poke around in my life some more?"

There was bitterness in my tone, the origins of which I wasn't sure of. Why be bitter? It wasn't his fault. Don't shoot the messenger and all that jazz. But that being said, I couldn't confront the source of my anger, resentment, and pain. He was gone. There would never be closure there.

Also, in one internet search, every plan of perfect vengeance just... disappeared.

I had no right to keep Luce anymore.

He hadn't done anything to me.

He had tried to do something that I actually found commendable.

In the process, he had set me free.

Sure, it hurt. It might always. But that was the price you had to pay for the truth at times.

And, truly, I had to set him free.

I turned away without anything else, going back up the stairs, and into my bedroom where I grabbed the key, then made my way back down again.

"Where's the laptop?" he asked, brows drawing together.

I moved over toward the door, pressing the lock, and turning, hearing the click, then the groan of the un-oiled joints.

"At your home," I answered, moving slightly to the side of the doorway to allow him to walk past.

"You're just letting me out," he half-asked, half-declared, leaning against the bars of his prison, crossing his arms over his chest, watching me like I had lost my mind.

"I can't keep you here. You didn't do what I thought you did."

"And if I had?" he prompted.

"Even if you had, I would probably let you go. Now that I know the truth."

"Gotta say, I'm liking the ability to be rational about this shit."

"Gee, thanks," I mumbled.

I wasn't exactly sure it was *healthy* to be rational about it all. Wasn't love supposed to trump all? Shouldn't a daughter be able to forgive the sins of the man who loved and raised her?

I didn't know about should, but I knew I didn't.

Because being good to me didn't undo all the bad he did to who knew how many others. If your bad outweighed your good, then you were bad. It was simple math really. And maybe if his crimes were just more murders of deserving people, I could have looked past it.

This was different.

This was horrific.

There was no excuse for his level of evil.

And knowing he had done it to other women while protecting me from the same fate? Yeah, no. The bastard.

"Look, I think it's good to be able to compartmentalize things."

"Says the robot," I agreed, wincing at the snarky tone, not liking that I was being cruel to someone who didn't earn it.

"Imagine how much shit I had to learn to box away in password protected files on an external harddrive, so the motherboard didn't fucking explode, Evan," he said, tone almost a little... sad?

It was right in that second, gone before I could fully appreciate the depth of it, that this strange vigilante, almost robotic guy showed me what was underneath.

And what was underneath was a well of hurt so deep that it made what I was feeling seem positively uplifting by comparison.

I didn't know the man.

I doubted he would want me too.

But regardless of all of that, I had the almost overwhelming urge to know what made him how he was.

Why?

I had no idea.

Maybe it was as simple as the fact that he knew all my darkness now, and I wanted things to be more even.

Though, a part of me thought that perhaps it was more than that, that maybe this enigmatic loner intrigued me now that I finally understood his motivations.

"Don't pity me, doll face."

"I'm not pitying you," I shot back immediately, shaking my head. That was as far from the truth as possible.

"What then?"

"I don't know. It's... curiosity, I guess," I admitted, shrugging, trying to seem casual.

"About me?" he asked, smirking, and it did wonderful things to his dark eyes. "I'm figuring that if you were able to track me down, that you already did a fair amount of research." His smile went wicked then, making the skin beside his eyes crinkle up slightly. "Tell me, did you come across all that fanfic erotica written about me?"

So, I had a tendency not to blush, but show discomfort somehow in my features. I wasn't sure exactly what the combination of changes were, but everyone I had ever met could read right into me when I was embarrassed.

And, seeing as I had not only come across, but read said erotica extensively, I was freaking embarrassed as hell.

I hadn't meant to read it, I swear!

But I saw it on some site called "Luce's Lovers" and I thought there might be information about his whereabouts. There wasn't, but there was a section for writing which I had opened in case it seemed like one of the writers had met Luce personally and could, therefore, point me in a direction if I was looking for him.

Then I started reading.

This woman, whoever she was, actually got pretty close description-wise to how Luce actually looked. Except she made him heavily tattooed and green-eyed. Personally, I preferred the real Luce. I was always a sucker for brown eyes. But aside from the slightly inaccurate physical description of him, yeah, she, well, she wrote a convincing anti-hero. Those sex scenes, too, yeah, they were, um, realistic.

Oh crap.

I shouldn't have been thinking about them right then.

Because a bright, vivid image of one of those detailed scenes flashed in front of me. But instead of the green-eyed, tattooed fictional version of Luce taking the lead, it was the real-life, flesh-and-bone version instead. Bending me over a sink in his killing room, hands clutching my breasts, fingers tweaking my nipples, hard cock pressing against my ass. And then...

"I'll take that as a yes," Luce's voice cut into the scene in my mind, pulling me backward out of it so fast I'd swear I got whiplash.

Holy shit.

Holy shit.

That did not just happen.

I did not just have a vivid sexual fantasy about the man who had planned to kill my father. A man I had been holding as a prisoner.

And I totally did not have that fantasy whilst standing in front of said man who happened to be the most freakishly observant person I had ever met in my life, and likely picked up on how my breathing went uneven, my skin flushed, my eyes hooded.

"Don't be embarrassed," he went on, his voice sounding closer. As I forced my head up, I realized that was because he had silently closed the distance between us, and was standing in the small space of the opened doorway with me.

"I'm not embarrassed," I insisted, trying to pull myself together, knowing I was failing epically seeing as there was a dull, but insistent, throbbing sensation of need between my thighs.

"No?" he asked, head tipping to the side slightly. "Then explain this," he said, running a finger across my cheek that felt heated. "And this," he went on, his finger gliding upward to stroke near my eye that did feel heavy-lidded. "And this," he continued, his finger moving lower, brushing over my lower lip. Hand to God, that motion sent a shiver through my system. And it was not a subtle one. No, it was one that shook my entire body. One that Luce not only saw, but felt. "Thought so," he said, voice deep. His eyes seemed deeper as well suddenly, something I couldn't quite peg for what it was until what happened next, well, happened.

His hand slid across my cheek, whispering over the column of my neck, then curling around the back of it. Gentle. It was all so gentle. That is until he yanked me forward, sending me colliding into his chest as he kept my head angled up by slipping his fingers into my hair and pulling.

And his lips crashed down on mine.

The shock of it sent a jolt through my body.

But the shock was replaced by something else entirely, something deeper, something clawing, needy, indescribable. It worked its way up from the base of my spine and slowly flowed outward, slipped into my very veins, warmed me in a way I wasn't sure I had ever experienced before.

So without thinking how warped it was, without questioning my sanity in doing so, my hands moved up and curled into his upper arms, holding his body close as my breasts pressed harder into his chest, as my hips lined up to his.

His teeth nipped my lower lip, dragging a ragged groan from me as they slid apart and his tongue moved inside to claim mine, his hand tightening in my hair. His other arm moved around my lower back, holding me ever-more tightly to him as his tongue raided, owned, then retreated, allowing his lips to sear into mine again.

My heart was a desperate pounding in my chest.

The pulsing between my thighs became almost overwhelming, an acutely painful unsatisfied need that had my hips pressing harder into his, feeling the outline of his cock, and there seemed to be an immediate hollowness within that needed fulfillment.

In response to it, there was a wholly uncontrollable whimpering noise from deep within my chest that pushed out from between my lips, making an equally needy-sounding growl rumble through Luce's chest.

I was sure the torment would come to an end, that his hand would slide between us and work me with his fingers until the pain became pleasure that became something else entirely.

But that wasn't what happened.

One moment, he was kissing me like the war was over.

The next, his lips tore from mine, his hands loosened their hold so I went back on my flat feet, and his forehead pressed into mine.

"Fuck," he huffed, somewhat out of breath.

It was the first time I really got to be so close to him without thoughts of sticking poisonous needles in him clouding my senses with a sulfur-scented, bone-deep hatred.

He smelled good.

I couldn't quite peg what it was, but it was outdoorsy, woodsy, a hint of pine, and dirt, and fresh air.

It shouldn't have been, but absolutely was, one of the most intoxicating things I had ever smelled on a man before.

Then he was no longer pressing his forehead to mine. His hand was no longer in my hair. His arm was no longer a reassuring anchor around my back.

One second, he was almost fully supporting me.

The next, he was a full foot away, watching me with those dark eyes, but there was a shutter down over them, making it impossible to read anything in their depths.

There was a pause, him seeming lost in his own thoughts. And me, well, I didn't seem capable of speech as I tried to shut down the live wire known as desire coursing through my system.

Then he nodded at me, shrugged, and declared, "Well, this has been a lovely detention. I am going to head out."

Of all the things he could have said, yeah, that was maybe what I would have anticipated the least.

"What?" I asked, my breath a husky imitation of itself.

"I have some sick bastard to look into. I got contacted about him right before you abducted me. Need to finish that job. Thank you for your hospitality," he added, moving toward the steps, then pausing at the bottom one. "Oh, and if you want to know who is trying to kill you, come find me."

With that, and not so much as a glance backward, he was tearing up the stairs.

Before I could even make it to the bottom one, I could hear the door to the outside slamming.

He was gone.

And I hadn't gotten the chance to tell him that the 'sick bastard' he was looking for was actually me. See, I never did track him down myself. But I tracked down someone who was a bit loose with their cell phone locking and was in contact with Luce. I cloned his phone, and had all the information I needed to page him, then created a robotic phone voice to tell him about a fictional serial killer who targeted girls.

But that wasn't what had my heart flying up into my throat.

Oh, no.

What the hell did he mean someone was trying to kill me?

SIX

Luce

Well then.

That was an unexpected turn of events.

Here I had been thinking someone was going to be carving up little pieces of my flesh and feeding it to their dogs, and I got off with a little flower poison.

Thank fuck no one else knew about that shit; I would never have lived that down.

Flower poison.

Jesus.

To be perfectly honest, I never thought she would believe the truth. Most people didn't. It didn't matter how much evidence was staring them in the face, they just shut down and believed what they wanted to believe.

That explained politics in our country, to be honest.

But, no, Evangeline Cruz, was not someone who was so set in her opinions that she couldn't see past them. It was such a rare quality anymore that I truly hadn't even factored it in as a possibility.

She had come down those stairs shattered. There was no other way to describe it. She looked absolutely wrecked. Her face was tear-streaked; her eyes were bloodshot; she looked pale.

I was so fucking jaded to all that shit, all that evil. Finding a rapist, a child molester, a serial killer, that was just my everyday norm. I had to troll through the shittiest of sites on the dark web. I had to see women being brutalized, children being violated, people begging for their lives uselessly. I was so desensitized to it all that I forgot what shock felt like, if I ever had the ability to feel it at all.

But it was clear that the one image she found, one I had found a while back as well, one that, to me, was almost PG compared to all the other depravity I was usually surrounded by, completely shattered her.

I hardly ever had the luxury of feeling love toward a parent. Not because I didn't have a parent that I should have loved, but because they never did anything worthy of love.

So I couldn't relate to her loss. I couldn't understand how his sins laid at her feet made her feel like they were hers to pick up. I couldn't understand her guilt for being safe from rape while her father was a rapist. I couldn't fathom why that would feel like a betrayal.

But she felt his sins, she felt guilt, and she absolutely felt betrayal.

I didn't have to understand to be able to sympathize, to feel something inside at the sight of a broken woman. I wasn't a fucking automaton. My knee-jerk reaction was to reach for her. My desire was to try to wipe all of that away. I didn't know her. I shouldn't have cared, not when I rarely cared for anyone, but I did. I cared. Maybe it was as simple as my honesty was what tore her world apart.

But, in my opinion, the pain of the truth would always be better than the bliss of ignorance.

Judging by her reaction, Evan felt the same way.

Then damn if she didn't go all heated at the memory of my fanfic porn. I mean, not that I blamed her. That shit was a lot sexier than I realized it could be. I finally understood why romance outsold every other genre. I was hard as a fucking rock reading it. And if that got the pussy all lubed up like it got my cock hard, yeah, women could just go right ahead and rev up those engines for their men to test drive when they got home from work. Fucking nothing wrong with that.

But seeing that look on her face, that heaviness in her eyes, that flush to her skin, that unevenness of her breathing, yeah, it did something to me. I didn't often think, let alone act, with my dick. There was simply no stopping it. Maybe it was the emotionally charged moment, or the fact that I found her ability to take me down and plan my imprisonment sexy as all fuck, or maybe it was a simple reaction to her desire.

Whatever it was, there was no fighting it.

Even if I had wanted to, that is.

As it was, there wasn't a single part of me that wanted to hold back. I had a feeling getting my hands on her would be something new, something heady.

I wasn't wrong.

It was just a minute, just a fucking kiss, but there was this pull inside, this strange sensation of it unwinding from its tight coil in my chest and moving outward, trying to tie into a similar string in her chest.

That shit, yeah, that was utterly fucked up.

That was what eventually pulled me away when everything within me was begging me to lower her down on that cold floor and bury inside her sweet pussy, to give her a memory of this day that was not pain and betrayal and heartbreak.

But that couldn't be.

I had to get out of there.

I flew up those stairs, then out the first door I came to which put me into what seemed to be the side yard of a classic 1960's ranch-style house with off-white siding and a small amount of brickwork out front beneath the bay window. It was the center house in a four-house cul-de-sac, the sound of a train coming from a few streets behind.

If we were still in Navesink Bank, I could find my way once I got to the train station. Even if we weren't still in Navesink Bank, the train would get me where I needed to be. I turned out of the cul-de-sac, swearing I caught sight of her standing in the bay window watching me as I quickly pulled up my hood and disappeared.

Ten minutes later, I saw the very familiar Navesink Bank train station. Taking a deep breath, knowing my walk was about to be long as fuck and it was late as hell, I just got a move on.

I had some shit to deal with at home.

First, the sick bastard I had mentioned earlier.

Second, I wanted to prove I was right about her, about her parentage. Alejandro Cruz may have been her father in the way of him raising her, but he wasn't in her veins, in her blood. No fucking way. Too much just didn't add up.

When I had the information, I would send it to her.

Send.

In the mail.

Because being close to her apparently made me lose my ever-loving mind.

"You look like shit," a voice said to my side, making me look over to find none other than Detective Lloyd of the NBPD leaning against his car outside of She's Bean Around.

Considering it was closed, that was weird.

I turned, seeing Jazzy moving around, rapidly trying to put things to rights, everything about the usually confident and carefree woman seeming just a tad frazzled and frantic. Like she was in a rush. A rush to... "No fucking way. You and Jazz?" I asked, shaking my head. And, judging by the way his face went all stoney, I was right. I usually was. "Damn. Try to deserve her, man," I said, shaking my head as Jazz cut the lights and practically ran out the door, barely remembering to turn back and lock it.

"Oh, Luce," she said, jerking backward, eyes going huge, like she was caught red-handed or something.

"Interesting choice of bedmates, doll face," I said with a tired smirk. Good for her. She deserved a good man. And Lloyd, while technically someone who could haul me in for a life sentence at any given time, was a good man.

"You look like shit," she said, smile teasing.

"So I hear. Rough night."

"Aw, what's the matter, L? Get kicked out of some woman's bed?"

"Right," I smiled. "Like any woman would want to kick me out of bed. Have fun, you two. Remember, the only good sex is safe sex."

"Leave," Jazzy said, big-eyeing me in a way that said I better cover my balls the next time I saw her, or she might be sporting them as earrings.

"Catch you around," I called, waving over my shoulder at them as I made my way to the edge of the town, then up the tall ass hill that I cursed seven ways to fucking Sunday and then twice more for good measure. My sleep-weary limbs were screaming by the time I made it to my door, still half-open from where I must have fallen into it when Evan knocked me out and dosed me.

Christ, even that thought send a rush of desire through my system, making my cock harden against my jeans painfully.

Then, because once the floodgates were opened, they could not be closed again, I went ahead and tortured myself with the idea that maybe she was still just as affected. Maybe she would take her pretty ass back to her bedroom, pull open her laptop, and go find some of that literary porn that had gotten her all hot and bothered before. Maybe she would strip out of her clothes, finding them itchy and suffocating on her body, painful to her hardened nipples. Maybe she wouldn't be able to stop her hand from sliding down her stomach and under her panties, stroking up her slick slit, and finding her swollen, throbbing clit, rubbing it until the emptiness inside was too much to bear, then shoving her fingers deep inside, raking over her G-spot until she came.

"Fuck," I growled, having to reach down to unfasten my jeans, finding the pressure painful.

My thumb brushed over the head of my cock, making me let out a hiss, knowing there was no going back.

I reached inside my boxer briefs, freeing my cock, stroking it hard and fast, imagining those dark eyes of hers looking up at me from her knees with need before sucking me deep.

"Fuck," I growled, coming harder than I had in months. Hell, years.

I dragged my tired ass to the bathroom, showering off the day, then falling into bed, figuring I would fall into an exhausted sleep.

But that wasn't what happened.

And that wasn't exactly rare.

Nighttime tended to bring up the memories. No matter how deeply I buried them, they always clawed their way up to the surface.

They always taunted me with their special type of horrors. Some nights, I could force them back where they came from. Then I could catch a few blissful hours if the nightmares stayed at bay.

This didn't seem like it was going to be one of those nights.

This was one of the nights where, no matter how much I tossed and turned, how many other memories I tried to use to fight those off, nothing would work.

So, eyes the consistency of sandpaper, I climbed back out of bed and went back down in the bunker, firing up a new laptop from my stash, and setting out to do some research.

I meant to look into this new bastard I needed to take out.

That was my plan.

Why then did my fingers type in Evangeline Cruz instead? Yeah, fuck if I knew. But that was what they did. And as soon as the search page loaded, I knew there was no going back.

That was just how I operated.

I was focused, methodical, painstakingly anal about details, thorough to the point of absolute obsessiveness.

But in my particular line of work, I couldn't afford to be wrong. Unlike our fucked up criminal justice system, I actually *did* give a shit whether or not the man I was going to kill actually committed the crime. I checked and double checked and triple checked every fact. I retraced every step. I tried to find receipts or proof of their location near where certain events took place. I made sure their traces online went right back to where they were supposed to, not diverted somewhere in between to make a false trail for some other sicko to use the person as a pawn.

I couldn't afford to fall asleep on the job.

Not one man who made it down into my bunker hadn't been checked out until there was not even a shadow of a doubt of their guilt.

Hell, just like Harold Grains, I often found proof of their crimes on their person. In their wallets or in their phones.

It was like they couldn't afford to be away from their depravity for any length of time. They constantly needed it with them, like a security blanket for vicious, bottom-feeding filth.

Statistically, one in twenty-five sentenced to death in the United States penitentiary system was innocent.

Me, well, that would be zero.

I've never fucked up.

I spent weeks, or even months, looking into these people.

I was hoping it wouldn't take me that long to find traces of the real parents of one Evangeline Cruz.

There simply wouldn't be that long.

She would be showing back up in no time.

There was no way she was thinking I was yanking her chain when I told her someone was trying to kill her. What's more, I was actually being honest. Someone was most definitely trying to kill her. The only reason I didn't insist we figure that shit out right away was that I knew it wasn't going to kill her anytime soon.

How she missed the signs were beyond me.

My best guess was that she was so consumed with finding me and bringing me in that she didn't stop to think about her own well-being. I understood obsession, so I could see how she maybe missed something that was, for all intents and purposes, rather subtle.

But she trusted my eye enough to know I wouldn't have been mistaken. And as soon as she maybe got some rest, got some food, and found some nerve, she would be back.

I only had until then to find her mother at the very least.

To do that, I had to trace her so-called father back to his whereabouts approximately twenty-two years before. If she wasn't his, if she was somehow stolen from her birth parents, it had to have happened before she was five, after which kids generally would remember something like being ripped from their mother. Hell, even five seemed like it was pushing it, but some kids just had crummy memories, and others had brains that needed to shut down and shut out that trauma, never to resurface again.

If only all of us were so lucky.

"Fuck," I growled, shaking my head at myself.

I didn't do that; I didn't go all woe-is-me. It didn't matter that I had genuine reason to be hiding in a corner humming for the rest of my life. Those things were a part of my childhood. I was a grown ass man. I refused to be a mother fucking victim. I locked that shit down in a vault and I never, ever, let it back out except in times when my guards were down too much to fight it- right before sleep, and during my unconscious moments.

Every other moment... Locked. The. Fuck. Down.

That was the way it had to be, so that was the way it was.

I took out whatever residual feelings, namely rage, that were left over, and channeled them into my own personal little mission in life. So far, so good. It kept me sane. It lifted a bit of the weight I had always felt knowing from such a young age what kind of vile filth existed within seemingly normal human beings. It felt like it was my responsibility not to expose it per se, but to exterminate it. I swear if I could round all the fucks up, stick them in a room, and set off a smoke bomb like you do to kill roaches, I'd do it in a fucking heartbeat. But with great fanfare came a greater chance of getting caught. And I needed to, as long as possible, keep going, keep ratting them out like a terrier, and taking them down one by one.

If not me, who?

That was what it came down to.

Sure, every so often a rape victim will go apeshit and tear off the dick of her abuser and shove it up his own ass.

But it was rare.

And they tended to get caught.

There were vigilantes spread out all over, operating right beneath the noses of local law enforcement. Hell, I knew of one who *was* a cop. Ten years on the job, and sick of there never being justice. So he took justice into his own hands.

He was a pretty vicious bastard too.

But while we did exist, we were rare. We had to be careful. It wasn't like when one cartel member gets taken out, another steps right in his place, getting his former boss's blood all over his shoes in his desire for power. When one of us was taken out, that meant more shitheads got away with what they did.

If I was taken out, there was no one to step up in Jersey.

I heard rumors of some new blood up in the city, but he had enough to deal with in that place. He wasn't coming down to Jersey to find child molesters and serial killers when he had plenty where he was.

The longer I stayed around, the longer I was able to keep doing what I did, the better it was not just for myself, but all the unsuspecting potential victims in the area.

I got up out of my chair, walking into the kitchen, and brewing a pot of coffee as I grabbed an energy drink out of the fridge and downed it while it brewed. I wasn't going to be sleeping, but I wasn't one of those people who did well without sleep either. My body never 'got used to it' as some claimed. It always brought about a general slowness and brain fog. So, to combat that, caffeine was mainlined until another day had passed, and it was time to try the sleep thing again.

In the meantime, it was all about Alejandro's travels in the five-year window I figured there could be.

African and Asian countries were automatically crossed off for obvious reasons. So that just left... shit.

Argentina. Bolivia. Brazil. Chile. Colombia. Ecuador. Guyana. Paraguay. Peru. Suriname. Uruguay. Venezuela. Falkland Islands. Mexico. Cuba. Dominican Republic. Costa Rica. Puerto Rico. Guatemala. Honduras.

And, well, let's not forget the lower United States just near the border.

Alejandro himself had duel citizenship for both Colombia and the United States. Which was how Evangeline herself was considered a US citizen, despite barely spending any time in the states. I had copies of Alejandro's passport, along with all other incriminating information I had on him before I brought him in burned on a CD amidst my massive DVD collection. As I did with all my 'victims' who I was more likely to call 'marks' since they weren't victimized by me; they were brought to fucking justice. I could track back those stamps. It would be easier still if I had Evangeline's, but that was asking for too much. And there was really no way to track someone's passport movements save for from countries with exit visas or sharing agreements like the US, Canada, and Mexico.

Bank statements could be used to track Alejandro, though he mostly dealt in cash, but that wouldn't help me narrow down when he started bringing Evan along with him.

But, no matter.

Everything, literally everything, could be found out about a person if you dug long enough.

Sure, scumbags like Alejandro were easier because they left a trail of victims. But I would find Evan's origins soon enough.

Preferably before she showed back up.

I figured I had about eight to ten hours.

Plenty of time.

I could even cut the time in a third if I maybe called in Barrett as well as some badass lady hackers he knew named Alex and

Jstorm. And, sure, they knew who I was. They knew what I did. I also knew I could trust them, especially seeing as Alex and Jstorm were known for doing some cyber justice themselves, siphoning out money from certain assholes' Bitcoin accounts, and depositing them into the accounts for charities. Between all four of us, we'd not only have Evan's mother, but her back story, her grandparents' back stories, what diseases she might be pre-disposed to, and full fucking genealogy reports dating back three-hundred years.

Yes, they were all that good.

But I didn't want to call them.

Why, you might ask.

It was the most fucked up thing actually.

I wanted the goddamn credit.

I wasn't some dick who would say someone else's work was my own. So if I called the others in, I would need to tell Evangeline which parts I found myself, and which parts they had helped with.

I wanted all the glory of finding out her origin story.

It wasn't like me, but I was figuring it had something to do with the fact that I was responsible for the pain she was going through. Mix in the fact that I was ridiculously attracted to her, impressed *by* her, and maybe just had a slight desire for her gratitude, and you could pretty much understand the motive.

Warped?

Yeah, probably.

Full of ego?

Most definitely.

But truthful nonetheless.

I was nothing if I wasn't honest.

The sun was streaking across the sky almost eleven hours later as the printer kept producing sheet after sheet for me which I was carefully stapling, arranging, and compiling into a folder. My hands were shaking slightly from the lack of sleep and overindulgence of caffeine. My eyes felt swollen and dry. My neck and shoulders had cricks. And, well, my stomach was twisted into a tight knot.

Because I was so sure she would show up, that she would know I was being straight with her.

But nothing.

As I shuffled the last page into what was, apparently, a complete waste of my sleepless night, I finally heard it.

See, I was down in the bunker.

Why?

Paranoia would likely be as accurate a description as any.

My line of work made it likely that the cops would come find me eventually. If they raided my house, I was somewhat safe in the bunker. If they found the entrance to the bunker, well, I was working on that. I was slowly but surely digging out a small tunnel. Not for escape, because, quite frankly, I was too far in the middle of nowhere. There was nowhere to escape *to.* It was more like a place where I could hide out if they found a way into the bunker. Found a clever fucking way to hide the door too. But it was just meant to be a hiding place, a last ditch effort to remain a free man, free to continue my work.

So I just... naturally gravitated to the bunker most of the time.

Which made it hard as hell to hear anything above.

But once the printer stopped spitting out paper, there was a definite tap tap tapping from a floor above.

It was actually fucking embarrassing how fast I kicked my rolling chair back toward the laptop to check the outside camera.

It was equally embarrassing, the ridiculous, borderline goofy fucking smile that threatened to split my face at seeing the ducked head of Evangeline standing there, her dark hair catching the sun, and making it look just as silky as it felt.

Christ, I couldn't even remember the last time I smiled hard enough for it to pinch the muscles in my cheeks.

Months?

Years?

Had I ever smiled that big?

I slammed the file shut, tucked it under my arm, and went for the door to the upper floor.

"You can't just tell a woman someone is trying to kill her, and then disappear, you jackass!" I heard her shriek through the door as her hand pounded into the thick wood. Actually, I was pretty sure I heard a goddamn kick too.

If that wasn't the cutest fucking thing.

"Keep your panties on," I called as I shut the door to the bunker, and moved across the floor to the front door. "Or, on second thought," I said, pulling the locks, "take them off, doll face," I added as I pulled it open to find her standing there, mouth parted comically.

And, damn, there was the freaking goofy grin again.

What the fuck?

"Who is trying to kill me?" she recovered quickly, shaking her head, swallowing hard.

I shrugged at that, leaning into the doorjamb. "Fuck if I know."

SEVEN

Evan

I had a hard, okay nearly impossible, night of sleep.

First, because, well, even when I tried to close my eyes, the image of my father and his buddies and those poor, abused women kept flashing across my mind.

When I had gotten back to my room, I had needed to close out the tabs of the image, making dry heaves rack my body almost violently for another ten minutes before I finally got myself under control.

Then, y'know, there was that other issue to deal with.

Someone was trying to kill me?

Of course, my knee-jerk reaction was to say he was bullshitting me, getting a bit of petty vengeance, screwing with my head further. After all, maybe that was just how the freak got his kicks.

After sort of having his way with me.

Ugh.

That part did not factor in. Nope. Not at all.

The sleeplessness was totally about the sudden and heart-wrenching reality of my father's life, and, well, the possibility of my far-off or maybe imminent death.

Because it was hardly more than five minutes of back-and-forth in my head about it, I knew Luce wasn't screwing with me. If anything, the man seemed truthful to a fault. If he was saying someone was trying to kill me, then someone was trying to kill me. So, if he could see that someone was trying to kill me, then the evidence had to be on me somewhere.

That sent me running into my bathroom, ripping my drying towel and robe off the back of my door to expose the long mirror standing there. With frantic fingers, I practically clawed my shirt, shorts, and panties off, looking myself over.

But I couldn't seem to find anything amiss.

That didn't mean it wasn't; it simply meant that Luce's eyes just managed to see more than mine did.

It was not easy to sleep while considering your own mortality.

I wondered how patients managed it when given only a couple months to live. I would be drowning in coffee and doing all the things I never made time for before I got sick.

All in all, my life was better than most. I got to travel. I got to see the most beautiful, winding, light-sanded, piercing blue beaches in the world. I have tasted fruit no one north of the equator even knew existed. I had learned, and forgotten, several languages. I had known the touch of a man who wanted nothing in the world but to bring me pleasure. I had had the satisfaction of turning away a man who only meant to bring me pain. I had danced in life-changing festivals. I had *lived.* I had, as the saying went, lived *deeply*; I was full-up of the marrow of life.

That didn't, however, mean I was ready to die.

Hell, I hadn't gotten laid in a year.

I couldn't go to my grave while in an epic dry spell.

No way.

And, you know, it would be nice to see my thirties.

Or forties.

Maybe explore the US a bit more.

Find someone to will Diego to, seeing as it was looking more and more likely that he might outlive me.

Ugh.

Pathetic, I decided as I climbed out of bed, the sun peeking through the blinds, Diego already squawking his morning 'give me food' scream, I was being absolutely pathetic.

What's more, it was for no reason.

There was no reason to stress about it like there were no answers. I wasn't suffering from some debilitating and unknown illness.

Because whatever was wrong with me, Luce had the answers.

I was going to drag my ass back up his hill, and get them.

After a shower, a clothing change, and making sure Diego couldn't cause too much trouble while I was away.

It was almost noon by the time I finally reached the top of his godforsaken hill, walking through the woods for a couple minutes before I came across the low, dark cabin. Oddly, my thoughts as I walked up to the door, were that it didn't seem like a place that suited him. He was the kind of man who should live in, like, a renovated warehouse, all cement floors, brick walls, drafty windows, and maybe one of those abandoned industrial areas they use to mix big vats of liquids. You know... where he could *dispose* of bodies. I figured he was of the melting, not burying, sort. Burying was too sloppy, too traceable. He melted the bodies; I was sure of it. So, yeah, those big vats would come in handy.

But yeah, this place was meant for some crotchety old man who drank shitty beer, and had the belly to prove it, while bitching about how the world was going to come to the end or some nonsense like that, some angry, backward loner with no one left in the world to care about them.

There was a weird sinking feeling in my stomach at that thought though, wondering if perhaps that was the life Luce was going to lead. He was absolutely a loner. Was there some buried anger as well?

How else would someone be able to do what he did in life?

Normal, well-adjusted people did not become what was, essentially, a serial killer. Sure, he perhaps did it for the right reasons, but a killer was a killer. And judging by what I had seen about him online, the number of people he had put in the ground, or down the drain more likely, 'serial' definitely applied.

I was starting to think he wasn't there, an idea that made my heart flutter at the possible repercussions of that, when I finally heard his voice from inside.

Telling me to keep my panties on. Then take them off.

Which, well, as you can imagine thanks to the kiss to end all kisses the night before, maybe sent a wild surge of desire through my system.

He looked like hell.

Sure, he seemed showered and changed. Though, how I knew he was changed when he was just in another pair of jeans and a seemingly fresh black hoodie with white hood pulls, was beyond me. But aside from that, he looked even more pale than usual, almost ghostly. His eyes were stained with red, and swollen. There was even a bit of scruff on his face which was sexy as all hell for some reason.

He clearly hadn't slept.

Weird, considering he had been through a lot.

"What do you mean you don't know?" I pretty much, well, shrieked. "If you don't know, then you can't possibly know that someone even *is* trying to kill me."

His lips tipped up slightly. "Don't know who would want you dead, Evan, but I know someone does."

"How?"

"There's no denying the symptoms."

"There *are* no symptoms," I insisted.

His smile went wicked then, making his dark eyes dance. "Stripped down and checked yourself out, did you?"

Oh, God.

Okay.

My lady bits didn't get the memo that I wasn't supposed to be into him. I had tried to reason with them just a moment ago about the panties comment, but let's just say, the message never quite made it to the target.

I had to press my thighs together to stem the chaos there.

"There is nothing off."

"No?" he asked, head ducking to the side.

"No," I insisted, rolling my eyes. He didn't know my body better than I knew my body for goodness sakes.

"Then what's this?" he asked, arm raising, reaching outward toward me, making his sleeve slide upward, exposing the smooth skin of his inner arm. Well, on a normal person, there was smooth skin. On Luce, there were dozens of scars.

But there was hardly a second to consider that because the next second, his fingers closed around the collar of my shirt, the tips of them brushing my skin, causing a small, involuntary shiver to course through me. His eyes moved from my neck to my face, watching me intensely, trying to bank the spark of desire there, but failing completely. Just as I was sure I was as well.

"What is what?" I forced out, pretending to ignore how my voice sounded more airy, more breathless than it usually did.

Judging by the way his eyes hooded all the more, he definitely noticed the change as well. But then his fingers yanked so hard at the material that there was the distinct ripping sound of the tight collar stitches pulling as he made the neck go wide. "This," he explained, then made the whole pretending-I-wasn't-turned-on thing go out the window when his fingers brushed across my chest.

"It's a rash," I explained, swallowing hard.

"Yeah, it is."

"I get them when I am stressed out," I explained. I'd been having that issue since I was a little girl. I got this obnoxious red rash across my chest, neck, sometimes even my face if the stress was strong enough for too long. Learning that your father was, I thought, murdered, then finding he had actually killed himself and was nothing like the man I thought? Yeah, that qualified as a lot of damn stress.

"Maybe," he agreed, eyes moving up from my chest to my face again. "But not like this."

"How would you know what my stress rash looks like?" I shot back, standing up straighter.

"Then there is this," he said, his hand moving downward, igniting a spark across my palm when his hand slid under it, and slowly started lifting my arm upward.

"This what?" I asked, looking at my hand. Again, I saw nothing amiss.

"You would think Alejandro, with all his years of experience with poisons, would never let you wear nail polish," he said oddly, making my brows draw together.

What the hell was he talking about?

"Why would he care about my nail polish?"

"Because it makes you miss this," he said, turning my hand, then holding my thumb between his and his forefinger. Stomach tightening, my gaze moved downward to the finger in question. "Your polish chipped off when you went upstairs. I noticed it when you came back down. See these white lines in your nail bed?" he asked. And, oh, I saw them alright. I saw them, and because I saw them, I felt a wave a nausea work through me again. I was, among a rash and Mees' lines on my nails, developing a bit of a weak stomach. Of course I was. Because that fit too. "These thick white lines..."

"Mees' lines," I choked out, heart tripping into overdrive, making me almost instantly lightheaded.

He nodded at that. "Arsenic poisoning."

God.

God.

How the hell could I have missed it?

It took prolonged exposure to said arsenic to cause Mees' lines to show up on nails. Where the hell had my head been that I had been so careless to miss my own goddamn poisoning?

"Don't pass out on me," Luce's voice demanded, sounding almost far away, like from the end of a tunnel, making me realize I was definitely too dizzy, that passing out was an actual possibility. "Evan..." he called again, sounding further away still. "Shit," he snapped, reaching for me just as I seemed to do the absolute most lame thing any person could do.

I freaking *fainted.*

"I have got to stop leaving my invisible spinning wheels right outside my front door. You must have pricked your finger."

That was what I woke up to.

And, even dazed, I couldn't seem to stop the laugh that came from somewhere deep. "Nice reference. What man knows *Little Briar Rose*?"

"Don't know what backward fucking world you were raised in, doll, but in the US, we call that story *Sleeping Beauty*, and it is a Disney classic."

"Disney. With the mouse," I recalled, finally opening my eyes.

"With the mouse," he repeated, sounding almost vaguely... offended?

"Yeah, you know... with the steamboat and the whistling. Mick."

"Mick*ey*," he corrected, eyes big, mouth catching flies. "How the fuck do you not know the name of Mickey Mouse?"

"I grew up in rainforests and deserts," I defended immediately. Was he really insinuating that my childhood was lacking just because I didn't know the name of some fictional rodent?

"You've seriously never seen a Disney movie?"

"I've really only seen a handful of movies ever. And all of them were Spanish."

"You can't be serious," he said again, looking downright mystified at the very idea.

"I read a lot," I defended, shrugging. Books were easier to carry around traveling than a portable DVD player and a set of DVDs. We had to travel as light as possible.

"Okay, we are going to lay those cinema sins of yours aside for another time," he said, shaking his head like he couldn't get rid of some niggling thought.

"How magnanimous of you."

"Magnanimous. Now that thur is that'a book learning talkin,'" he drawled in a thick accent. "Gettin' all kinds of thoughts in that thur head, making ya' think yer good for anything more than cookin' and stuffin.'"

Okay.

So Luce had a sense of humor.

And I maybe found it hilarious because I had totally encountered a man while moving through the south that spoke exactly like that.

"There you go," he said, a small smile spreading, making his eyes brighten. "That put a little color in your face." He reached out then, touching my forehead. "No fever. Probably just from the hike and the surprise." He paused, lips twitching. "Or maybe you were just overcome with how fucking good looking I am."

"Yeah, that must be it," I laughed, though maybe more than a small part of me was in complete agreement about his attractiveness. But all humor aside, I had passed out. From *shock?* My lip curled. "I can't believe I *fainted*."

"Evan, you've had a fuck of a couple of days. Judging by how pale you are, you haven't been sleeping. Or eating. Then you trek up this hill, and realize you've been dosed with arsenic. It's frankly pretty astonishing that you haven't taken to your bed in dramatics over all this shit."

Well, that made me feel marginally better.

"Neck is hot though," he said, the cold brush of the backs of his fingers touching the skin of my neck and upper chest, making a shudder course through me.

"It's just hot out," I allowed.

"Yeah," he said, trying to hold back a smirk, likely seeing it for what it was - desire - but letting it drop. "That must be it. Alright. Stay put. I'm getting you some electrolytes and something to eat."

With that, he was gone, his absence seeming to allow whatever pressure was on my chest to ease, and for me to take my first deep breath in several minutes.

And it was also the first chance I got to look around his place.

And, well, it sort of solidified the idea of the loner old man I had thought earlier. So much so that I was pretty sure next to nothing inside actually belonged to Luce. It probably all came with the cabin. From the olive-colored and too-firm couch I was laying on, to the scuffed and wide coffee table, to the dusty-looking window treatments, built-in cabinets, and the framed wall art of what seemed to be military pictures, but it was hard to tell from far away.

The only things that seemed likely to be his were the huge flatscreen TV and a giant collection of DVDs.

So Luce was a cinephile.

No wonder he seemed to almost take an affront to my lack of exposure to movies. Window treatments aside, and likely because I couldn't think of a single straight man who would think to vacuum or wash those like a woman would, the place was clean. Spotless almost. Hell, the coffee table, while scuffed, was super shiny like someone had recently taken Pledge to it. As if to prove that fact, even with the sun casting across it, I couldn't make out a single fingerprint.

Which was strange.

Who didn't touch their own stuff?

There was a slamming sound from behind me as I pushed myself slowly upward, careful to make sure that I pushed the lightheadedness aside because I wasn't some southern bell for whom fainting was sweet and delicate.

I was not sweet and delicate.

I had seen men gunned down in the streets of Colombia.

I had seen monks flagellating themselves in the Philippines.

I had seen babies be stillborn to mothers who died soon after in huts in Africa.

I was not some shrinking violet.

I took another deep breath, swiveling my head to where the noise Luce was making was coming from. I could see a partial doorway and a window showing me some of the woods out back, but that was it.

It was another full five minutes before Luce reappeared, two bottles tucked under an arm, and plates in his hands.

"I can't make some bomb ass burrito," he said, shrugging. "But I make a pretty mediocre sandwich. Which you are gonna fucking eat. I don't care if my tastebuds are mistaken about it being palatable, and it actually tastes like sawdust. You need to eat." With that, he dropped the plate none-too-ceremoniously onto my lap, revealing a sandwich that could have easily fed me for two meals, a cut up apple, and a handful of chips. Apple aside, it was total man-food. And it was utterly charming to be perfectly honest.

"Where'd you get your medical degree, doctor?" I asked, watching as he put an energy drink on the table. The last thing it seemed like he needed was caffeine. He needed sleep. But then again, so did I, so I had no place to talk I guess. Then he did the damnedest thing. He put what I assumed was my bottle of light blue Gatorade on his knee... and opened the cap for me.

It was such a little thing.

And maybe I even should have been offended that he thought my little girly hands couldn't open a bottle.

But I wasn't.

I was completely, almost foolishly charmed by the action.

"What?" he asked, making me realize his hand was extended to me, and I was just staring at him like an idiot.

"You opened the cap," I explained, not knowing what else to say.

"Yeah, you a germaphobe or something?" he asked, completely in the dark.

"No," I said, smiling a little.

"Then what's the problem?"

Nothing.

There was absolutely no problem whatsoever.

Except maybe I was beginning to really find him interesting. It was likely not smart or healthy, but it was just how it was. He was a fascinating character, case closed.

"No problem," I insisted as I took the drink with a hand that was, admittedly, a bit weaker than was usual, and brought it up to take a sip.

"You eat. I'll load up *Sleeping Beauty*," he informed me, reaching for a remote to turn the TV screen from black to some weird app screen instead. "Then after you eat, we have some shit to discuss."

"Right," I agreed, reaching for the both soft and crunchy sandwich bread, noticing he had taken the time to slice lettuce and tomato onto it, not just slapped on meat and cheese and called it a sandwich. "Like who is poisoning me, and why."

"Well, that," he agreed, not looking at me as he scrolled through a page of movies so fast that it was nauseating. "But more so the fact that I did some research last night."

"On?" I asked bringing the sandwich up to my mouth, and taking a healthy bite.

I should have waited until he answered.

I realized this when I almost choked on my mouthful when he spoke again.

"Think I have a lead on when Alejandro picked you up and claimed you as his own."

"What?" My shout was muffled by the aforementioned mouthful, making him turn to see my assuredly bulging cheeks as I frantically tried to chew.

"Yeah. But right now, we're eating, and watching a Disney classic. Please hold all your questions until after the feature," he added in a very cinematic voice, making me smile.

I choked back my questions, varied and desperate as they were, acknowledging that I did, in fact, need to eat. If small shocks were enough to make me *faint*, then I definitely needed to make sure my blood sugar levels were evened out before I received any more news that I needed to mull over.

Besides, I was actually maybe a little excited about the idea of watching a movie. I had been too busy traveling most of my life to really sit and enjoy one. And since I had been back in the states, I had been doing nothing but grieving the loss of my father, looking for leads on what might have happened to him, burying an empty casket, and then finally finding Luce, and tracking him down, building the cell in the basement, working out all the kinks.

It simply never seemed like a priority.

And maybe I was a little old for Disney fairytales, but as the opening scene started, I couldn't seem to bring myself to look away.

Sometime during the movie, I had brought my legs up on the couch, crossing them, absentmindedly eating the sandwich that was not 'mediocre' in any way. In fact, instead of a bottled condiment, I was pretty sure he swiped fresh pesto onto the roll.

"So?" Luce asked as the credits rolled.

"It's... cute."

"That is lacking enthusiasm."

"Does Disney ever, I don't know, make movies that aren't so insta-lovey? I mean, she's in a coma, gets kissed, and then it's love? Get real."

He chuckled at that, tossing his chips onto my plate. "Modern Disney sometimes doesn't make the chick have a love interest at all. They're smashing that patriarchy, man. I bet you'd love a little Merida, Moana, or Elsa."

"Oh!" I said, excited. "I've heard of Elsa."

"Of course you have," he said, reaching for his energy drink, and popping the top. "I think you could be in a cave ten miles away from civilization, and that goddamn soundtrack would still come creeping through the walls somehow." He raised his hand, taking a long swig of his toxic-looking bright green drink. "So have I made a movie lover out of you?"

"I could maybe consider watching something non-animated sometime."

"Feeling less fainty?"

"I'm pretty sure 'fainty' isn't a word."

"Sure it is; I just said it. If they can add the word 'cray' to the *Oxford Dictionary*, then I can fucking say fainty all I want."

"Can't fault that logic, though I have no idea what 'cray' is. Is it an abbreviation for crayfish?"

That, apparently, was hilarious to Luce.

I knew this because one minute, he seemed mildly amused by me. The next, he was throwing his head back like a little boy, letting out a sexy rumbling laugh that seemed to somehow slip inside my skin, swarm around my insides, and turn my belly to mush.

"It means crazy," he told me recovering. "Christ, you really have been sheltered from the modern world, huh?"

"Tell me one good thing I have truly been 'missing out' about in the modern world."

"Aside from movies?" he asked, and waited for my nod even though it seemed rhetorical. "The internet. Online shopping. Never having to leave the house if you don't want to."

"Why would you not want to leave the house?" I countered, genuinely curious.

"Have you *met* people? They suck. Most of them anyway," he said, knocking his knee into mine in a way that implied that present company was excluded.

"I think you spend too much time holed up in your old man cabin, Luce."

"My old-man cabin?" he repeated, brow quirked.

"An old man definitely lived here," I shot back, sure of it.

"Died here too," Luce agreed, nodding.

"Not on this couch, right?"

He chuckled at that. "No. Downstairs. Watched it happen."

"Wait... what? Oh," I said, remembering again who he was, what he did. "Did you kill him?"

"You know, doll, I don't fucking kill everyone I come in contact with. No, I didn't kill him. He was this survivalist doomsday nut job who had this vlog on the dark web full of asinine conspiracy theories anyone with brain cells would know are complete crap. Anyway, he was raging out one day, getting all red, then dropped dead of a heart attack right there in his cellar."

"So... you ended up here because..."

"Because I saw an opportunity. My job might be for the greater good, but the payout, especially at the beginning, wasn't great. So I dragged my ass to Navesink Bank, I climbed up that hill, and I broke in. I filled out a fake will, forged his signature, and left it in an easy-to-find drawer. Took me for-fucking-ever to figure out the secret door to downstairs to find him though. And I don't think I need to tell you how rank a week-old body is. Set him up in his kitchen. Left. Called the cops saying I was concerned because I was used to seeing him around, and knew he lived alone. They found him and dealt with the body. The public administrator came in to investigate for wills or heirs, found the fake one, voila, I have a home, and land, a sinful amount of MREs, and a small nest egg to use to invest in lye."

"And black hoodies," I observed.

"Exactly," he said with a smirk.

"What is an MRE?"

"Meals, ready to eat. They are military rations. They're supposedly good for just about ever."

"Wow, must be tasty," I laughed.

"Hey, nut jobs gotta eat, man." There was a short, but strained silence before he reached to put my plate on the coffee table. "So, you ready now? Feeling all fainted-out?"

"I think I should be able to withstand the shock. What did you find?"

"Not as much as I would like. Actually, do you have your old passports on you?"

I did.

That was likely weird for normal people. I spent so much time traveling that I always had my current one. But I kept my old ones on me as well, as tokens. They almost felt like a security blanket. It felt almost irrationally wrong to be without them. "Yeah. Why?" I asked as I reached for my purse that must have slipped off my shoulder outside to be retrieved by Luce.

"Just want to compare something," he said, reaching for a folder on the table.

As I handed him the little blue fold with the little circle cut out of it, indicating its expiration, I saw another appear from the file, making my skin immediately chill, and my stomach twist. "Is that my father's?"

"It's Alejandro's, yes," he said, nodding, as he flipped mine open to the first page, then went several pages longer in my father's. "Yep. I thought so."

"You thought what?" I asked as he just kept looking at the stamps.

"McAllen, Texas."

"What about McAllen, Texas?"

"Alejandro has a stamp in here for Dallas on June 11th of this particular year. And then I found an article about a suspicious poisoning in McAllen on the 18th. Some pain in the ass sheriff who was getting to close to figuring out how the cartel operated. Then just two days later, he has an entry stamp for Mexico. And suddenly you do as well." He stopped, looking at me, looking for me, I was sure, to agree with him. "You would have been three here. Why was this the first time you showed up on paper?"

"Maybe I lived with my relatives. That's what he always told me. His life wasn't conducive to dealing with a screaming infant. He took me when I would be less work. Which sounds horrible repeated, but I mean... I understand that logic."

"Sure. Maybe. But I think it is more likely you never met Alejandro Cruz until sometime between the 11th and 18th of June."

"I think Old Man Loonybin must have left some of his residual conspiracy theory energy around here. And you, my dear, have soaked it up or something."

"Just, hear me out," he said, reaching for his folder.

"Well, I guess I owe you that after drugging, abducting, and holding you prisoner."

"How... *magnanimous*," he threw my earlier word back at me. "Anyway. McAllen, Texas. It is one of the most immigrant-packed border towns there is. And thanks to local churches being, well, all churchy about opening their doors, they often become asylums. Especially to women and children."

"You think my mother traveled in with me from Mexico? You know how long a walk through the desert that is, right? How hot? How many adults don't make it all the way? How would my mother make it with me in tow?"

"People can be weak, singularly. A mother, on the other hand, I don't think there is a fiercer creature on the planet. Depending on what she was trying to escape, what life she was trying to provide for you away from that, she could have done it with you strapped to her back for an extra week if that was what she needed to do. Besides, you're being pretty literal about 'crossing the border.' There are plenty of underground tunnels as well. For the right amount."

"Okay, so let's suspend reality for a moment and say she crossed over with me into McAllen, Texas. What then? What next? Your trail is cold from there."

"My trail is cold online from there, yeah. Records from Mexico are hard at best to get. Many areas aren't as... digitalized as we are here."

"So you're proposing I visit McAllen, Texas? Go knock on the doors, and ask anyone if *twenty-four* years ago they remember a mother and her young daughter? Get real, Luce."

"There's also this," he said, looking grave, like maybe he was hesitant to share it. He reached for a scanned copy of a newspaper, handing it to me."

"Oh, fun. A parade!" I mocked enthusiasm.

"Smartass, one column below."

And there it was.

And maybe it was a bit of a long shot.

It happened every day. It happened every *three minutes* in the US alone.

But considering the other evidence, it was hard to deny the probability.

"'An unnamed immigrant was severely beaten and assaulted,'" I started reading, feeling the sandwich roll around in my stomach.

"Alright, there's that paleness again," he said, ripping the page out of my hand. He had literally ripped it too; a corner was still between my thumb and forefinger. "The gist is, she was treated, and released. Reports said she maybe went to the St. Christopher Church in McAllen. But that was all there was. I know it doesn't sound like much, but if there is anything I have learned in this line of work, it's that if something looks fishy, it is. And if you keep digging, you'll find that rotten fish."

"So you think I should go to Texas and... dig."

I could do it.

Fact of the matter was, my father left a lot of money. True, in most cases, you needed a death certificate to get a dead parent's money. And when there is no body, to get a death certificate in absentia, it takes seven years.

You know, if you did things legally.

If you used banks.

My father didn't exactly obtain his money legally. To avoid getting into trouble with the IRS, he just stashed it every time we crossed into the states, just keeping out enough for the next leg of our travels.

I never actually went with him when he pulled into the storage center in the wee hours of the night, so before he went missing, I had no idea how much he had stored there.

But, well, poisons experts the likes of his skill set and knowledge were rare. And rarity, in every single aspect of life, was rewarded handsomely.

So when I ferreted out the key, found the storage locker, and stepped inside, I wasn't overly shocked with the stacks of money, jewels, and even a stash of diamonds I found.

It was enough to set me up for the next fifteen years with me doing nothing but sitting on my ass.

It was certainly enough to get me my modest home, get some furniture, build a prison in the basement, and maybe take a trip to Texas to look for answers.

"You really think it's wise to be doing any digging into your past on your own with your newfound fainting condition?"

"It's not a condition!" I squeaked, shaking my head. "I've just been... overwhelmed is all."

"Think it is going to be any less overwhelming to find out the truth about your mom and Alejandro?"

He had a point there.

"I'll... invest in some smelling salts and wear them around my neck," I said with a smile.

His deep eyes watched me for a long minute, unreadable, as they almost always seemed to be.

"Just ask me to come, Evan."

Whoa.

Don't ask me why, but those words, and maybe the depth with which he said them, sent a weird fluttery feeling across my belly.

Ask him to come?

Of all the insane, asinine, yet somehow completely appealing ideas.

Did I want him to come? I sort of did.

Was that pretty nuts? Ah, hells yeah.

Then again, the whole situation was nuts.

So, what could it hurt, right?
"Come with me, Luce."

EIGHT

Luce

Don't fucking ask me why I asked her to ask me to go with her.

I was not that guy.

I didn't go on road trips to solve mysteries.

I didn't make friends with practical strangers.

In fact, the only time I traveled was to find my marks and bring them back with me. And that was only when I couldn't find a way to trick them into coming to me, which was rare. Usually, I could just make a post for the perverts about some new den where they could get their rape on with underage boys or girls, and they just came running. Paying an upfront fee for entrance too.

Fucking suckers.

Truly got what was coming to them.

But yeah, I didn't do random trips to random towns in fucking Texas to go dig up twenty-four-year-old dirt.

Yet somehow, I was doing just that.

What can I say, I fucking liked Evan.

She was different.

There were equal parts silk and steel to her.

On top of that, I just got this weird feeling like she needed a friend. Normally, I'd just ignore that urge to forge bonds, calling it what it was - stupid and reckless. I just couldn't seem to make myself do that in this situation.

A part of me wanted to claim it was just the story, just the untied ends, just my almost compulsive urge to know the truth, to know I was right. But the other part of me seemed to acknowledge that it was something more than that.

Though, whatever *more* it might have been, was just going to be friendly.

No more kissing.

No more imagining her touching herself while thinking of me.

No more rubbing one out and thinking about her begging for my cock.

Fuck.

Seeing as even thinking those things had me half-hard, yeah, this whole part of the plan was going to take some real goddamn willpower.

"So, when are you free to go?" she asked after what must have been a tense silence with me all lost in my own thoughts.

Ah, yeah.

We were doing this shit.

Planning.

Comparing schedules.

I had never had to plan shit except traps and escape routes before.

"Ah, I just have some fucking shithead to deal with first," I said, realizing I had spent the whole day researching Evan's shit and not working on my own.

What the hell was wrong with me?

"Oh, yeah. About that," she said, nipping into her lower lip slightly, looking guilty as hell.

"About what?" I prompted when she didn't go on.

"That shithead isn't real. That page and that robot voice on the phone..."

"No shit," I said, finding myself smiling when I should have been raging mad. First, because a connection was compromised. Second, because that contact didn't think to *tell me* they were compromised.

"I needed to lure you out so I could follow you," she admitted. "And maybe get your mind occupied, so you didn't see me coming."

"Mission accomplished," I said, unzipping my hoodie slightly, so I could pull the back down and show her the nasty ass bruise I had across the back of my neck.

"Ow," she hissed. "Sorry. I, ah, really threw all my rage into that swing. I've never hit someone before. I had no idea how much force it would take to take you down."

"More force is usually the best bet," I agreed, zipping my hoodie back up. "Well, then... my schedule is clear. I don't exactly have a nine-to-five here."

"It might be good for you to get out of here too."

"So the Old Man Loonybin conspiracy theorist energy stops getting soaked in through my pores."

"Exactly," she agreed with a small laugh. "Oh," she said, suddenly looking crestfallen.

"Oh, what?"

"Oh, Diego."

"Yeah, I'm gonna need more than that, doll."

"My bird," she explained.

"Your macaw," I specified, still feeling pretty damn proud of myself for calling that one.

"Yes, my blue and gold macaw, Diego. I can't bring him. I mean, he's been on a plane before. But there was always an RV or van or something on the other end where he could move around. And I don't think hotels let you bring birds. I just... I don't know anyone who would be willing to take him on. And I don't want to board him."

I rubbed my chin, feeling the stubble, making a mental note to shave that off before we left. "I might know someone."

"Do they like birds?"

"Sure," I agreed, nodding.

I was sure he maybe had, you know, enjoyed the look or sounds of a bird from afar at some point or another. Then again, maybe not. He was a weird fuck.

But considering I had done him and his friends a big fat favor a while back, I was going to go ahead and call in the marker.

Barrett might have been trapped in his own head a lot, too smart for his own good, and anti-social, but he was a good guy. He would probably spend ten hours researching macaw care, and Evan would come home to the healthiest fucking parrot on the east coast.

"Do you think they could do it on short notice?"

"Yeah, he's not busy. I can swing by and let him know to expect him whenever you are ready to leave, and then you can come and drop him off."

"Okay, well. I need to go and look into flights and stuff. But if we can maybe get going before the weekend..."

"You give me the day and time, and we can make it happen."

"Alright, um," she said, looking around for something else to say, but there wasn't anything. "Thanks for the catching me when I fainted thing."

"Super leading man of me, right? That shit should make its way into that erotica."

Fuck.

I shouldn't have said that.

Because her eyes got heated, man. And I was trying to be all noble and keep my dick in line with the 'just friends' idea.

"Very dreamy," she said, voice blank, recovering quickly. "And thanks for the food and movie and company and... you know..." she trailed off, shrugging.

"I know?" I prompted, wanting to know whatever it was she thought I could silently pick up on. I couldn't.

"For, I don't know, kinda... being a friend," she said, sounding strained.

"Doll," I said, standing as she did as well, "if you're happy to have me as a friend, you got some pretty fucked up ideas about what constitutes a good friend. But you're welcome for the food and movie and, you know, the pleasure of my company," I said with a smirk, trying to lighten the mood.

"Do you, um, have a cell I can contact you on? You know... without having to use the pager system?"

That, well, that was asking for a fuckuva lot.

I didn't give a direct line out to anyone.

Literally no one.

"Ah, one sec," I surprised myself by saying, walking into the bedroom and grabbing one of the boxes off the dresser. I bought burners by the fucking cart-full. "Alright, this one, this will be just for contact between you and me. Give this number out, and you will have to be the next body melting in my tub," I warned, but there wasn't a drop of sincerity in the threat and we both knew it.

"Like I have anyone to give it out to anyway," she said as she typed it into her phone. And her voice when she said it, well, it was sad. Hollow, almost.

It was a pretty awful thing to realize that a vigilante serial killer who melted bodies in tubs and couldn't seem to have any normal relationships with people was your only goddamn 'friend' in the world.

"Okay, all set. I will text you about the flights. Text me when you get an answer from your friend."

"Will do."

"You need to install a slide or something on this hill," she informed me as I walked her to the door, and watched her eye the hill in question with distaste. "Oh, and you might want to, I don't know, pack some t-shirts or something. It's hot in Texas."

With that, she was gone.

Well, not gone.

In fact, she wasn't out of sight for almost half an hour, and my crazy fucking ass stood there and watched until she pulled away.

Once she was gone, I locked up, and made my way down the hill as well, walking my ass all the way into town and to Barrett's office.

"Yo," I called when he looked at me from his periphery, then just went back to work, likely thinking I was just there to use the john to make a call.

"What's up, Luce?" he asked, reaching up to scrub his hands down his face.

He looked like he had lost a night of sleep too.

I felt bad for the fuck sometimes.

It couldn't have been easy to be the younger brother to the best PI in town, always having to work so much harder to get even a fraction of the recognition that he did. The crazy thing was, Barrett was about a thousand times better than his brother in the computer and research department, but with Sawyer's special forces training, there was no way Barrett could come close to his hand-to-hand skills. It was a shame the two of them never could figure out how to work with each other without wanting to kill one another. And they had tried.

"Calling in a marker," I explained, leaning against the wall, my arms folded over my chest.

"*You*?" he asked, not even pretending to hide his astonishment. I never needed help. I always worked alone. "You need to call in your marker? I swear I was sure your headstone would say: Barrett, you still owe me."

"Yeah, well, this isn't work-related. Personal favor."

"Well, seeing as you're every bit as good at computers as me, and seem to have no interest in learning Polish... what? Do you need me to water your plants and take in your mail?" he asked, voice full of sarcasm.

"I need you to bird-sit."

I swear there was a solid five beats before his brows went back down. "Bird-sit?"

"Parrot actually. Blue and gold macaw."

"Since the fuck when are you a bird person?"

"I'm not. It's for a, ah, friend of mine."

"I wasn't aware you *had* any friends."

"Right, because your social calendar is booked solid."

"So, you're serious. You have a macaw you need me to watch."

"Yep."

"When? For how long?"

"Um, I don't know yet, but soon. And for however long a trip to Texas is going to take."

"Do I want to know?"

"It's a long story," I said with a shrug.

"Then, no, I don't want to know. This thing isn't going to take my finger off, is it?"

"Fuck if I know. I've never even seen it. Just heard it while I was locked in a basement cell last night."

"Basement cell," he repeated, brows drawing together.

"Misunderstanding about a murder that was actually a suicide."

"Ah," he said, like he knew exactly what happened.

"Oh, wait," I said when my phone rang in my pocket. It was such a foreign thing for me that I actually jumped. "Might have more details in a sec," I explained as I swiped the screen.

"Is that... a cell? That was... ringing?"

"It's looking like the day after tomorrow at, say, ten AM. She will come by and drop off all the stuff he needs. I will keep you updated via text on when we might be back. So I need your... what?" I asked when all he did was stare at me.

"Who the hell are *you*?" he asked, shaking his head. "You suddenly have a friend who you are going on some road trip with. You have a cell, and you are actually programming numbers into it. What the hell happened in that basement Luce?"

That was actually a pretty valid question, one I knew I would have to mull over myself. Sometime. But not today.

"Dunno man. I'm evolving I guess. So you'll do it."

"I, ah, well it gives me some time to research."

What did I say?

In a day or so, Barrett was going to be the foremost blue and gold macaw expert in the country. He was a prime example of why some seemingly cold, robotic people could actually make good assets in life. Maybe he wasn't going to kiss the fucking bird's beak or some shit, but he would feed it right, make sure it slept, shit, exercised, and behaved like it was supposed to.

A day and a half later, I was standing in Barrett's office with a huge smirk.

Because it wasn't his office anymore. Not really. Sure, his desk was still there, and his office equipment was where it always had been, but all of the limited free space had been turned into a mini bird jungle.

No shit.

There was stuff hanging from the ceilings and huge tree limb play stands all over. There was an overhead light that he explained was full-spectrum because, apparently, if birds didn't get enough of the right lighting, they actually stopped seeing color. Which, he went on to explain, would make their eating habits change for the worse because they couldn't see what they were eating properly.

I swear to fuck he told me all this shit in the three minutes between when I showed up and when Evan walked through the door.

She did so with the bird in question sitting on her hand. It was looking around curiously, but not seeming the least bit spooked. "Oh wow," she said, stopping short, looking at me with big eyes for a second, questioning, then looking at Barrett. "I think you're going to take better care of him than I do," she said, sounding almost a little guilty about that.

"I did some parrot research, but are there any specific things I need to know about him?"

Oh, Barrett. All about the facts. He didn't even know her name. Or the bird's.

"Ah, well he isn't clipped, so he flies all over. He screams at sun up and down, but only for a little while. If you give him cauliflower, he will throw it. If you give him blackberries, he will... just don't give him blackberries. Trust me. He talks and he only nips when you are trying to get him to do something he doesn't want to. He's pretty good, all in all. And he's used to moving around and strangers, so he shouldn't be nervous or self-destructive being away from me for a few days."

"His diet?"

"Pellets, seed as treats, and fresh veggies and fruit when he will eat them."

"Alright. That's all I need to know."

"Well, his name is Diego," Evan said, brow lifted. "You might need to know that."

"Figured he would tell me himself," Barrett said, approaching the giant bird with a massive beak, and offering his hand without even an ounce of fear. I wondered if that was part of Barrett's thing, his whatever-it-was that made him just a little different from everyone else. Did it also make him foolishly fearless?

But the bird responded to his confidence and stepped right up, letting out a caw that made me wince.

"Alright. We will keep you updated via text," I reminded him, as he seemed to completely ignore us, bringing the bird over to his new jungle, and introducing him to the places where the food dishes and water were. "Might as well get going now, doll. We lost him."

She looked at me, then back to Barrett who was giving Diego scratches, then back to me. "Ah, yeah, okay. Let's get going. Do you have everything?" she asked. I reached down, grabbing my backpack, and picking it up. "That's it? Really?"

"That's it, really," I agreed, nodding. I didn't exactly have an extensive wardrobe.

"Are you seriously wearing the hoodie on the plane?" she asked as we headed outside toward her car, storing my bag in the back with her modest duffle. Moving around as much as she had, she must have known how to economize with her carry-on.

"I'd be more worried about the recycled air, MRSA armrests, and screaming babies than my hoodie, Ev," I said, giving her a small smile.

"Oh, you're gonna be a fun flight-buddy, huh?" she teased, rolling her eyes. We climbed in and made our way to the airport.

"I told you not to wear the hoodie," she said after the TSA guard made me take it off to look me over and pat me down. I guess I looked like a criminal. You know, because I was one.

"Yeah, yeah, yeah," I said, shrugging back into it like armor. "You done 'told you so'ing? Can we get on the big metal germ incubator now?"

She laughed, the sound warm and musical.

"You're ridiculous," she declared, whacking her shoulder into mine as she said it, like she was saying she liked that about me.

And that, yeah, I liked that too much.

This trip was going to be all kinds of revealing; not just for Evan but me as well.

I couldn't decide if that was a good thing or not.

NINE

Evan

I think he was insecure about his scars.

That was why he had insisted on wearing a hoodie on a flight that was going to land somewhere that would make both of us break out into a sweat in minutes.

I had gotten a peek of some once before, but I had no idea they were as extensive as they were until the TSA agent made him take off his hoodie, leaving him in a simple black tee instead, his arms on full display.

And there were scars.

There were *a lot* of scars.

Some looked like deep gashes, like maybe the people he had killed had scratched him. Others though, they looked odd. Round. Very perfectly round. And I had the bone-deep feeling that they were cigarette and cigar burns. The skin was raised and puckered like it did with the remains of burns like that. My father had had one on the top of his hand in the triangle between the thumb and forefinger from some gang leader who got their hands on him once.

There were others too, ones that weren't as superficial as the scratches; they looked like gouges had been taken out of his flesh, then left untreated so that the skin had needed to try to grow over the missing spots, not being sewn together with stitches, making them neat.

Painful.

Whatever had done that had to have hurt like a mother.

I couldn't imagine.

And whatever had caused them was obviously not something he wanted to talk about. That was why he kept them covered at all times.

What darkness must he have known?

"Nope," he said suddenly, making me jump, so long lost in my own thoughts that I realized I had followed him on auto-pilot into the plane and down the aisle without noticing.

"Nope, what?"

"Nope, I want the aisle," he clarified, bumping my shoulder, and effectively almost sending me falling into the seat.

"Such a gentleman," I said, rolling my eyes at him as I dropped down.

"That's me, regular fucking Ashley Wilkes. You should know that reference from all your book learning," he added, fastening his seatbelt.

"*Gone With the Wind.*"

"That's the one. Another good flick. If you have four hours to spare."

"You're totally going to make me watch the in-flight movie, aren't you?"

"Well, look at that," he declared, smirking. "We can watch *Moana*," he said, sounding excited. "And by 'can,' I mean 'will be,'" he declared.

A couple minutes later, we were.

And it was cute.

But I was maybe a little more distracted than I should have been by the fact that we were kinda sharing an armrest, that I could feel his body heat through the material of his sleeve, that he didn't pull away when mine moved there. It was like being sixteen all over again.

Which, apparently, meant I totally had a - and I cringe using this word as a grown ass adult - crush on the strange, scarred, occasionally hilarious, always mysterious, very skilled kisser known as Luce.

Really, there was no denying it.

Not when I was hyper aware of tiny, inconsequential things like his arm brushing mine, his body heat, and the way his eyes danced when he said something funny. That all added up to crush, no matter what way you tried to work the equation.

Smart?

No.

Logical?

Well, of course not.

But there was the feeling nonetheless.

I figured maybe the trip was good. Maybe being around him for a couple days straight in stifling heat while in a somewhat emotionally-charged situation would cure me of it.

Or, you know, maybe we would end up a tangled pile of sweaty limbs after intense world-shattering orgasms.

Either way.

I was willing to take that 'risk.'

"So?" he asked when the movie ended, reaching over to pull my headphones off.

"I want a pig," I declared, making him chuckle. "Puaa means pig in Hawaiian. That didn't take much imagination."

"Like Heifer from *Rocko's Modern Life*. Oh, yeah," he said, sighing, "I forgot. Your childhood never taught you that r-e-c-y-c-l-e song. How the hell did you ever learn how to spell 'conserve' without that show?"

"Um... a dictionary?" I suggested.

He snorted at that. "Nerd," he accused. "So, from Houston, where are we heading?"

Luce had literally left every little detail of the travel planning to me. I knew he was normally an almost alarmingly meticulous stickler for details in his work, but maybe because this wasn't his work per se, he was alright with riding passenger, and letting me handle all the plans.

"I have a car rental from the airport. It is a five-hour drive from the airport to McAllen where we can crash for the night. We're gonna be beat by then."

"And where are we crashing?"

"Well, I did do my best to try to find a cabin in the woods on a hill with old man vibes, but, alas, Texas is flat and not big on the woods department. Plenty of old men, though. Maybe one will have left his energy in the walls of your hotel room. It is very, ah, southern decor-wise. I'm pretty sure I saw framed pictures of cowboy boots on one of the walls. It's a nice place. And only fifteen minutes from the church you mentioned."

"Sounds good."

"Maybe you'll be able to get some sleep there," I said at the strained silence, making his head snap over to look at me curiously. "Come on, not even all the caffeine can hide the fact that you're not sleeping."

"I go through phases," he evaded, shrugging like it was no big deal.

"Well, maybe a change of scenery will help."

"Yeah, maybe."

There wasn't even a shred of optimism in his voice.

And I couldn't help but wonder what his phases were, what caused them, what made them go away again. Was it simply all the darkness he had involved himself in? Behind his lids when he tried to rest at night, did he see men begging for their lives, taking their last breaths, dead bodies melting in a tub?

These were all questions that would seemingly go unanswered because for the rest of the flight, he cold-shouldered me. He wasn't outwardly all that difference except he kept his focus out toward the aisle so I couldn't catch his eyes to start another conversation.

I had a feeling he was being touchy because I hit a nerve. Maybe between seeing his scars earlier and calling him on his sleeplessness, he was feeling a little exposed. A man like him, living behind his guards, behind his long sleeves and hood, hiding in his woods away from the world, I was pretty sure he wasn't used to having anyone even attempt to get close to him.

I mean, even his private investigator friend Barrett didn't exactly seem like a friend. The two men interacted like two people who used to hang out when they were teens and hadn't seen each other in a decade. They were both equally odd characters, sure, and maybe that had more to do with it than Luce's inability to connect. For all I knew, maybe they watched sports together and hit the town to pick up chicks every week.

That last idea made my belly wobble slightly, completely irrationally, I knew, but it happened none the less.

I needed to get ahold of those crushy-type feelings for the man.

This would prove nearly impossible, though, once we got through a very tense car ride where I drove, and Luce played captain of the radio. This was fine by me because, well, I didn't know any of the damn songs anyway. I could feel Luce's eyes on my profile when a song he must have found particularly popular, poignant, good, or all three, looking for some sign of recognition. When he found none, there was a quiet sighing or tisking.

Other than this, and the occasional directions from the English-sounding GPS lady on my phone, the ride was painfully silent.

We didn't talk.

He didn't make jokes at my expense.

And me, well, I couldn't think of anything to say.

Oh, look, another horse, seemed a bit lame.

The outside of the hotel was a warm sandy-colored stucco, very Spanish villa styled, massive, and there was a fair amount of greenery that I found impressive given the oppressive dry heat.

Me, I had experienced all kinds of heat in my travels.

In my humble opinion, nothing was worse than dry. It pressed down on your chest and made breathing more like an idea than an actuality.

We grabbed our respective bags and moved into the lobby where I let out a snort because, not only was there a framed picture of cowboy boots as I had insinuated, but there was also a framed picture of a cowboy hat, one of a spur, and one of a cactus. Sure, they were kinda modern with bright primary colors, but they were still incredibly, almost offensively southwestern. Were the locals even into things like that? Who knew.

"I'm sorry, Miss Cruz," the young woman at the service desk said, looking up from her computer, looking competent and professional in her crisp white shirt. How she didn't sweat through it on the way to work was beyond me.

The blood thins was something someone once told me in Alabama when I complained about a particularly bad heat wave.

Maybe people who grew up in certain climates weren't as affected by them as people who visited them were.

"But I have you down for one room with two queens, not two rooms with a queen in each."

"What? No," I insisted, shaking my head, feeling like an idiot. "No, that's not possible."

"It can be hard on the online form, ma'am," she went on, looking apologetic and seemingly unconcerned with how my lip curled at the word 'ma'am.' I was hardly a *ma'am*, damnit. I was still squarely within the *miss* category. "Those two options are stacked. You probably just hit the wrong button."

Ugh.

I guess that was entirely possible.

"You done fucked up," Luce said, low, leaning on the desk with his back to the woman. It was maybe the first time he spoke directly to me aside from helping me read street signs since the plane. And when my gaze went over, he looked amused at said fuck up.

"Right. I'm sorry for the misunderstanding," I said, giving her a smile. "Is there any way... what?" I asked because halfway into my speech, she was already shaking her head at me.

"I'm sorry, ma'am." Oh, she was really digging her grave with the ma'am shit. I was hot. I was stiff and irritated from travel. My stomach was growling. And I was almost irrationally irritated with the distance between myself and my travel companion. In short, I was grumpy, and I was not in the mood for hospitality nonsense. "There is a convention in our event room this week. We are full-up."

"Of course you are," I grumbled, closing my eyes, taking a deep breath, trying to not flip on her since, sins of the 'ma'am' aside, it was not her fault. "I guess we will go somewhere..."

"Just check us into the room you have us down for, *ma'am*," Luce said, making my eyes snap open to find his lips twitching, like he knew I was pissy over that word, like he knew exactly what he was doing saying it to the woman who was at least two or three years younger than me.

I had to press my lips together when she immediately stiffened, her smile falling for a beat, before it got replaced by a glacial hospitality-fake one.

"You get grumpy as fuck when you travel, huh?" he asked as she clicked away at her computer.

"Says the guy who has had his panties in a bunch for five hours and wouldn't speak to me. The silent treatment is childish, Luce. In case you weren't aware. If you have a problem with me, you tell me."

I could feel his eyes on my profile, almost surprised he didn't bore holes into my skin with their intensity. But I kept my focus on the woman at the desk as she started her little spiel.

When I was handed the keycards, I thanked her, turned on my heel, and started toward the elevators she had pointed to, not bothering to wait for Luce to see if he was coming or not.

He did, however, catch up and slip into the elevator with me, following me down the hall on our floor.

The room was nice, if a bit unusual. The wall behind the beds was a somewhat bright lime green. The wall where the windows overlooked the pool in the back was covered in fake white bricks. The window dressings were sheers and terra-cotta curtains. The carpet was clean, plush, and a medium brown. The beds each had faux leather brown tufted headboards, white sheets, and comforters of white, the bright lime green, brown, terra-cotta, and aqua. It was almost very beachy considering how far inland we were.

But it was pretty.

And I smelled bleach, disinfectant, and a trace of fabric softener, so it was clean.

That was what mattered most.

I walked over toward the bed closest to the windows, dropping my bag down there, and sitting down on the edge of the bed with a sigh.

I had higher hopes for the trip.

That was silly, maybe. I had based it on one afternoon's interaction in his house, watching TV, eating sandwiches, making plans. It wasn't like I could get a full idea of how a person was from one afternoon.

I just figured, I don't know, that there would be more of his humor, his interesting conversation, something. I didn't expect a complete cold-shoulder. Or having to share a room with someone who was obviously not my biggest fan right about then.

I was vaguely aware of Luce dropping down on the edge of his bed as well, but facing me.

"Alright," he said with a sigh in his voice. "I'm not used to people trying to get to know me, or even giving a fucking shit about anything about me. Even something as small as me being tired." My head swiveled over my shoulder to find him watching me, still in his damn hoodie. As if sensing the thought in my head, he went on. "As for the hoodie and the scars, Ev, that shit is not something I am going to talk about. I'm not the kind of person who opens up. My past is fucked up, and it's ugly, and it has no place in that pretty little head of yours. Because then neither of us will be sleeping. Okay?"

Really, what more could I expect?

We were still practical strangers.

It would be nuts to want more than a vague answer to personal issues.

"Okay," I agreed with a small nod.

"So," he said, smirk pulling at one side of his lips, making his serious face look wicked. "You really got an issue with the ma'am thing, huh? Clock ticking or some shit like that?"

"I have at least three more years before someone can start calling me that."

"Think it might be more about southern hospitality than your age, doll. But that is interesting. You pissy because you're hungry?"

"Don't worry," I said, smiling. "I won't be fainting on you again. But, yes, I'm hungry."

"Well, there's an Olive Garden next door."

My face twisted up. "An olive garden? Like... we go and pick olives? I mean, I'm going to need more sustenance than that. What's so funny?" I asked when he did that throwing his head back boyish laugh that made my belly go liquid and a fluttering sensation to start between my thighs.

"Olive Garden is an Italian chain restaurant, Ev. Pretty fucking popular one too."

"In Texas?" I asked, squinting at him. "Wouldn't traditional American food or, honestly, Mexican food be more appropriate for the region?"

"Christ, you're a trip. You're like a fucking alien coming to a new planet," he declared, shaking his head at me. "If there is one thing you should know about us Americans, it's that we want every single ethnic food available to us in every town we visit. Did you not notice that Navesink Bank had about five Italian places, three Chinese, sushi, Mexican, Vietnamese, Indian, and Cajun around it?"

"I thought it was just a quirk of that town," I explained. "I mean, I guess I am just used to eating Mexican food in Mexico, and Indian food in India, and Sushi in Japan."

"Ah, but we're the Great Melting Pot."

"I believe that is in reference to ethnic diversity."

"Exactly," he agreed. "And each of those ethnicities brings their food to share with the rest of us."

"Oh, yeah? And what do Americans literally bring to the table?"

"Well," he said, pretending to really mull it over. "There's high fructose corn syrup, and fruit roll ups, burgers with donuts as buns..."

"So basically... food-like products," I said with a smile.

"Highly, highly addictive, sugar-filled, food-like products," he agreed. "I mean, if you've never dropped into a diner at midnight and had a full stack of syrup-soaked pancakes with a big ol' glob of butter, a side of toast with jelly, and a bottomless coffee full of cream and sugar, quite frankly, you've not experienced all this country has to offer."

"I can't imagine that would ever sound appetizing. Unless maybe you're drunk."

"Oh, you've got a lot to learn. Don't worry; I'll make a sugar addict out of you yet. You want a shower to wash off that shitty mood before we get some food?"

"I, ah, yeah," I said, standing quickly, reaching for my bag. "I'll just be ten minutes."

"That's girl-speak for forty minutes, right? I can get a power nap in."

I genuinely did mean ten minutes. I wasn't very high maintenance. I had showered that morning. The only reason I wanted another was to wash the day off and, well, maybe deal with a particularly strong, pulsating need between my legs. If I didn't handle it, I knew all I was going to be thinking about the rest of the night was the fact that we would be in a hotel room together where anything, including tangled-limbed, wild sex, could happen.

I turned on the shower as I tied up my hair and stripped, taking a deep breath as I stepped under the spray, leaning slightly against the side wall of the shower as my hand moved down my body, slipping between my thighs, and wasting no time trying to put an end to the throbbing desire there.

It was going to be a long, long trip with the sexual frustration seemingly right under the surface just waiting for a smirk or a laugh or some witty comment.

I bit into my lip to keep any sounds in.

But as I got closer, as the image of Luce in my mind got stronger, as my sex tightened painfully in the suspended nothingness, then crashed through the waves of the orgasm, an almost pained whimper ripped from somewhere deep inside, unstoppable, but hopefully muffled by the sounds of the shower and the closed door.

Feeling slightly more level-headed, I redressed in something less constricting than I had worn earlier, deciding on a simple deep blue sundress with the hopes that I wouldn't feel nearly as hot with some air circulating all over.

I had barely stepped out of the bathroom before Luce was right there. As in *right* there, toe to toe. And his eyes were full of something that I couldn't quite place.

He took a step in.

Not knowing why, I took a step back, and hit the wall.

My chest felt weighted again.

My heart started pounding wildly.

This proved an appropriate response.

Because the next second, without even the slightest bit of warning, his hand slid up, and pressed hard into my clit, making me let out a strangled whimper at the unexpected contact, somehow feeling the desire completely reignite like I hadn't already doused it just moments before.

His forehead pressed into mine, his eyes closing for a long moment as his fingers kept working me. Expertly. Relentlessly. Until my hands had to go up around him to hold on because my inner thighs started shaking. Until my forehead slid from his to bury in his neck as the whimpers became moans.

Until he backed me up to the edge, then pushed me over without hesitation, making me cry out his name as the waves crashed through me, his free hand having to slam into my hip to press me against the wall to keep me upright.

His hand moved away as I sucked in a deep breath, trying to come back down, trying to understand what the hell just happened... and why.

I lifted my head, forcing my heavy-lidded eyes to open.

I found him again watching me, but this time I understood the look for what it was - desire.

"Sounded good from behind a closed door, doll, but sounds a fuckuva lot better up close and personal," he declared, hands moving up to give my hips a squeeze before he moved back and away. "I have the keycards. Don't forget your purse. And shoes," he added, almost sounding amused as I just... stood there, too overwhelmed to move.

But then he moved out into the hall, giving me a minute, and I snapped out of my stupor, moving over to my bed and sitting down for a second, mind racing as fast as my heart.

Holy crap.

Okay.

So... that happened.

It happened, and I was apparently supposed to act like nothing at all went down. I was just supposed to walk out of the room, go have a meal with the man, and just somehow forget he had given me an orgasm.

And, well, I was a grown ass woman.

I couldn't actually do it, but I could fake it.

I took another deep breath, grabbed my purse, and slipped into shoes before going to the door.

"Italian?" he asked, pushing off the wall where he had been resting.

"Yep," I said, raising my chin slightly.

Then we had dinner.

We talked about Navesink Bank, about the food, about Texas, about what time we were going to get moving the next day.

Nothing personal.

Which made it at little easier to slip back into friend-mode.

We got back to the hotel, and Luce slipped into the bathroom to shower. I waited until I heard the water, then quickly stripped and changed into my pajamas, which I had packed thinking I would be sleeping in privacy, so yeah... it was shorty shorts that my ass almost hung out of and a silky tank top that the air made my nipples poke through the fabric of.

So I scurried up the bed, flicking off the overhead light, leaving just one by the door to the hall on, pulled up the blankets, and attempted sleep.

You know, until the door creaked open and my half-open eyes caught sight of white. As in the white towels from the bathroom.

And, well, there was no way I wasn't going to look.

I was only human.

He was half-turned away, digging into his bag, giving me a completely unobstructed view of his back, showing a bit more muscle tone than I had expected given his general thinness.

But that wasn't what had my stomach dropping as I forgot all about faking being asleep.

No.

That was because if I thought his arms were maybe from his own victims before, I knew right that moment that I was completely mistaken.

Because *Luce* had been a victim.

His back was a map of horrors.

Each scar told a story that I was pretty sure would make me ill.

And there didn't seem to be a single square inch of skin that was unmarked.

What had happened to him?

Was that why he lived in a cabin in the woods, cut off from people? What kind of monster did that to another person?

"Luce..." I said, sitting up, everything in me seeming to reach out to him.

His entire body jerked, like he had truly thought I had been sleeping. And in his shock, he turned to me fully, revealing another, different array of scars. But these were all in one spot across his chest. And they weren't just random scars. They were a word carved into his flesh.

Before I could say anything else, he turned, and disappeared back into the bathroom. I could hear something slam, then nothing.

And I mean nothing.

There was no noise from in there for nearly an hour.

He came back out after that, flicking off the light, but not before I could see he was in a tee, like maybe he accepted that there was no hiding anymore.

But he kept his eyes away from me as he slipped under the sheet, and stared up at the ceiling.

I felt like I couldn't let that moment hang, couldn't just... pretend something didn't happen.

I pushed up, sitting up off the side of the bed. "Luce?" I called, but he just shook his head, still staring upward.

I took a deep breath and stood, walking over to the side of his bed, watching as he forced his eyes to me, trying to bank the vulnerability there, but not before I saw it.

"I won't ask," I said, reaching down, touching his forearm, my fingers meeting one of the round burns, raised, but oddly smooth at the same time. "Okay? I won't ever ask."

I don't know what I had been expecting.

But it certainly wasn't what actually happened.

One second, I was just standing there.

The next, he half-folded up, grabbed my arm, and yanked me down onto his bed. I had barely landed before his arm wrapped around my back, and curled me onto his chest.

"Okay," he said, voice barely audible.

And then we slept.

Well, he slept.

Which was good.

He needed it.

Me, well, I stayed awake realizing we had somehow, without hardly even speaking, jumped what was a giant hurdle between us.

Which meant we took the whole 'we're only friends with the occasional benefit' thing, and tossed it out the window.

At least, I was pretty sure that happened.

Time would tell.

Eventually, lulled by the steady fall of Luce's chest beneath me, his heartbeat, and his arm holding me tight, a luxury I hadn't been afforded in far too long, I drifted off to a dreamless sleep.

TEN

Luce

Shit changed.

Don't ask me exactly when.

I was pretty sure it started in stages.

Stage one, kissing her in the basement.

Two, agreeing to go on a trip with her.

Three, feeling shitty about shutting her out, then giving her an evasive answer about why I was doing so. That shit was new for me.

Four, relaxing on that bed, minding my own business, when I heard her come from behind the closed door. The surge I felt inside was different. Sexual? Sure. But it was more than that as well. It was primal and possessive, something that made me want to be the only reason she ever made those sounds again.

Five, actually getting to make her make those sounds, feeling the warmth and wetness of her sweet pussy, feeling her warm breath catch and exhale on my neck, her fingers digging into me to hold her up, crying out my name as she came... yeah, that shit was unexpectedly overwhelming.

Six, well, six was a whole new territory entirely. Six was her seeing something no one, not a single person had seen in years. The scars on my arm, I knew they weren't always hiding, that my sleeve slipped up and showed them occasionally. But no one got to see my back and chest. No one got to speculate how those marks got onto my skin. Hearing the horror in her voice when she said my name after seeing them made a coil of dread fill my stomach. Because I couldn't go there. I never went there. I wasn't sure I could come back intact if I even tried. Everything within me screamed to shut down. That was exactly what I had tried to do.

Then she had come over to me, touched me, and said the one thing that could have made the situation better.

She wasn't going to ask.

She was *never* going to ask.

The relief was of a strength I had never experienced before. If I had been standing, it might have brought me to my knees. As it was, it made me want to at least give her some sign of how much that vow meant to me.

So I pulled her down on the bed with me, I tucked her into my side, I felt her head rest over the shriveled, dark, broken thing that was my heart.

And me?

I slept like a goddamn baby.

I was pretty sure I had never had a night of such dreamless sleep.

I even woke up before her, finding her almost completely sprawled across me. Her leg was thrown over my hips, her knee resting on the mattress on my other side, which put her torso covering me like a blanket. Her face was buried in my neck, her arm resting casually on my shoulder.

I was a grown ass man, but this was something I had never experienced before- waking up with a woman.

Hell, most of the sexual encounters I had had barely involved getting undressed. Usually, if we could just hike a skirt and drop my pants, I was a happy fucking guy. It wasn't worth it to have to answer questions about my scars just for a fuck.

I certainly never stuck around afterward.

I never opened up to the point where things like my past could matter.

There was the distinct, heavy feeling in my chest that said it was already far too late with Evan.

Somehow, though, I wasn't overcome with the desire to slide out from under her, and run the fuck away.

No, instead, I felt my hands start to roam, across her shoulders, her back, the flare of her hips, her plump ass, where my hands stopped to squeeze, making her grumble and wiggle in her sleep.

Apparently, she slept like the dead.

My cock was half-hard from running my hands over her body before she finally stretched, her body doing a quivering sensation that brought another stab of desire through my system. Then there was a long sigh.

"Are your hands on my ass?" she asked, sleep-groggy.

"What? These hands?" I asked, giving her another squeeze that made her giggle into my neck. "Nope. Not on your ass at all. You are a hard woman to wake up."

"Nuh-uh. I'm a light sleeper," she insisted, doing another stretch, then rolling off of me to go onto her back, staring at the ceiling.

"Bull fucking shit. Whoever told you that is a liar. Not only did I get to feel you up, but the door slammed so hard next door that it shook the bed, and what seemed like twenty rowdy kids tore down that hall five minutes ago. A coma patient would be easier to wake up."

She made some sort of noncommittal grunting. "What time is it?"

"Almost ten," I said as I folded up to reach for my cell, something that was foreign to me. I never had a cell that required checking. It was always my pager. But I had left that at home figuring that I was due for a vacation away from all that. Also, I knew there would be no secure ways to check on things like there were in Navesink Bank.

"And breakfast is over at eleven," she said, practically throwing herself down the bed to pop off of it. "We gotta hustle," she declared, grabbing her bag, and disappearing into the bathroom.

I smiled at her retreating body, thinking that a woman that excited for breakfast was the kind of woman I could get behind.

I stretched, found my hoodie, and slipped it on, as well as my shoes. I was rational enough to realize that once we were out in the heat, there would be no more hoodie, but I was going to avoid curious looks as long as possible.

"Alright, all yours," she declared, rushing back out, tying her hair into a messy knot at the top of her head. She didn't have a stitch of makeup on, but she was still stupidly gorgeous. "Come on, go brush your teeth. I have a sudden urge for pancakes," she declared, making me smile big.

"That was supposed to be pancakes at *midnight*, but at least you are *trying* to acclimate to American culture," I said, moving past her to go through my quick morning ritual.

We had breakfast, talking about the food (which she loved, though made sure she told me that food like pancakes were a *treat)*.

"Dollars to donuts, doll, you'll be eating pancakes at least twice a week from now on."

"Hardly," she said, rolling her eyes as she cleared her plate. "You ready?" she asked, standing.

"Nervous," I remarked as I followed her out toward the lobby.

"I'm not..."

"You're nervous," I cut her off, touching her hip as we squeezed together to fit through the door. "It's normal," I assured her as we got into the car, and I finally gave up on the hoodie, and pulled it off. "You didn't even know there were questions that needed answers until a few days ago."

"I just... want to get this part over with," she said, and I could feel the palpable tension moving through her the whole drive to the church which was a surprisingly large structure of old stucco, curved stained glass windows, and huge wooden doors. To the left, surrounded by seemingly freshly painted white picket fencing, was a small, ancient-looking cemetery with crumbling headstones, the words on them long washed away by time.

"Come on," I said, reaching for my door, knowing that sitting and trying to 'prepare' was only going to make her life more difficult. "Let's hope for old nuns and priests or whatever the fuck they are called."

Religion, as a whole, went over my head.

There was too much evil in the world for there to be some kind of supreme, loving being out there supposedly looking out for us.

I had spent too much time as a kid crying, screaming, begging for some higher power to intervene.

But none came.

So I had to get myself out of it.

Any faith I had died that day.

The first time I took a life.

"What? Afraid you'll burst into flames?" she teased, making me realize she was a few steps above me as I stared up at the cross on the roof.

"Doing 'God's' work, taking out these bastards. I think the carvings of angels will sing when I walk in there," I quipped, trying to cover my dark mood.

"Can I help you?" a voice greeted us when we were halfway down the aisle.

"Hi, I'm Evan. This is Luce. We actually just have a question about an immigrant who might have been here." She paused at that, looking back at me, waiting for me to hand her the newspaper article she knew I had on me. "It was a long time ago, I'm afraid," she explained, handing the young man the paper.

"Oh, yeah, this was before my time," he explained unnecessarily since I was pretty sure he wasn't even legal drinking age yet. "Let me get Sister Maria. She has been here longer than I've been alive. She might remember."

He handed us back the article, and retreated back behind the doors situated to the sides of the altar, leaving us almost uncomfortably alone for several long minutes.

As such, it made us both jump when a female voice declared. "*Gabriela?*" she gasped, immediately crossing herself, her eyes huge.

I was apparently a bit outdated in my nun-knowledge because I was expecting the long black robes and that box-type thing on her head. But this nun was dressed in a long blue skirt with a blue vest over a white long-sleeve button-up. A cross hung from her neck, and a blue veil covered most of her hair, showing only a small amount of white at the top of her forehead.

She was what you expected from a nun who had been at a church for almost thirty years- older, a bit wrinkled, with green eyes framed in metal glasses, and a general air of kindness, but firmness as well.

"But no," she said immediately, squinting at Evan. "My eyes must be playing tricks on me. What can I help you with today, my dear?"

"Hi, sister," Evan said, giving her a warm smile. "My name is Evangeline. This is Luce. We actually just have some questions about a female immigrant who may or may not have been here twenty some-odd years ago." Hell, even I could hear the defeat already in her tone. But she handed her the paper regardless.

Sister Maria barely even glanced at the article before she looked back up at Evan, recognition plain on her face. "No wonder," she said, shaking her head. "No wonder I thought it was she," she explained, curling up the paper like it offended her. If she was left to deal with the aftermath of Alejandro's rape of the poor woman, it likely did. "You are Evangeline," she declared, sure as if you asked her if God existed. "Gabriela's daughter. Oh, you look *just* like her."

"You knew her? Gabriela? The woman from the article."

"Your *mother*," Sister Maria corrected. "You might not know her, dear, but she was your mother. You are her mirror image from the day she came here, so skinny from the journey that all her bones were poking out of her dress, with a three-year-old chubby baby girl strapped to her back. *Evangeline* Luana Santos."

This wasn't the moment to say it aloud, but I fucking *knew* it.

Evan fumbled to find words, swallowing hard, shaking her head.

"Can you tell us what happened on the night she was assaulted?" I asked, knowing we needed the answers, even if it sucked to have to ask a goddamn *nun* those kinds of questions.

Sister Maria's face went pale, looking somehow both sad and enraged simultaneously. "She went out to work, as she always did, at a local motel. She brought you," she said, nodding at Evan. "She used to let you come and watch TV while she cleaned. Her boss looked the other way, knowing it is hard around here for single immigrant mothers." When she continued, her tone went sour. "When it happened, she was in the bathroom. The man came back, turned the TV louder for you, and followed her in. That *savage*," she growled, closing her eyes tight, shaking her head, trying to clear the image. "The things he did to her."

"I can't," Evan said, shaking her head, turning, and running outside.

A part of me, maybe even the larger part of me, wanted to follow her, wanted to comfort her. The other part, however, knew one of us needed all the answers.

"Let me guess, when she returned, Evan was nowhere to be found."

"She could barely walk, but she searched everywhere for weeks, begging everyone she came across on the streets for information about her missing daughter. No one ever found out what happened to her."

"What happened was, her mother's rapist took her, raised her like she was his own, and unbeknownst to Evan, raped women across several continents. He recently died..."

"I know I am not supposed to say this, but good riddance."

"May he rot in hell," I agreed, though I didn't believe in it personally. "And she finally learned the truth of him. We found some information linking her to McAllen, so we came here for answers. Whatever happened to Gabriela?"

"After two years, so broken, just a shell of a woman, she went back."

"Back to where? Mexico?"

"Brazil."

"Do you have any reason to believe she is still alive?"

Sister Maria gave me a small smile. "We bonded. While she recovered. While she raged at God for the loss of her daughter, we became close. She still sends letters occasionally, asking for updates, or simply saying hello."

"Is there any chance we can have the address?"

"Twenty-four years of suffering and wondering?" she asked, shaking her head. "Of course you can have that to unburden her of the misery of uncertainty. She will be beside herself."

With that, she moved to go retrieve a letter, pressing it into my hands. "Evangeline," she said, holding my gaze. "Will she be alright? This can not be an easy time for her."

"She's a lot stronger than she seems. She just needs to process it in her own time. Thank you for this. It means a lot."

"For a change," she said, smiling kindly, "I will be looking forward to Gabriela's letter. She will be so happy."

"We will make sure we mention your help," I said, giving her a smile, then moving back down the aisle to go back outside.

I found Evangeline sitting on the lowest step, knees to chest, elbows on knees, face buried in her hands.

I dropped down next to her, our bodies pressing from shoulder to shoes, not caring about the oppressive heat.

"I have her address," I told her, tapping her bare knee with the letter from Sister Maria.

"I was *there*," she said back, voice thick. "I was in the other room."

"Ev, you were three years old. It's not like you could have known..."

"I was in the other room, and that *fucking bastard* did that to my mother? And then *took me?* For what? Some goddamn souvenir? Like some teeth from a corpse? How, Luce?" she asked, looking at me, eyes pleading. "How could I have not known how evil he was? *How*?"

"Listen to me," I said, tucking away the letter, and turning fully to face her. "If there is one thing I have learned doing what I do, it is that it doesn't matter how evil someone is, without fail, everyone around them is shocked when they learned what they did. They have to adapt. They have to put on a good show."

"For twenty-four *years*?" she snapped, swatting at a tear that slipped down her cheek. "He never once let it slip in front of me in all that time?"

"Even if he did, Ev, you wouldn't have had any context to put it in. You would have shrugged it off as him having a hard day with his job, knowing that brought some level of darkness into his life. This isn't on you. It's really fucked that you are feeling even a tiny bit of guilt about this. You were *three*. Of course you don't remember any of this shit, and he could create any story he wanted to. And, I hate to say this because I think rapists are pretty much the vilest of shitheads, and I know my shitheads," I added, shrugging. "But the fact that you never *did* see that side of him did show that there was some goodness in him. You grew up loved. You loved him enough to want to murder me for killing him."

"I know!" she snapped, swiping both her hands under her eyes. "That's the worst part! I loved him. I loved him, and he violently raped my mother with me in the next room watching cartoons! Then he stole me. And I *loved* him!"

Her voice cracked hard at that as my arm moved out across her lower back, pulling her against my chest.

I had a feeling it was going to go along these lines, but it was clear Evan hadn't been quite convinced when we started on the journey. She wasn't as prepared for this inevitability as she could have been if she considered the possibilities sometime between Jersey and Texas.

"I hate him," she told my neck, body shaking with silent sobs.

I knew she wanted to believe that down to her marrow. And maybe it was true for ninety-nine percent of her, but no matter what, I was pretty sure there would always be one-percent that still had feelings toward him that weren't blind hatred.

Because he *had* taken care of her. He had protected, fed, educated, exposed her to the world, and provided for her even upon his death.

Did that make him a good man? No. Of fucking course not.

But he had learned to be, it appeared, a decent father.

And that was going to be a hard reality for her to come to terms with eventually.

"Well," she said, pulling away, self-consciously scrubbing at her face, keeping her head ducked. "At least I know I don't have his evil in my DNA."

"I coulda told you that," I agreed, moving to stand when she did. "The nun told me that your mother still writes a couple times a year to check in, and ask if anyone had heard anything about you."

Evan stopped walking, took a deep breath, and looked over at me. "From where?"

"Brazil."

"Brazil?" she asked, eyes squinting like that didn't make sense.

"Yeah. Makes perfect sense to me. Brazilian women are hot as fuck."

She laughed at that, shaking her head. "Thanks, I think?"

"So, what now? Are you going to write her? Go visit her? What?" I asked when she looked sharply away at the tail-end of that.

"I'd like to visit her," she confessed.

"That's great. I'm sure she would be excited to..."

"But I don't think I am going to go."

"Now, that makes no fucking sense. Why not? I'm sure you've been to Brazil before. You've been everywhere." And that's when it hit me. She had been everywhere with her father. "What's up, Ev? Parts of Brazil are rough, but it's no more unsafe than walking around Mexico on your own."

"That's just the thing though, isn't it? I've never walked around... anywhere alone. Except for a couple places in the US after my fath... after Alejandro went missing. There was always the bubble that his protection provided. I mean... I can't even smuggle in any of my own poisons or anything to protect myself with. He was the one who knew how to pull all that off, pay off the right guys, or hide it in plain sight. He taught me a lot, but not that."

"You're afraid to travel alone," I guessed, surprised.

She turned back at my tone, giving me a hard look. "If you have seen the underbelly like I have in all these countries, you wouldn't feel safe going alone either."

"You do know that the underbelly in the States isn't really any better, right?"

"It's not as blatant. I've seen men gunned down in Columbia right in front of the police. Sure, people get gunned down in the US too, but I have never seen the police laugh and walk away."

I took a breath, wondering how Barrett was getting on with the bird, if he was cool with taking him for another week or so. Knowing Barrett, he probably wouldn't give a shit.

"You want me to take you to Brazil, Ev?" I asked.

I could feel the area around my eyes and jaw loosen when she shot me a look full of hope. "Really?"

"Really," I agreed, nodding.

"Like... now?"

"Like once we get back to the hotel, and look into flights and shit, yeah. No point in putting it off. What?" I asked after a long silence where she was just... looking at me.

"You're a really good guy, Luce," she surprised me by saying. "It's really a shame you don't let people see that."

Affected perhaps more deeply than was appropriate, I covered by snorting. "Doll, I think the heat is getting to your weak lady-brain. Did you forget that I kill people for a living?"

"My weak lady-brain?" she said, smiling big because she knew I didn't mean it.

"How the fuck else would you explain that asinine idea?"

"Objectivity," she said with a shrug before turning, and walking back to the car.

Lord fucking help me.

I had at least another handful of days with the woman.

It was bound to get messy, I decided as I climbed in the car and we drove back to the hotel.

At the time, though, I had no idea just how fucking messy it was going to get.

And soon.

ELEVEN

Evan

It was stupid to be nervous.

I had been on planes countless times.

I had been to Brazil on at least three different occasions.

And I wasn't alone.

Luce had been sitting next to me, watching some cinematically dark, bloody vampire movie that was like the fifth in a series or something, so I had opted out of watching along. Besides, my mind was too all-over-the-place to be able to concentrate on a movie. And I had a feeling that Luce would ask me about it afterward, and wouldn't be happy if I came back with 'oh, it was very action packed' as an answer.

Things after the church had been... different than before the church.

There was no more flirtation, no hints at flirtation, and certainly no more touching.

In fact, after I showered, he was already sprawled out on his bed texting Barrett. So I brought my cell up and looked into flights. We ordered food to the room. Luce put on one of his favorite action movies, a really interesting movie about, essentially, a heist and an off-duty cop who put a stop to it. While I liked it, I very much doubted that he was correct in calling it the greatest Christmas movie of all time.

Men.

But then, yeah, we booked the flight to Brazil the next morning... and just... went to sleep. In separate beds.

That left me tossing and turning a lot until, almost at sunrise, I finally drifted off.

We were more than halfway to our destination. From there, we had to take two buses. Then we would crash at the closest local town with a motel. After that, well, there would be some walking. Apparently, Gabriela Santos lived in a rural village in the middle of nowhere with a dirt road that turned to deep mud that no local car would attempt to drive down lest it get stuck.

Luce had taken all this information like a seasoned world traveler. Though, I had gotten a look at his passport stamps earlier, and all I had seen were Mexico, Canada, and, oddly, China.

Because the little flirtation thing between us had been gone all morning, I had felt weird asking. But as I watched him pull off his headphones, his movie rolling credits, in my nervousness, I couldn't help but blurt out, "Why China?"

"What?" he asked, looking taken aback.

"Your passport said Mexico, Canada, and China. Why China?"

He gave me a long look, so long that I wasn't sure he was going to answer. "When I first started my... business," he said carefully, giving me a pointed look, "I wasn't as skilled or careful as I am now. Things got hot. I decided to get lost for a while. Didn't last long."

"You missed your melting pot food," I guessed, making him smile.

"Something like that, yeah." He paused, looking down to where my fingers were thrumming against my thigh. "What's up, Evan?" he asked, putting his hand over mine.

And the action was so unexpected that my gaze went to the top of his hand, and stayed there for a long moment, having to physically force my fingers to stay flat, to not slide between his.

"I'm nervous," I admitted.

"Your mom is going to love to see you. I hope you speak Spanish."

"Portuguese," I corrected. "They speak Portuguese in Brazil. But it is a lot like Spanish. I should be able to carry on a conversation easily enough."

"Then what? She obviously wants to see you if she is still looking for you." He paused as I looked out the window. "Is this because Alejandro raised you?" he asked, and I felt my stomach twist painfully, making me almost wonder if I needed to reach for an airsickness bag. "Evan, you had no idea. She is not going to blame you, or look at you any differently. If anything, she might want you to reassure her that he never put his hands on you."

Ugh.

I hadn't even thought of that.

Of course, as a mother, and as a woman who had been brutally raped, she would worry about a similar fate happening to me. Hell, with the amount of trafficking in the world, maybe she even worried I had been sold into a child sex ring.

I couldn't imagine how much she had worried about me.

Meanwhile, I had been traipsing around her rainforests several times in my life. With her rapist.

What a fucked up situation.

"Look," Luce tried when I stayed silent, lost in my own swirling thoughts. "Worst case, if it sucks, if you are uncomfortable, it's just an hour. We can say when we get there that we have plans or some shit. You can tolerate anything for an hour, right?"

That was true.

"Right," I agreed.

And then I didn't have to force my fingers to stay straight anymore, because his curled inward and held mine.

Somehow, I felt instantly a lot better.

Which was crazy.

But true nonetheless.

"I don't think we thought this out enough," Luce said, swatting at a swarm of gnats around his head.

"Why?" I asked, somewhat amused by his discomfort.

He might have been a vigilante, a stone-cold killer, but he was not the outdoorsy type. He was what I might call *indoorsy.* He was thin and had more muscles than I had been aware of under his hoodie, but it was clear that a long, hot, exhausting hike was not his thing.

"Because your feet hurt in those converse?" I suggested.

"Because... where the fuck are we going to stay overnight in the middle of Bumfuck, Nowhere?"

Okay.

He had a point.

"We will just have to walk back to the motel," I suggested, shrugging.

"You want to walk this in the dark?" he asked, waving at the wide open landscape. "I mean, what are the local predators?"

"Oh, nothing really. Caiman near the rivers and such. You might see some wolf occasionally. And, you know," I said, trying to fight back a smile. "Just some jaguar."

"Did you just say fucking *jaguar?*" He asked, stopping.

"I'd worry more about the puma, I think."

"Jesus Christ. Can we go back to fucking Jersey now?" he asked, shaking his head. "We had one, *one* coyote loose once and every animal control officer and cop was hunting that mother fucker down."

I laughed at that, used to the threat of wildlife. Though, even I could admit I was more afraid without my fath... Alejandro and his blow darts around.

"Look, this is farming land," I said as we kept moving. "The big cats would be around farms with animals that they could pick off. I haven't seen a farm with any animals for almost an hour. We'll be fine in the dark. Plus, it will be a little cooler, so we can move a little faster."

He nodded at that, but there was a definite grumble, like maybe he thought this pace was fast enough.

"Hey, didn't they say blue with red trim and roof?" Luce said, stopping, and pointing toward the side of a hill where, sure enough, a blue wooden building was half-hidden by said hill. There was a large garden out back and, even from a distance, I could make out a few chicken walking around.

In the US, they would call this small, squat, rectangular, typically one-room dwelling a 'shack,' or something equally low-brow. In most countries, however, this was how many of the people lived.

"Yeah," I agreed, stomach spinning. "That looks like the one they described."

"You ready?" Luce asked, moving back a step to stand shoulder-to-shoulder with me as I reached up to self-consciously swipe a sweaty brow.

"Not really," I admitted truthfully. "But it's just an hour, right?" I asked, bringing up his words from the plane. "I can tolerate anything for an hour."

"Sure as fuck can," he agreed, elbowing me in the side a little in a 'let's get moving' kind of way.

So we did.

And fifteen minutes later, we were standing outside the door to my birth mother's home.

I could feel Luce's stare on my profile, but I couldn't seem to force myself to raise my hand to knock.

"Allow me," he said, taking the whole thing out of my hands by knocking twice on the old, shaky door.

There was some shuffling for maybe only five seconds before the door pulled open, and there she was.

I got an eyeful of what I would look like in about twenty years. Sister Maria was right; we were very similar looks-wise. We had the same skin, the same hair, the same eyes. I was taller, but we both seemed to carry our weight in our lower bodies. She was dressed in a simple blue dress with a white apron tied around her waist. Her hair was in a loose braid, with tendrils floating around her face. There were some wrinkles beside her lips and eyes, but she looked young still somehow.

I could have sworn I heard Luce mumble something about 'good genes,' and I had to agree.

There was only one part of her face that didn't match mine, an unevenness beside her right eye that might have pointed to a broken eye-socket at one time.

I think we all knew how that got broken.

"Oh minha filha!" she gasped, making a steeple of her fingers in front of her mouth. "Oh minha filha!" she said again, eyes filling as she reached for me, and yanked me against her chest.

Really, there was nothing to do but hold her back, this woman who had never given up, who had constantly written to ask for updates on my search, even when she herself was forced back to Brazil.

Before too long, she was sobbing into my neck, letting out a string of Portuguese so fast that I was struggling to make it out, if it even made any sense to begin with.

I caught bits and pieces about how she never thought she would see me again, how her heart hurt every day, how she never gave up the search.

Finally, what seemed like a lifetime later, she pulled back, reaching for her apron to wipe her face, then looking at me for a long minute. Her hands rose, cupping my face. "English, yes?" she asked.

"Mostly," I agreed. "Though I can understand most of what you're saying."

"I can speak the English," she said, giving me a smile. "And who is this?" she asked, giving me a look that, while I was raised motherless, I could completely interpret as a maternal excitement to meet her daughter's boyfriend.

"Oh, sorry. This is my friend, Luce," I offered, touching his arm. "Luce, this is Gabriela," I said, feeling awkward. "My mother."

"Luce! Nice to meet you. I'm glad Evangeline has such nice *friends*," she said the word heavily, like she knew it was more than that, though there was no way she could, "to bring her all the way down to Brazil."

"He was the one to actually find you and sort of... bring me here," I offered, wanting to give credit where credit was due.

"So, I have you to thank!" she said, turning her hugs onto him. And Luce, well, he looked hilariously uncomfortable with the contact. His eyes were huge; his hands were awkwardly patting her back; his body was stiff as a board. "Come in, come in. You must be starving. I didn't see cars. We had rains last night," she explained. "The mud, impassable."

Yeah, they weren't kidding about the cars not being able to handle the mud on the dirt roads. We saw three of them stuck with mud that literally would have come halfway up my calf if we hadn't been walking on the grass.

"Thank you," I said as we moved inside to find pretty much what I had expected. It was a one-room space with only the bathroom separate. There was a bed pushed against the wall beside the side window, nothing hanging to cover it, letting the light shine in to, I imagined, wake her at sunrise so she could get to work on the garden out back.

I always envied the lifestyle of the small village gardeners. It was an homage to our ancestors to wake up with the sun, tend your land, eat what you grew or killed, spend time with your family and community, then go to bed. Shower, rinse, repeat.

What a simple life.

Only maybe three feet from the end of the bed was a small straight kitchen with a stove, sink, lower cabinets, and shelves of dishwear above, pretty pieces in bright colors, likely made locally, which gave me the urge to make sure we hit a local town square so I could pick up a few pieces to remember this trip by.

To the opposite side of the room, there was a dining table, worn lovingly with time, and I inwardly wondered how many generations of my ancestors had sat there and broken bread together, how many stories were shared, laughs had.

I felt a deep pang inside at the idea of never having experienced that. It also struck me that I had never actually been given any history from my fath... from Alejandro. Why that had never struck me as odd before was completely beyond me. How had it never crossed my mind to ask about my grandparents? My cousins? Especially on holidays. He had, after all, told me that relatives raised me. Relatives I would never meet.

God, I had been so so blind.

Granted, for all intents and purposes, I didn't know any better, but still. While he had exposed me to so much, so many cultures, so many different pockets of the world, it had also left me very insulated and ignorant of what was a more normal relationship to have with your family.

You would think in this golden age of technology, that would no longer be an excuse, but when you spent a lot of time in areas with little or no cell reception, and even when you had it, you had no friends to connect with on social media, well, you learned to do without things like that.

"Thirsty?" she asked, going to the fridge before we even answered, reaching inside, and pulling out a pitcher of not-quite-clear liquid that I knew to be coconut water, something I drank almost exclusively the last time I was in Brazil. It had done amazing things to my skin.

"Yes, please," I said, moving with Luce over to the table she gestured to.

"Food?" she asked, filling three glasses with liquid.

"No thanks," I answered, then shot Luce a guilty look.

"It's too fucking hot for food," he whispered back at me.

She came back over, passing out the drinks which we both took long, almost embarrassing swigs of thanks to the fact that we each finished our water less than halfway into the trek.

It only took all of five minutes before it happened.

We got the part about Sister Maria out, and then she asked what led us there.

I could have lied.

It would have made life easier.

But I didn't want to.

She was the only actual relative I was aware of having. I felt I owed her honesty at least.

So I told her.

"Ele te machucou?" she asked, voice completely shattered. "Ele te machucou?"

Did he hurt you?

"No," I said, voice firm, reaching across the table to place my hand on top of hers which was worrying a rag that had been on the table. "No, not at all. Never once. He never let anyone else hurt me either," I added. "He just... I don't know if maybe his plan had been to hurt me or let others. That's possible. But he never did. I guess I brought out the very small human side of him. Because he wasn't good, Gabriela," I said, watching as she winced slightly at that, but I wasn't at the point where I could call her Mom yet. "The things he did to you, he did that to many other women across several continents. I... I had no idea. He never..." I said, shaking my head, feeling the tears sting at my eyes again.

"He never let her get wind of the evil shit he was doing," Luce supplied. "It wasn't until after he died that, well, I told her."

"And you know because?"

I took a deep breath then rushed on before he could answer. I wanted to be truthful. But, y'know, without getting thrown out of her house.

"Luce is someone who... finds bad people, and gets them off the street."

"I'm not a cop, Evan," he said behind me, making me want to elbow him to shut up, but my mother was watching too closely.

"You are a... what is the word... a vigilante."

I didn't have to look to see the smirk Luce had on. "Exactly."

"I know he was like a father to her," she said, ignoring me completely, "but I hope he suffered."

"He took the chickenshit road and downed some cyanide," Luce countered, sounding so casual about the whole thing, reminding me how much darkness he had seen. Hell, it was etched on his skin.

"Good riddance," she said, shaking her head. Then she reached for me, rubbing my hand. "I'm sorry, Evangeline. I know he was..."

"Don't," I implored, shaking my head. "Don't apologize. It was all his fault any of this happened."

"Okay. Okay," she said, shaking her head. "Let's not talk any more of him. Let's talk of you."

So then we did.

For almost *three hours*.

I had never met someone who wanted to know every teeny, minuscule detail of my life from my first date to what languages I spoke to my faith, my dreams, my life in Navesink Bank.

And during all of this, I was acutely aware of Luce behind me, hearing every word, knowing about Emanuel who had taken me to a local faire, bought me a flower crown, and kissed me for the first time when I was fifteen, and he also learned that I had no idea what I wanted to do with my life now that I was done traveling.

He knew almost everything about me.

"It's getting dark," Gabriela said much later, looking out the window. "You should be getting back before the wolves come out."

"Told you," Luce growled at me, making me laugh.

"Will you visit again? Can you stay for another day or two?"

I looked over my shoulder at Luce, knowing it wasn't just me who had to make that decision.

"We can stay as long as you want, Ev. It's not like my job is missing me."

"Okay?" she asked, sounding hopeful.

"Okay," I agreed, smiling. "We can meet? In town? Tomorrow?"

"Perfect," I agreed, smiling. "I wanted to check out the town."

"Okay. Here," she said, standing suddenly, and grabbing a bat she kept behind her door. "You take this," she said, thrusting it at Luce. "And you protect my girl."

Luce looked at me, eyes warm with... something I couldn't explain. "I will bring her back to you safe and sound, I promise."

With that, I was hugged like I was going off to war.

Then so was Luce.

Which was, again, hilarious.

And we were off into the night.

"You alright?" he asked fifteen tense minutes later, both of us a little out of breath because we heard a howling that made us simultaneously start to run-walk.

"That was... heavy," I admitted, looking for the lights of the motel, still a while off, but visible.

"So if Emanuel was your first kiss..." he trailed off, sounding amused.

"I was nineteen," I supplied, shrugging. "And he was from Spain. It was on his boat," I added, shaking my head at my young naivety. I thought, like most young women did, that it meant something. And while the whole experience was lovely, leaps and bounds better than most women's stories, it didn't go beyond that night. I had been a sullen, unhappy girl all through Italy and then Cambodia before I finally shook it off.

"Nice."

He didn't offer any information about his first time and, quite frankly, I had a feeling that that was completely off-limits.

"Thank God," I groaned thirty minutes later when we finally walked into the motel room.

It was nothing like the one in Texas. There was no funky, modern color scheme or fancy bathroom accessories. The walls were a mustardy yellow. The floors were tile. The beds were only fulls.

The bathroom had a stall shower, vanity, sink, and toilet. All of it was the kind contractors get in bulk, cheap and nothing to write home about.

But it was clean.

And it was near where we needed to be.

And it wasn't the "Free Love" motel we passed on the way in that Luce had raised a brow at.

"It's for prostitutes and Johns," I supplied, explaining why I was walking right past it. "There is a huge economy in Brazil, but flesh will always be a bestselling cash crop here."

That was a sad reality of the country, of many countries.

But Brazil, unfortunately, was second only to Thailand in the epidemic of child and teen sex trafficking. I had seen them myself on the streets, fifteen and sixteen-year-old girls dressed in a way that made my twelve-year-old self uncomfortable. When I had angled my head up to question my father, he had given me a grimace. "Income inequality in a country always affects women and children the worst," he had explained. "Sometimes, the mom is out working the streets, leaving her kids at home, and they get snatched and sold into sex rings. They never get out. Women have bodies that are marketable. And in a bad economy, they sell the only goods they have to keep food in their stomachs."

Maybe that should have been a warning sign too. Maybe a topic so heartbreaking told so clinically should have made me give pause. But I was hardly more than a child, and then time long buried that conversation until I had reason to think of it again.

And while, as someone who had traveled a lot and had literally broken bread with prostitutes in countries where it was a legal, safe, and less frowned-upon profession, I saw nothing wrong with a woman who sold her body. That was her choice to make.

Children, however, had no choice.

It made me sick that there were people who profited on their misery.

"Alright, go ahead," Luce said, tossing a towel that hit me in the chest because I was too lost in my own head to pay attention. "I'll go after."

Really, as tired as I was, there was no way I was going to bed as sticky and disgusting as I felt. That was one thing I had apparently forgotten about the endless traveling I used to do with my fath... with

Alejandro. You were always sweaty, sticky, just shy of dirty, and always hyper aware of that fact.

So I nearly ran into the shower, keeping the water somewhere between warm and cool, shivering slightly, my nipples hardening as I scrubbed soap over my skin and into my hair, almost moaning at the feeling of cleanliness.

I was so lost in that good feeling, that I almost didn't hear the quiet tapping sound at the door. It almost seemed... hesitant.

I rinsed my hair, shut off the water, and reached for a towel just to hold in front of me. "Yeah?"

The door opened slowly.

And there was Luce.

With that deep look in his eyes that I couldn't read.

But they were focused on me.

And the next thing I knew, he was kicking out of his shoes, then reaching for the hem of his shirt, lifting the dark material slowly. There was no denying the surge of surprise and desire that coursed through me, realizing what was happening. My heart leaped into overdrive, and a heavy pressure settled in my lower stomach.

He tossed the shirt to the floor, something I knew took effort for him, took a show of trust that he likely had never demonstrated before, baring those scars he was so protective of.

His head cocked to the side as his hands moved to the waistband of his pants. As he popped the button, a fast, furious, fluttering sensation started between my thighs. Anticipation. Need.

The pants hit the floor, leaving him in a pair of black boxer briefs that did nothing to hide his straining cock.

The fluttering became something entirely different then, something stronger, something borderline painful.

Then his hands reached for the elastic waistband of his underwear, pulling it down.

And I swear I almost came right then and there.

His cock was straining, larger than you would guess from his deceptively thin body.

Forget breathing. My chest felt constricted even as I forced my eyes to move upward to his face, even as his eyes warmed slightly, maybe feeling relief that I hadn't shrunk away. But the reality was, the last thing on my mind right then were his scars.

Seeming to sense the acceptance, he moved forward across the small space, pulling open the stall door, and stepping inside, making me press back against the wall to make room for him.

His hand rose, resting over the one that I had in the center of my chest, holding the towel in place. My eyes on his, seeing a desire there so thick that I felt completely enveloped in it, my hand slipped away, letting him hold the towel for a long moment before he pulled it down and dropped it to the side.

I don't know what I was expecting next.

But he reached out and a cascade of cool water hit me, making me let out a strangled yipping noise in surprise, making his lips curve up.

"Come here," he said, moving backward under the spray, putting his hands on my hips to pull me with him.

The cold water moved across my suddenly heavy breasts, making a shiver course through me.

But then his hands on my hips pulled, making my pelvis meet his, making his cock press into my belly, and, yeah, that shiver had nothing to do with the cold.

"Don't worry," he said, leaning down to run his lips up my neck. "Once I'm done here, I'm gonna take care of you," he said, like a promise, like a vow. That was how serious his tone was as he reached past me for the soap.

"Can I?" I asked, surprising myself, I think, more than him.

His smile went a little wicked even as his eyes got heavier, but as my hand rose to touch the edge of the scar on his chest, his entire body stiffened. "It doesn't matter," I said, pressing closer to him. "Whatever this is," I went on, brushing the soap across the whole thing, "it doesn't matter right now, okay?"

There was a long moment where he was staring at me, his eyes blank, lost somewhere. Lost, I was sure, in the moment when those scars got carved into his flesh.

But then he came back, slowly at first, like he was thawing.

"Between us," he said, ducking his head a bit to keep intense eye-contact, "it never matters, okay?"

I could understand the need for that, guessing that whatever put them there was horrific, was something dark and ugly that he didn't want to put between what was growing with us.

"Okay," I agreed, nodding, doing another swipe across his chest that didn't make him stiffen so hard.

By the time I was scrubbing his back, noticing for the first time lash marks across the backs of his thighs, swallowing hard, trying to show no signs of my shock, even though he was facing away from me, his entire body - cock aside- had relaxed.

"Think I'm clean now, doll," he rumbled as my hands moved over his ass.

"I'm just being extra sure," I said, pressing my breasts into his back, enjoying the little rumbling growly noise he let out at my hardened nipples pressing into his skin. "You know," I teased, hands moving across his belly and *down*, "I think I maybe missed a spot..." I added as my fingers teased down the deep V of his Adonis belt.

The soap dropped, forgotten, as my hand closed around his cock.

I barely got to stroke him once before he whipped around. His wide-palmed hands closed around my wrists, dragging my arms up, then slamming them back against the shower wall over my head as his lips crashed down on mine.

Everything else simply fell away.

All there was was his tongue in my mouth, his teeth in my lip, his cock against my belly, his hard chest against my breasts.

His lips ripped from mine, making a pained whimper escape me before I felt his lips work their way down the column of my neck. He released my wrists and my hands raked down his back, making him hiss as his teeth nipped into the skin right below my ear.

"Luce... please," I groaned, leg raising to his side, wrapping half around his back, practically climbing him in my need for more.

"What? You don't like being tortured?" he asked against my ear, nipping into the lobe. "I've been thinking about this shit for over a week."

I dropped my hips, feeling his cock brush against my clit, making a whimper escape me.

"I've been thinking of you inside me for over a week," I admitted, making his head raise, his smirk wicked.

"Well, that's too fucking long." His hands went down my back to sink into my ass, yanking me up by it, forcing my legs around him as he stepped out of the stall, stopping for only a second to dry his feet because falling and breaking something would have made the moment a helluva lot less sexy.

The next thing I knew, as I was busy trying to torture his neck as he tortured mine, I was free falling backward before I bounced on the bed, making me let out a loud laugh for a moment before he moved to the foot of the bed, reaching down to touch my ankle.

It was chaste, but it sent off an electric current up my calf, thigh, then between.

"Nice fucking view," he rumbled, voice low as his knees pressed into the edge of the mattress. His hands moved up my calves to grab my knees, sinking in, and spreading my thighs wide on the outside of his hips.

"Luce," I demanded as he just kept looking down at me, eyes downcast.

"Never done a fucking thing in my life to deserve this," he said, tone heavy, as his hands drifted up my belly, stroking across the sensitive undersides of my breasts. "But I'm gonna show you just how fucking appreciative I am."

Then he was down on the mattress.

And I could barely pull in a breath before I felt his tongue slide up my slick cleft and circle around my seemingly throbbing clit.

My hand slapped down on the back of his neck, holding him to me, but there was no need; he didn't need to be held there. He had no plans to stop, to bring me to the brink, then take it away.

He was devouring me, working my clit in circles as his fingers slid between and slipped slowly inside me, working with small, gentle strokes.

My hand slid upward, curling into his wet hair as my hips started moving against him, wanting more, needing more, needing *him.*

"Luce, please," I whimpered, reaching for his shoulders, trying to pull him upward.

His tongue left my clit as he angled his head up, but his fingers kept their thrusting. "How can I show you how much I appreciate you if I don't make you scream before I get to feel your tight pussy take me in?"

Then he tipped his head back down.

But his tongue didn't move out.

No.

His lips closed around my clit and sucked hard just as his fingers curled and stroked over my G-spot.

That was it.

That was all it took.

The orgasm ripped through me, making my thighs shake as the waves crashed, as I screamed. *His name.*

"Fuck," he growled as he released my clit and kissed up my belly, his scruff scraping at the overly-sensitive skin deliciously.

It didn't matter that he had just given me a powerful orgasm. It didn't matter that it was more than I had had in far too long.

It wasn't enough.

It wasn't anywhere near enough.

Nothing would be enough until I felt him slide inside me, until I felt him move within me, until we both shattered together.

As if sensing this, he took his time.

His tongue traced under my breast, making a shiver move through me a second before his lips closed around my nipple, and sucked hard. He moved across my chest to suck the other hardened point in, then nipped so viciously that I saw stars as an unexpected surge of desire shot between my thighs.

Frustrated, I whipped upward, slamming a hand into his shoulder, sending him flying onto his back with a grunt.

"Like to play rough, huh?" he asked, smiling up at me as I moved to straddle him.

"Two can play that torture game," I informed him as I lowered my face down toward him, making sure my breasts teased into his chest.

I kissed, licked, sucked down his neck, his chest, his stomach.

"Evan..." his voice warned as I nipped into his inner thigh.

I smiled as I turned suddenly, sucking his cock deep before he could even anticipate the motion, making his hips jerk upward as his hand slammed down on the back of my neck.

"Fuck, doll," he growled, moving to grab my hair to curl it in his fist so he could watch as I started to work him. *Slowly.*

He liked torture; I could torture.

"Jesus Christ," he growled as my fingers teased over his balls. "Okay, okay," he chuckled. "I get it, Ev," he said, yanking hard enough on my hair to make me lose his cock completely. "You want my cock," he added, looking devilish as he curled to the side of the bed, shuffling around in his bag, and coming back with a condom. "That's the point you're trying to make, right?" he asked as he reached for my wrist, grabbing, and sending me falling down on the bed.

I rolled to my side facing him as he rolled to his, pulling up the condom to nip at the edge and rip it. "That's definitely the point I've been trying to make," I agreed, sliding my leg up over his hip as he protected us.

"Well, I can't deny such a request, huh?" he asked, hand sliding up my thigh, curving around until it settled on my ass.

"No, you wouldn't do that," I agreed as he rolled me onto my back, moving over me, sealing his lips into mine.

His cock pressed hard into my slit, making my legs raise up, wrapping around his lower back, inviting him in as he nipped my lower lip.

"Luce, please," I groaned, hips grinding up into his, nails digging into his back.

His eyes flashed as he raised up to look down at me. "Sounds fucking good when you beg for my cock, doll," he growled as the head of his cock finally pressed where I needed him most, creating a pressure that made me let out a whimper of desperation. "Know what will sound even better?" he asked as his hips pressed forward, as his cock slid inside me, making me let out a loud moan. "Yeah, that," he agreed, cock twitching as he settled deep.

"Oh my *God.*"

True, it had been a while, but I was sure in that moment that nothing had ever felt anywhere near as good before.

"Only gonna get better, doll," he said, voice low, as his hips shifted back, then pressed deep again.

And then it did.

His eyes were on mine as he slowly, gently, almost, dare I say it, lovingly thrust within me, driving me up slowly, almost excruciatingly, seeming to take his joy in leisurely building an almost painful amount of pleasure in me before allowing it to finally crest.

"Okay, baby, okay," he crooned as my whimpers became actual cries, the need so strong it was a painful pressure that felt like there would be no end to. "You want to come for me?" he asked, shifting slightly so his hand could slide between us, pressing into my swollen clit. "Yeah?" he asked. I nodded as my entire body stiffened, as he pushed me into that nothingness. "Come, Evan," he demanded as his cock pressed forward, as his finger did another swipe.

My cry got caught, strangled in my throat as the first waves slammed through my system, seeming to start at the base of my spine, and explode outward. But then I did find my voice again, and there was only one thing to say.

His name.

"*Luce*," I cried out on the last waves as he buried deep and hissed my name into my neck as he came with me.

He stayed buried deep as we both struggled to find our breaths, as my body shook gently in aftershocks, as our hearts slowed.

"Worth the wait," he said as he pressed upward, looking down at me with eyes that seemed heavy, as they often did, but this time with something that wasn't scary or dark. It was something else, something I couldn't quite place, but something that seemed good, something that made a warmth spread through my belly.

"Yeah, it was," I agreed, hand going behind his neck to pull him back down, kissing him long until his lips were smiling against mine, making me let him up. "What?" I asked, smiling back.

"Tell you what... ask me that again tomorrow, okay?" he said oddly as he pulled against my hold to stand.

"Why?"

"Got my reasons. Ask me tomorrow," he demanded again, giving me a lazy grin as he moved toward the bathroom.

Intrigued, I forced my lazy limbs to move, climbing off the bed that we had soaked with our shower-wet bodies.

"Here, Ev," Luce said as he came back out, holding a fluffy towel. "Your hair is still dripping," he explained as I took it and started drying. "Hungry?" he asked, fishing out a new pair of boxer briefs, and slipping them on.

"I could eat," I agreed as he slipped into jeans and a tee.

"I'll drop into that place down the street again," he said, tying on some shoes. "That stew last night was pretty banging," he added, and I had to agree. "Gotta keep your strength up," he went on, closing in on me, reaching behind me to run a finger down my spine. "Because there's going to be a fuckuva lot of that from now on," he said with a wink as he gestured toward the bed.

"Promise?" I asked with a smirk that he returned.

"Fucking vow," he agreed, lips crushing to mine for a long moment before he moved toward the door. "I'll be back in twenty."

With that, he was gone, leaving me to change into a pair of lightweight shorts and one of Luce's tees.

"You forgot your key you idi..." I started as I opened the door following a few short knocks.

The smile fell from my face though as soon as I had the door open.

Because it wasn't Luce who had been knocking.

And my stomach dropped painfully, something in me screaming that things had just taken a sharp turn downward.

The man's smile was slow, slick, evil.

"Been waiting years to send a message to your old man," he growled as I moved backward, trying to find the bat we had walked home with. "Now, what better way than taking his perfect, protected little angel?" he asked as my hand closed around the long, hard, cold handle of the bat, my heart thrumming so hard that I couldn't seem to even think past the pounding, not even enough to do the smart thing and *scream.*

My arm raised, but before I could even swing the back, it was ripped from my hand, raised, and just as I remembered to scream, as my mouth opened, as the first sounds came out, the bat descended and all I saw was blackness.

TWELVE

Luce

I wasn't lying when I said I didn't do anything to deserve her.

My entire life was ugly, filthy, dark, and awful.

The only thing I touched was evil, with the soul purpose of getting rid of it, sure, but there weren't any gloves thick enough to keep that shit from touching you, from getting under your skin too.

I didn't have any right to touch anything beautiful, knowing damn well that I risked ruining it with my filth.

And Evan, yeah, she was fucking beautiful.

I had no business putting a finger on her.

But there was no going back for me from that first time she told me she wouldn't ask about the scars. I had tried to fight it here and there; I knew it was best for her to see that I was not the man for her, to want to put some space there.

No matter how I tried to pull away though, there was simply no denying the connection, the way her eyes went bright when she talked to me, went hungry when she looked at me.

I knew I should have regretted it; I should have been coming up with ways to untangle myself from the situation for her good, but no, I was going to the little all-night convenience store that served food that was better than half the restaurants back in Navesink Bank to bring some sustenance back to her, so she could gain her strength, and we could go another round or three before morning.

Fact of the matter was, I didn't fuck around a whole helluva lot. The not wanting to get undressed shit limited the options for dipping the wick. But I was no starry-eyed virgin. I had been around the block. So when I say I know that nothing, fucking nothing had ever felt like that before, I knew what I was saying.

I wasn't a romantic. I didn't even understand the concept of flowers and candy. I didn't have the words that many men did.

But I wasn't walking away.

I always walked away.

It was *smart* to walk away.

It was better for her that I walk away.

I just couldn't, and didn't want to, do that this time.

It was probably going to blow up in my face. Some day, after I likely got in way too goddamn deep, she was going to see all the ugly, she was going to realize she didn't want it mucking up her life, and she was going to leave.

That, well, I was in-touch enough with myself to know that shit was not going to feel great.

But those were the consequences. And I was thinking I was maybe willing to face them up.

Some day.

After I had gotten to enjoy the fuck out of her for as long as she would allow it.

Which was why I caught myself smiling like a fucking fool as I closed in on the door to our room, a bag full of dinner, drinks, and snacks to hold us over until we hit town the next day to meet her mother.

Nothing seemed amiss.

I walked in, figuring she was in the bathroom.

But then I moved to put the bags down on the small desk just inside the door.

And my eyes caught sight of the bat, laid out across the floor where it most definitely did not belong.

The bags dropped from my hands, the tops slipping off the stew containers and spilling dinner all over the floor.

But I was barely even aware of that.

Because that bat... it had fucking blood on it.

And Evan was missing.

"*Fuck!*" I yelled, slamming my fist backward into the wall, the pain ricocheting up my arm, somehow managing to ground me.

I moved across the room, getting my cell, grabbing my hoodie, and a wad of cash, and heading out, knocking on the doors to the side of the room, clearly waking everyone up.

No one had heard a thing.

Of course not.

I tore back down the street, my heart hammering in my chest, trying not to get too ahead of myself. Wherever she was, whoever had her, they couldn't be far off.

I needed to fucking focus.

I needed to keep my cool.

We were in mother fucking *Brazil.*

I didn't know how shit worked. I didn't know who the major players were. I didn't know why someone would take her. I didn't know how not to get caught if I went sniffing around. I didn't know dick.

But I did know one thing.

I couldn't do shit without the right tools.

"Yo," I called to a group of men standing outside the convenience store I had just left. Every town had the type. Didn't matter if they were black, white, Latino, Asian; it didn't fucking matter. You knew the type when you saw them. They could be in wifebeaters with their underwear hanging ten inches out of their jeans, or they could be in tracksuits, or dress shirts. It didn't matter. You could spot them. There was just a vibe in the air around them. There was a laid-back cockiness to criminals. "Yo, anyone speak English? Falar inglês? No?" I asked when they all turned, giving me a once over. "Fuck. Alright. I need a gun. A... arma," I tried, reaching into my pocket to wave the money. "Jesus Christ. Tell me who can get me a mother fucking gun."

"Hey, amigo, you need to take a breath. A aí?"

A aí?

What's up?

"My girl was just taken from my mother fucking motel room. I need a gun, and I need to know the players in this bumfuck backward jungle town. That's what's up. So if you're not who I need to be talking to, point me where I need to be."

"Or what?"

"Or I will pick up that broken beer bottle right there," I said, pointing to the ground near my foot without looking, wanting to keep my eyes on the trio, "and I will slit your jugular," I said to the main guy, "take that knife you have in your belt and stab the other two of you. My reputation might not precede me in this place, but trust me when I say you do not want to fuck with me. So I will repeat myself *one more time*. I need a gun, and I need to know who might have a problem with Alejandro Cruz."

There was a hush following that name, making me realize maybe I should have brought it up before right that moment.

One of them men in the back mumbled *estuprador*.

Rapist.

The other said *envenenador*.

Poisoner.

So my reputation didn't mean shit, but his sure as shit still did. Apparently, word hadn't made it this far that the rapist poisoner was long dead.

And, if I wasn't mistaken, and I fucking wasn't, there was a certain level of fear in their voices when they said those words.

"You work for Cruz?" the leader asked, looking me over again.

"And Cruz's daughter was just taken. You want me to go back, pull him away from business, and tell him you stupid fucks wouldn't help me get a gun, and point me in a direction? That what you are telling me? I'd be happy to go get..." I started, turning to walk away.

"Whoa! Wait. Okay, amigo. No need to call o chefe. You want a gun? You can have my gun," he said, reaching behind his back to pull it out of his waistband.

"Does it work?"

As an answer, he raised it above his head and fired off two shots.

You knew the people inside were used to these guys because they barely even flinched at the sound of gunshots.

"It works."

"Bullets. And information," I demanded, slapping the pile of cash into his hand as he handed me the gun with the other. "Who wants Cruz to suffer around here?"

One of the guys in the back snorted. "All the fathers of the girls who he put his hands on maybe?"

"Yeah, I get it," I said, tucking the gun away. "He's got a bad rep. But I think you shitheads know that if you don't start giving me some answers, that if one goddamn hair is out of place on that girl's head, that he will drag his ass down here, get each of you strapped to a chair, then get his jollies off by finding new and inventive ways to make you pay for *her* pain and suffering."

"Fuck, man," the leader said, holding up his hands in a defensive gesture, letting me know just how bad a rep Cruz actually had on the streets. When you looked around online, you had to figure that at least half of the shit was hearsay, was embellished.

In the case of Alejandro Cruz, apparently, all the information was on point.

"Talk," I demanded, pointing the gun at him. "Or I start with the dick and work my way around other, more vital organs for such an ugly fuck."

"The Diaz crew," he rushed to say, voice actually fucking shaking. So whoever they were, they were low level. Dealers or pimps, not people used to having guns pointed at them.

"Who are they? Where are they? Why would they want her?"

"Cruz came through, I don't know... ten years back or something. He was hired by some nobody dealer with a big ego to take out the leading cartel around here."

"Let me guess," I said, putting the gun down, "the Diaz crew."

"Took out Luis Diaz," the guy agreed, nodding. "But not before he held down his wife and daughter and raped them in front of the man."

I felt my jaw tighten, wishing I could have resuscitated the fucking bastard so I could have killed him myself.

"Who would be left? Who would come for her for revenge?" I asked, teeth grinding so hard that a pain shot up to my temples.

Because if the crime was rape and murder, the revenge would most likely be the same. Eye for an eye.

I needed to get to her.

Five goddamn minutes ago.

If that mother fucker touched her...

No.

I couldn't go there.

I had to shut it down.

I had to keep a clear head.

The only reason I had survived so long in the criminal underbelly was because I kept my feelings out of shit. I went in cold and calculated. I kept my head on straight. I handled my shit.

I could *feel* later.

Right now, I needed to shut it the fuck down.

"The crew disbanded, went on and joined the new o chefe to keep food in their stomachs."

"All except who?"

"Diaz's only son. Miguel. He was seventeen at the time, out on a job. Comes home to find his mom and sister broken, his father murdered."

"Where do I find Miguel?" I asked, raising the gun when they paused, looking at each other, pointing it at his dick, and cocking it.

"Whoa! Okay. Calm down, amigo. Back the way you came, you saw that big house on the hill on your way? That is Diaz's place. His father's place."

I turned to go walk away, but then turned back. "Where did Cruz kill Diaz?" I asked, figuring if this was going to go, it was going to go exactly how it did a decade ago.

"Guest house out back," one of the guys in the back supplied.

"Good. Now if I find out that Diaz got tipped off about me coming, what you imagine Cruz would do to you will mother fucking pale in comparison to how I will make you suffer. Got me?"

"Compreendo!" the leader said, holding up his hands.

Convinced they were scared enough, that I had enough headstart, I reached out, took the knife from the guy's belt, turned, and fucking *ran.*

Try as I might, as I ran, the thoughts swirled, the ideas of what could be happening to her rushed through my mind. I knew she had already been bashed, likely on the head, by the bat. For that and that alone, the bastard was going to get what was coming to him.

But it had been at least twenty minutes.

The shit that could have happened to her in twenty minutes...

No.

Fuck no.

I couldn't let my mind go there.

Because for the split second that it did, my vision flashed so red that I had to stop moving because I couldn't see a goddamn thing.

I took a deep breath and pressed forward, completely shutting down my brain. It was something I was good at. It was something I had needed to do countless times in my life. Not when taking out scumbags. No. I was fully present during all that. No. I'm talking about before that, before all the killing, before taking up the cause of vengeance for all those people who couldn't fight back.

Like me once upon a time.

If I could shut it down back then, then I could shut it down again. Just for another eight minutes, tops. Eight minutes of keeping my mind blank. Then the second I got inside that guest house, I was opening everything back up.

While I understood Diaz's desire for vengeance, while I respected wanting an eye-for-an-eye for shit as whacked as what Cruz pulled on Diaz's sister and mother, you did *not* get that revenge by hurting other innocent women.

You did not get an eye-for-an-eye using your cock as revenge on someone who never did a goddamn thing wrong. You know, or at fucking all.

Because there was no other word for that but evil. Marrow deep evil.

If he was willing to do that shit then, well, he was every bit as big a dirtbag as Alejandro.

And he was going to die a slow, painful, brutal death for even thinking he could do something like that to Evan.

God help his ass if he actually accomplished any of it.

The red flashed over my eyes again, making me need to shake my head, and take a deep breath before I could move on, rushing past the massive three-story home belonging to the dead Diaz.

A house like that was built to be protected, was built on a hill so guards could see for miles all the way around.

But since his father's business collapsed, Miguel Diaz obviously could not rebuild the ranks, thanks to them jumping ship, and likely a heavy presence from the rival cartel that took over.

There were no fucking guards.

All there was was the far-away sound of wolves, some night insects, and my thundering heartbeat.

I heard it as I rounded the small guesthouse. It was set back from the main house by about an acre. It was a small, rectangular building the size of Evan's mother's place, squat, with only two windows and a door out front. Nothing fancy, but as I crouched down beside it, I heard it.

A scream.

Evan's scream.

At that point, there was no keeping the anger down, no keeping a cool head.

The rage bubbled in my veins as I rounded on the door, taking the gun into my right hand, and the knife into my left, then raising a foot, and slamming it into the door, sending the shitty thing flying open.

"*Fodssse*!" the man who must have been Miguel Diaz yelled, springing backward from the crumpled form of Evan on the floor.

Miguel Diaz was darker-skinned with long black hair, dark eyes, and a medium build. And maybe if he didn't have Evan's shorts around her ankles, maybe I could have said he was reasonably good-looking.

But being as her shorts *were* around her ankles, all I saw was ugly.

"Yeah, fuck is right," I agreed, voice low and vicious. Because not only were her shorts around her ankles, but she was openly bleeding from her temple where, I assumed, the bat had struck her hard enough to knock her out since no one had heard any screams from her as he dragged her away. Her other eye was blackened, her lip split and swollen. There were bruises around her wrists from, I assumed, being held down.

"Think you're lost, amigo," he said, standing fully, and I wasn't sure if I could feel relief yet that his pants were fastened.

I could have simply been too late.

"Luce?" Evan's pained, desperate voice reached my ears, making my eyes move to find her frantically trying to drag her pants back up her legs, furious tears streaming down her face.

"Can you walk?" I asked through gritted teeth as she shakily moved to stand. I took a breath as she stumbled slightly, knowing I needed to keep it together for her sake. "Come here, doll," I said softly as she started moving across the floor. "You take this," I said as she got close, pressing the gun at her.

"You..."

"Take this gun and go outside," I said, voice soft, but firm. I needed her to follow orders. I needed to get her safe.

Because I was about to blow.

And she needed to be as far away from that as possible.

"And if you see anyone but me, you fucking empty the clip into their bodies. Okay?"

Her eyes went up to mine, making my stomach clench hard when I saw her bottom lip tremble as she moved to take it.

"Okay?" I repeated as her hand closed around it.

She gave me a tight nod, and moved almost robotically toward the door.

"What now, amigo? You have no gun."

"I don't use guns, *amigo*," I said, switching the knife to my right hand. "I like working with my hands."

"As you can see from your little girlfriend out there," he said, his head tipping to the side, "I do too."

"Oh, shithead, that was the wrong fucking thing to say."

I let it out then, the rage.

He must have underestimated me because when I flew at him and plunged the knife into his side, just under his lowest rib, just deep enough to hurt like a mother fucker, but not deep enough to cause any actual damage, his eyes went round as hell.

People did tend to underestimate me.

I wasn't a huge guy. Tall, sure, but thin, wiry, unassuming-looking.

No one thought the skinny guy in a hoodie with pale computer-geek skin was any kind of threat.

But, fucking hell were they wrong.

They were always shocked when the bag went over their heads, or the garrote around their throat, or the knife to the jugular.

It was like they all thought I was a bunch of talk.

Just some shithead who got off scaring people.

So it was always a shock.

"Just an inch deeper, and angled upward, and I'd be hitting lung. They'd fill up with blood, and you would suffocate from the inside out. It's a particularly awful way to go. So that seems like a fitting end," I told him. "Just not yet," I added, yanking the knife out, twirling it into my hand, cocking a fist, throwing every last bit of strength I had into the blow to his jaw, sending him flying to the floor.

"You protect her?" he screamed from the floor. "After what her bastard father did?"

"Key words there being *her bastard father*," I said, standing over him, waiting for him to make a move to stand. "She wasn't the one who put her hands on your mother and sister."

"He needs to pay for what he did to them!" he shrieked. "My sister, she killed herself three weeks later. Slit her wrists so deep that there was no repairing them. My mother died from the heartbreak! He needs to know that pain."

"See, now," I said, shrugging back into the coldness, the darkness like a favorite shirt, feeling much more comfortable in it. "That is why I am the vigilante, and you are just some two-bit schmuck so blind with rage that he can't see all he is doing is hurting more innocent women."

"Vigilante," he hissed, spitting a molar and a healthy mouthful of blood on the floor as he pushed up to stand. "Yeah, right."

"See, given the proper time, I'd let you stand a little mock trial, give you a chance to come clean, to turn yourself in, or choose death. I would take the time to get some lye, heat it up, melt you down. But I got a woman outside who needs me. So we are going to do this the fast, brutal, bloody, messy fucking way."

Then I charged, plunging the knife into his chest and stomach six times before he could even cry out.

I didn't often use knives.

They were a torture instrument unless it was a quick slice to the jugular so they could bleed out in a matter of seconds.

I didn't get off on pain.

I wasn't a fucking psycho.

I wanted people to pay with their lives for the misery it had brought to the world.

Usually, it was done as painlessly as possible.

Not this time.

This time it was personal.

This time it was about him putting his ugly hands all over the most beautiful fucking thing I had ever been lucky enough to have in my life, something I didn't deserve, but cherished nonethefuckingless.

For that, for putting those marks on her perfect face, for putting those tears in her eyes, for putting that quiver of fear in her voice, yeah, he had to *pay.*

It was a testament to my own darkness that his cries, that his begging, that his useless apologies, that the sounds of him literally choking on his own blood, blood that was saturating my hoodie, did nothing to me.

It simply didn't penetrate.

Because all I could see was Evan's face.

All I could hear was the desperate way she called my name.

All I could think was what thoughts she must have had swirling through her head when she woke up alone, with a throbbing head, in an unfamiliar room, with a man there who didn't even see her as a person, just a body he could exact vengeance on. She had to have thought of me, maybe even cried out for me while his hands struck bruises into her flawless skin. And there had to have been hopelessness. Because Evan was a smart woman. She knew it was a foreign country. She knew I didn't have contacts here. She knew the only parts of the language I knew were the parts I had heard her say, or the people on the TV say. She knew that I would have no idea who took her, or where, that she was completely and utterly alone, and at the mercy of a man who, as he was peeling off her clothes, she knew wanted to rape her.

Maybe, for a split second, maybe she even thought she deserved it. Because her emotions were still raw about Alejandro. Because there was guilt there for the atrocities he had committed while she blindly followed him around the world. Maybe she thought it was a fitting punishment for her ignorance.

That. Shit. Would. Not. Stand.

If he made her think that way, if he made her question her own right to say no, to not have something forced upon her, then he deserved every moment of agony I inflicted upon him.

"*Paula?*" he gasped, eyes going huge, wondrous.

He thought he was seeing his dead sister.

That was a surefire way to know they were close.

The brain misfired in the last moments, brain cells dying off, creating visions that weren't real.

"Afraid not," I said, pulling the knife back, ready for the final blow, done, beyond done. "There is no afterlife; you just die." With that, with that last, final, brutal blow to not only his psyche, but his heart with my knife, Miguel Diaz had joined the ranks of Alejandro.

And good fucking riddance to bad fucking rubbish.

There wasn't a guilty bone in my body as I wiped the knife clean of fingerprints with his shirt and left it, as I walked to the sink to wash most of the blood off my hands.

There was nothing I could do about the fact that my shirt was literally saturated with blood. But it was dark out. Even if we happened upon someone on the way back, they wouldn't likely be able to see.

The evidence, well, that would have to be dealt with later.

Right now, what mattered was Evan.

On that thought, I turned, moving back toward the door, and stepping out into the humid night air.

I heard a click.

"Ev, it's me," I said, voice soft, moving toward the sound, coming from the side of the guest house where I had crouched just twenty minutes before. "It's me, doll," I added as I stepped into view, reaching to place my hand on the top of the gun, pushing it so the barrel was facing the ground before pulling it out of her shaking fingers.

I tucked it into the back waistband of my jeans, lowering myself down in front of her, not reaching for her yet because I wasn't sure if that was the right move. "It's over, okay? It's all over."

"He... he..." she stammered, shaking her head, trying to take a deep breath, but it made her entire body shake with the effort.

"Ev," I said, softly, but even I heard the pleading in my voice. Hearing it, maybe understanding how unusual it was for me, her gaze rose. Her eyes were red, the lids swollen, but she was holding back another wave of tears. I didn't want to ask. It felt wrong. It felt like I was asking something that was none of my business. But at the same time, I needed to know. I needed to know because I needed to know if I was going to be enough, or if maybe I needed to bring her to her mother's, to get help from someone who would understand. So I had to ask. "Did he rape you?"

The words tasted like battery acid on my tongue.

They made her cringe backward too even as her eyes closed for a long second and she swallowed hard, making my stomach lurch, sure what her answer was going to be.

But then her eyes opened, clear, her voice when she spoke was even. "No," she said, tone firm. "He was going to," she said, nodding a little frantically, losing the small bit of control she had over her swirling emotions. "He even told me he was going..."

"Sh," I said, shaking my head, reaching out for her face, tilting her chin up. "I was never gonna let that happen, okay?"

"You didn't know where..."

"Well, I found out," I said, forcing a small smile that I didn't feel in the least, but knowing my own dark mood was of no use to her.

"How?"

"Can we maybe talk about that back at the motel, doll?" I asked, stroking my finger down her cheek. "I need to do something about this cut to the side of your head, and you gotta be wanting some pain medicine right about now. Think we can get moving?"

She nodded, taking my hand when I offered it to help her up. "You smell like blood," she informed me, tone a little empty.

"Yes."

"He was screaming."

My stomach tensed as we started walking.

I knew this day would come.

I knew that at some point she would see beyond the guy who made her laugh and think and would take her on cross-countries adventure.

I knew that she would only be able to accept me for a short time before she saw who I really was.

Maybe I had been hoping, though, that it wouldn't be quite so soon.

"I know, Ev," I agreed, keeping my eyes forward as I tried to press the pace faster, wanting to get back to the motel and out of sight as soon as possible.

I knew that someday, someway, somehow, I was going to end up in jail or dead for my actions. I did very much prefer, though, that the jail wasn't in fucking Brazil.

"Am I a terrible person for being glad he's dead?" she asked after a long, drawn-out silence that had my heart thrumming hard against my ribcage.

I stopped short, turning fully to her, noticing it took her an excruciatingly long moment to make eye-contact. But I wouldn't answer until I had it.

"Evan, he wanted to *rape* you. He wanted to shove something inside your body. If that something was a *knife* instead of a dick, would you be questioning your right to wish him dead right now? I don't care if you wanted to slice off his cock with a dull butter knife, then shove it up his ass, and make him write a twenty-page dissertation on the concept of consent while he writhed in un-lubricated agony. I still wouldn't think you were a terrible person. Rabid dogs can't be tamed, Ev. They need to be put down."

"So you put him down."

"Yes."

"Do they bother you?" she asked, feet planting, seeming to need to hash this out, right there on the side of the street.

"The men I kill?" I clarified.

"Yeah."

"I have a lot of demons that bother me, doll. These men are not one of them. I believe in what I do. I believe in ridding the world of people who only bring evil into it, even if that makes me evil in turn."

There was a long, excruciating silence following my words where Evan was just watching me with eyes I suddenly couldn't read.

Then she spoke, and her voice had more conviction than I had ever heard before. "You're not evil."

"Doll, you don't...."

"You *saved* me tonight," she cut me off. "You didn't have to do that. And you told me the truth about my fath... Alejandro. And my mother. You made me come here to meet her. You took time out of your life to make my life better. Evil people don't do that, Luce. Evil people just get off ruining peoples' lives. You might exist and work within a gray area, but you lean more light than dark."

With that little nugget, she turned, and started walking again, leaving me there standing dumbly for a long minute before I pulled it together and followed her.

"Shower," I demanded as soon as we walked in the door.

"I'm so tir..." she started to object, and my heart dropped.

I wanted to tell her that it was okay, that she could just climb into bed, that she could nurse her pounding head, and get a good nights' rest.

But I had to keep my head on straight.

In Navesink Bank, I could have called in someone else to do what had to be done that night so I could stay with her. In Brazil, I was on my own. If we wanted to get out of this country without spending a decade in prison, I needed to do everything by the book.

"I know, babe, I know. But you need to wash off the blood and evidence. Scrape under your nails. And I need your clothes."

It hadn't exactly escaped me that she was in my shirt. It was one of the first things I had noticed when I burst in that room, after the injuries and missing shorts.

She put on *my* shirt.

She had plenty of her own, but she wanted to wear mine.

I wouldn't claim to be an expert on women, but I was pretty sure that shit was clear.

"Oh, right," she agreed, eyes clearing a little. "You're..."

"I can wait until you're done," I said, nodding at her to go ahead, figuring she wanted a few minutes.

Honestly, I did too.

I needed to figure out how to get rid of the body. And our clothes. I needed to handle any possible loose ends.

Evan came back out a few minutes later, wet, and so much more pale than before. "Wait," I said when she went to go to the bed. "I know," I said when she whined. "I know, doll. I just need to put something on that cut. It's gonna get infected."

I pulled her back into the bathroom, finding some peroxide in the cabinet, watering it down, and pressing it into all the open cuts on her face.

"You're leaving," she mumbled as she watched me.

"Not for long," I promised. "An hour. And you're keeping the gun and the door locked. I just want to make sure we don't end up spending any time in some backward Brazilian prison."

"Okay," she said, giving me a nod, understanding even if she didn't like it.

"One hour," I promised, walking with her back to the bedroom, pulling the blankets up when she laid down. I placed the gun on the nightstand, rummaged in my bag for some aspirin, and handed it to her.

I grabbed clothes, running into the bathroom, showering so fast that I was pretty sure I scratched my own damn skin in a rush to get the blood off. I took the liner out of the trash, throwing both our clothes in it, and went back out.

She was already out cold.

With a lump in my throat, I made my way out, making sure the door was locked, and making my way back to the Diaz house at a dead run.

I stripped his body and threw it into the bath, running the water toward scalding and pouring half a bottle of bleach on him. I didn't plan on the body being found until it was good and decomposed. But you could never be too careful.

I took all our clothes into the small top-and-bottom laundry in the closet, putting them in with about a third of what was left of the bleach as well as twice the laundry detergent that was actually needed. The bloodstains would turn orange. But I wasn't worried about that. The purpose was destroying the evidence. Once it was gone, the clothes were going to be burned.

As they washed and dried, I cleaned up the blood on the floor and walls, finding the familiar action almost comforting.

Body cleaned, clothes dried, I grabbed a wheelbarrow, tossed him in, took the clothes in another bathroom liner, grabbed a shovel, and made a move toward the woods behind his property.

So maybe I lied to Evan when I said an hour. It took me almost an hour to clean. It was going to take another hour to find a location, dig a grave, then discreetly burn the clothes at another location.

Then and only then could I make my way back.

"Here," I said, stopping outside the convenience store, getting more food, discreetly dropping off the other hoodie I was wearing in the dumpster out back, then approaching the men from the night before. "All yours. Don't worry, I didn't use it," I said when he eyed me. "Turns out she was out for a fucking walk," I said, rolling my eyes. "At two in the goddamn morning."

"Candelas são loucas," the leader snorted. "Making you run all over like a maniac. Hope her father beats her ass."

"Careful," I warned, making them all stiffen. "You don't want that talk getting around to Alejandro."

With that, I made my way back to the motel, finding Evan still passed out, the bruises even deeper after time, and yet again stripping, then washing and bleaching my clothes.

I was finally, finally content that things were handled at least enough for us to be able to spend a few hours with her mother, then get the hell back onto US soil.

As soon as fucking possible.

I didn't like not knowing the major players. I didn't like not having backup. True, I never used it in Navesink Bank, but it was there if I somehow *did* need it; no questions asked. There would be Barrett, Jstorm, Alex, Pagan... any number of people I had helped over time. They would step up with their various skills and help me in any way I needed.

I needed to get back to that.

But I knew I couldn't just wake up Ev and force her to hop two buses and a plane when she was just hours away from a beating and almost-rape. She needed time. She needed sleep. She needed to keep her plans with her mother. She needed a little softness.

I was beginning to know her, so I knew she wouldn't need a week before she would crawl out of bed. She was going to get some sleep, get some food in her stomach, talk it out with her mom, then she was going to be ready to compartmentalize that and move forward.

She was resilient.

And, as much as I hated to give the bastard any credit, it must have been at least in part from the way Alejandro raised her.

I had barely gotten in bed with her, closing my eyes, when I felt her fingertips hesitantly touch my bare arm.

"You're here."

My arm slid around her hips, pulling her closer, keeping her against me tight.

"Yeah, doll. I'm right here."

And I had the oddest, strongest, almost overpowering feeling that that was where I would always want to be.

That shit?

Yeah, it was insane.

But I let myself think it as I fell asleep with her in my arms.

THIRTEEN

Evan

I hadn't lived a sheltered life. I had seen so many things. And not all of those things had been pretty. I had seen malnourished babies dying of starvation. I had seen bodies dead in the road from civil and gang wars. I had seen child prostitutes and grown women brutalized by the very male relatives who were supposed to protect them from such horrors.

The world could be a beautiful place.

But it could also be inhumanely ugly.

And, unfortunately, the recipient of most of that ugliness was women.

I had never been unaware of that fact.

But I had personally been sheltered from having those ugly fingers touch me before. I had always been protected by my fath... Alejandro's reputation, by his hovering presence.

It had never occurred to me before that I could be in danger *because* of him.

I barely had a chance to actually think anything through.

First, I was knocked cold within a minute of the man showing up at my door.

Second, when I woke up in an unfamiliar room, in pain, confused, towered over by a man I knew wanted to make me hurt worse than he already had, I was too worried about trying to de-escalate the situation to think about how Alejandro's sins were coming to haunt me.

I don't think it ever really clicked until he had me on my back, until my face was nothing but throbbing pain from his fists, that it finally clicked what he was doing.

He was going to rape me because my father raped people he loved.

And that was a whole new level of twisted I had never even considered before.

Who raped to avenge a rape victim?

Twisted people.

People that my fath... that Alejandro had twisted to be that way through his actions and the repercussions of them.

There was maybe even a moment of character weakness where I wondered if maybe I deserved it, maybe it was only right.

But then his hands moved to pull my pants and panties down and... I shut that shit right down and tried to hit, kick, scream, anything.

Then there was Luce, looking like some dark, avenging angel, gun raised, knife catching the moonlight in the other.

As I sat outside with the gun clutched so hard that I had marks in my hand for several long minutes after I let it go, I could hear almost everything inside.

I could hear the hisses of pain.

I could hear the begging, the crying, the calls to God.

And mixed with that, I could hear Luce's calm, almost eerily controlled voice through it all.

But then he came out, he got me home, he got the evidence off me, he got me medicine, and he got me in bed.

He was a true dichotomy if I ever saw one.

He was capable of such coldness, but such warmth at the same time.

When I woke up to find him curled up with me, his hair still wet from another shower, the sun starting to peek through the windows, there was a strong, almost overwhelming warm, swelling sensation in my chest.

I had only felt touches of it before in my life, just vague, pathetic facsimiles of what I was feeling right then with Luce.

But I had felt it enough to know exactly what it was.

I was falling in love with him.

Was it crazy?

Absolutely.

Was he someone I should have chosen?

No, of course not.

But that was the thing, wasn't it?

Love wasn't always a choice.

Sometimes it came to you slowly over time, getting to know someone for months and years before that sensation blossomed across your chest because, quite frankly, you knew them too well not to love them.

But sometimes the choice was out of your hands.

Sometimes it happened in a moment.

Sometimes the universe chose for you.

That's not to say you don't have a choice. There is always a choice. To stay. To walk away. To make the decision that was smart, not just the one that felt good.

You couldn't pick the feelings, but you could choose what to do about them.

The problem was, I didn't know what to do.

The smart decision was, of course, to stop it before it got out of hand. He was a wild card. He was a vigilante by profession. He didn't make connections with, well, anyone but me. He hadn't opened up to me about his past. Perhaps he never would.

That being said, this was a man who hadn't held a grudge about me kidnapping him and holding him hostage. He had given me the truth about my parentage thanks to his obsessive brand of need-to-knowing. He had accompanied me with barely a pause. To Texas. To Brazil. He had sweated in misery with me. He had made my body come alive with his touch.

He had *killed* for me.

Maybe his past didn't matter.

Maybe all that mattered was the way I felt more myself around him, how I felt *safe* with him, how I felt free to be someone other than who Alejandro Cruz had made me to be.

"See this?" Luce asked, making me shock back. I had thought he had drifted back off to sleep.

His hand was holding mine, eyes watching intently. "See what?"

"This," he said, chipping my nail polish back more than it already was.

"What am I looking at?"

"Your new nail growth is clear; no Mees' lines. Whatever had the arsenic in it, you've been away from it for a bit."

"Well, I'm glad I'm not dying," I admitted with a small laugh.

I had almost forgotten about the arsenic. So much else had been going on.

"Me too, doll, but that is still a mystery that needs solving when we get back home."

That was true.

But that was a problem for another day.

If the lines weren't growing in, I was relatively safe. I needed to do a heavy metal cleansing as soon as possible, but plenty of people survived arsenic poisoning in their lives with little to no negative effects.

I would be okay.

"You need to get some sleep," I said, feeling his fingers curl between mine and squeeze.

"I'll be fine."

"You'll make yourself sick."

"Worried about me," he said, his hand turning mine so his knuckles could graze my cheek. "Can't say I hate that," he added. "How you holding up?"

"I've been better," I admitted because it was honest. "But I could have been a lot worse."

"No, you couldn't have," he said with so much conviction that I actually believed him, like he had some kind of superpower that would have stopped the attempted rape and murder no matter what.

"Thanks to you."

"Don't thank me," he said, voice a little hollow. "It shouldn't have happened in the first place."

"Right, because you totally should have known that my father had enemies here that might want to hurt me. That was totally your job."

"You got this," he said, releasing my hand to touch my face, "on my watch. That's unacceptable."

"It's over," I said, trying to diffuse the situation, noticing the way his jaw was tightening. "And after we see Gabriela today, we can head out, okay? Get away from this. Get back to our lives."

"If you want to stay and spend some time..."

I was shaking my head before he even finished. "I don't really want to be here a minute longer than necessary. I can, I don't know, I can have her come visit me, right? That's what people do. They take turns visiting."

"Maybe now that she has a reason, doll, she would consider moving back to the states. That was always her plan, obviously."

Was that possible?

Maybe.

I definitely felt a connection with the woman, and I had only known her a few hours. She had been looking for me for decades. If it meant she could make up for lost time, maybe she would consider coming back and starting over again.

"I could get her papers," Luce said, seeming to sense where my mind was going. It was a bad time for immigrants to try to get into the US. "If she wants to come, and she can't get in through the legal channels, I know a forger who has been doing shit like this for longer than I have been alive. Hell, longer than your mother has been alive. If that's the route you want to take, Ev, all you have to do is say the word."

See?

Good.

True, his colors would never be white; it was all gray and black for him, but that didn't mean there wasn't goodness underneath the shields he wore.

In fact, even his job, as brutal, as awful as it may have seemed, had at its core the right idea - saving those who couldn't save themselves from predators they didn't even know existed.

If there was anything I learned from this whole ordeal, it was that you never knew who was hiding evil. It could be your next-door neighbor. It could be the father of one of the kids your daughter is friend with. It could be *your own father*.

You never really knew.

Hell, at least Luce wore his darkness, didn't try to hide it or pretend it wasn't there.

"Where are you?" Luce asked, making me snap out of my thoughts again.

"Nowhere important," I said, feeling a bit guilty because it was a lie, but it was a small one. "How long is it going to take us to get to town?"

"Twenty if we take our time," he said, rolling onto his back to check his phone for the time. "We still have an hour and a half before we need to head out."

"Gives me time to check flight schedules," I agreed, rolling so that I was half on Luce's chest. "Among other things."

So maybe it wasn't exactly 'normal' to want to hook up just hours after you were kidnapped, beaten, and almost raped. But with my head still doing a steady, uncomfortable pounding, my lip sore anytime I tried to speak, and scratches on my thighs that burned slightly when anything brushed against them, I just wanted to feel something *good*. I didn't want my only memory of being with Luce to be slightly marred by what happened almost directly after.

And maybe, since realizing I was falling, I just plain wanted him.

It was that simple.

"Other things, huh?" he asked, carelessly tossing his phone toward the other bed, still mussed from our rolling around in it, and moved his hand down my back to rest at the lowest spot of my back, his pinkie and ring fingers grazing the swell of my ass. "Have anything in particular in mind?" he asked, eyes already getting heavy-lidded.

"Oh, I can think of a few things," I offered, sliding my thigh up and over him, feeling his cock pressing into my flesh. "What?" I asked when his eyes went a little... sad?

His hand raised, touching just outside my lips. "Can't kiss you."

I winced slightly, disappointed too.

But I wasn't going to let that ruin the moment.

"Oh, but I have *so* many other areas that can be kissed," I said, smile going wicked.

"Mmm," he growled, hands moving to my hips, pulling me until my legs were straddling him, forcing me to press my hands down beside his body so I could lift up and look at him. "Like where?"

"Hmm," I said, leaning my head to the side, and balancing on one arm so I could trace a finger down my neck. "Like here."

"Well, that does look like a good spot," he agreed, leaning in to run his lips, tongue, teeth over the sensitive skin, moving up with me as I pressed back to a seated position to give him better access. "Anywhere else you have in mind?"

I took a deep, shaky breath, pulling back, then slowly lifting up my shirt, discarding it to the floor. "Here, maybe?" I asked, running a finger between my breasts.

"Definitely there," he agreed, ducking his head, his soft hair brushing over my painfully hardened nipples as his tongue traced between my breasts.

His head shifted, his wet tongue tracing my hardened peak with soft, excruciating caresses, making the heavy, almost oppressive weight of desire settle down low in my belly. He moved across my chest to torture my other nipple before resting his face between my breasts, angling his head up. "Anywhere else you can think of?"

"Well, there is *one* more place," I agreed, feeling his hand slide behind my back to support me as I moved to lay flat, lifting up my hips. "I just need to get these shorts off to show you exactly where."

"I think I can help you with that," he agreed, sliding my legs from around his back and reaching for my hips to grab the material. "Legs up, doll."

My legs lifted straight as he slid the material up then off my ankles, running his fingers down the backs of my calves, knees, thighs. Then they slid between, almost at the highest point, pressing, and spreading them wide onto the mattress.

"So," he said, sounding a mix of clinical and amused, but his eyes were molten, "where was it you needed kissing?" he asked, smirk devilish.

"Well, I seem to *need* you here," I said, hand sliding down my belly, watching as his eyes followed the motion aptly, before pressing my fingers over the triangle of my sex.

"Here?" he asked, brushing my hand away, using his fingers to spread my lips even further. "On your sweet fucking pussy?" He looked up for affirmation, though he damn well knew what I wanted. "Well, twist my arm, why don't ya'?" he asked, dropping down and, before I could even draw a breath, his mouth was on me.

He didn't tease.

He didn't drive me up slowly.

He feasted.

He sucked my clit.

He thrust his tongue inside me.

He moved back up to work my clit with his tongue as two fingers thrust inside, turned, and raked over my G-spot.

Just when I thought the orgasm was never going to come, he pressed hard into my G-spot as he sucked in my clit.

And I freaking... shattered.

He worked me through it, dragging it out, then slowly released as my clit became over-sensitive, moving across to bite into the soft flesh of my inner thigh, up my belly, under my breasts.

It didn't matter that I had just come, it didn't matter that it should have been enough to stem the desire. As soon as he rose up and looked down at me, eyes scorching, smile wicked, the urge to have him inside me was almost painful.

I moved up, pushing him backward until he was flat on the bed again, going almost frantically for the waistband of his pants, working them and his boxer briefs down far enough to free his cock.

"Hold on, Ev," he said, sounding both husky and amused as I went to straddle him. He half-rolled away to the side of the bed, digging in his bag, and coming back with a condom. "Okay," he said a second later after protecting us. "Have your way with me," he demanded with a smirk as he held his cock at the base to allow me to move to lower myself down on him.

There was no pretending to go slow, to make it last, to, essentially, make love.

I was too needy, too far gone with the need for him inside me.

I dropped my hips, taking him deep on a loud moan, my head thrown back as I tried to pull air back into my lungs.

"Fuck," he growled back, hands sinking painfully into my hips. "Ride me, Ev," he demanded as I took a second to try to pull it together.

And, yeah, screw trying to pull it together.

I'd much rather fall apart.

With him.

"Great fucking view," he groaned as I started riding him, my breasts bobbing with the wild, frantic motion of my body.

One of his hands stayed at my hip, anchoring me to him, making sure my movements didn't get too haphazard. The other moved inward and down, pressing into my clit. It stayed motionless, but as my body rocked, it rubbed with perfect pressure, making my pussy tighten around his cock, making me get closer.

"Already?" he asked, looking pleased.

And it was right about then that the first deep, hard pulsation of my orgasm started where our bodies were connected. "Fuck yeah, already," he growled, thrusting upward into me as the orgasm came crashing through my system, making me half-collapse forward onto him, crying out his name as I did. "Nope, not done with you," he said as I tried to lay flat and nuzzle in, enjoying the tingly aftermath of my orgasm.

With that, he rolled, so I rolled, landing on my back, losing all contact with him as he jumped off the edge of the bed. Reaching up, he snagged my ankles, and dragged me to the foot of the bed, slamming back inside me before I could even gasp.

That was when Luce let go of his carefully-held control.

I don't know if it was the worry for me the night before, or the violence following it, or the hours (I imagined) of dealing with the aftermath... or what, but he was wild, borderline savage. He *fucked* me with every bit of primal instinct in him.

And I loved every brutal, deep, hard stroke.

I loved the loud, rumbling sound of enjoyment in his chest.

I loved the way that no matter how lost he was in his own need for release, he still reached between us, he found my clit, and he made sure I got mine another time before he found his own release, cursing out my name as he came deep inside me.

It was a long minute before he pulled out of me, disappearing into the bathroom for a second, then coming back out, pulling off his shirt I never got around to discarding.

"Too rough?" he asked, coming up to the side of the bed where I was just a pile of useless bones and flesh.

"Nuh-uh," I said, shaking my head. "It was perfect."

"Scoot," he demanded, smiling softly down at me.

"Can't. Can't move," I said with a small smile.

He chuckled at that, the sound turning my belly liquid.

But before the feeling could settle, he was reaching down, yanking the blanket underneath me, and sending me rolling with a laugh.

"Oh no you don't," he said, grabbing me as I almost rolled off the bed, pulling my back against his chest, cocking his legs up under mine. "Are you sure?"

"Sure?" I asked, too caught up in how good it felt to have a man like Luce spooning me to remember what we had even been talking about.

"That that wasn't too much. I don't usually..."

"Hey," I cut him off, wrapping my arm around the arm he had across my chest, and giving it a squeeze. "If I'm not into something, Luce, I will tell you I'm not into it. You don't need to, like, hold back with me because you're afraid of freaking me out."

"Anyone tell you recently that you're pretty fucking amazing?"

"Nope."

"Fucking sin," he said, giving me a squeeze as he leaned in to plant a kiss to my neck. "Where you going?" he asked, making a grab for me as I made a grab for my cell.

"I just need to check the flights."

"In a rush to get out of here?" he asked, voice oddly guarded.

Not understanding that reaction, I turned with my cell to face him. "I don't want to be in this country any longer than necessary after last... after everything. I don't want to run into any of my fath... any of Alejandro's old enemies. The safest place is back in the US where, as far as I can tell, he didn't really do much business. You would know better than me, I guess."

"He was careful in the US," he agreed, tone still guarded for reasons I couldn't fathom. "It's harder to bribe people to look the other way while you poison men and rape women." I felt the wince, but didn't know it was so visible until Luce's face fell, until he sighed. "Fuck. Sorry. I don't mean to be a dick."

"Then why are you being a dick?" I asked, not one to mince words.

"What's the plan, Ev?" he asked oddly.

"The plan? For today?"

"For when we board a plane, land in Jersey, and drive back to Navesink Bank? What then?"

"Oh my God," I said, unable to stop the smile that pulled at my lips. "Are we doing this?" I asked, too amused to find myself in this situation to remember to be delicate.

"This?"

"This... the *talk*. The *relationship* talk? Is that what this is?"

Luce rolled onto his back, scrubbing his hands down his face. "No. Yes. Fuck, I don't know, Evan. I don't like not fucking knowing things. This has been great, but is this it? Did you want an adventure and a taboo fuck from some guy who kills people for a living and has a past he won't even tell you about?"

"Luce..."

"Tell me," he said, turning his head on the pillow to look at me, seeming to hold me frozen with those deep eyes, and the seriousness in them that I didn't quite understand. "Are you going to go back to Navesink Bank and start your life over, doing your best to forget about me?"

"I'd never forget about you," I said honestly. It wasn't even a remote possibility. "It doesn't matter what does or doesn't happen, there's no way I could forget you. Or this," I said, waving a hand around.

"I'm not saying it's gonna happen today or tomorrow or a week from now, but I'm saying..."

"What? You're saying what? Because right now, you're saying a whole lot of nothing, Luce," I said, moving to sit up, forgetting all about my nudity in my annoyance.

He angled his head up to look at me, the slightest twitching of his lips showing a sign of amusement that didn't meet his eyes.

"I guess I'm saying I'm no fucking good for you." He paused, but there was a heaviness in the air around us that told me it wasn't my place to speak yet. "And that you would be smart to get back to the States... and forget all about that time you went slumming it with some scar-covered killer in Brazil."

Oh, the good old-fashioned 'it's for your own good' argument. Usually, it was a dickhead's way of 'letting you down easy.'

I just didn't think that was true of Luce.

I genuinely believed he felt I was better off without him, that he thought so lowly of himself.

I had a feeling, too, that the phrase 'scar-covered killer' was key. Not so much the killer part, because that was always clear from the beginning.

I think it was about his scars.

I think it was about his past.

I think whatever he had been through had made him feel unworthy.

And that was ridiculous.

But he would never believe that I meant that because he knew I didn't know his past.

The problem was, I promised I would never ask.

I took a deep, steadying breath, holding it, then exhaling.

My hand dropped the phone, and reached out to touch the center of the ugly word on his chest.

"I won't ever ask," I repeated. "And it *doesn't* matter."

"You don't know that."

But I did.

And when he opened his mouth to tell me, it didn't prove me wrong.

It was horrible.

It was sickening.

But it didn't matter.

Whether he would believe that or not.

FOURTEEN

Luce

I was twelve-years-old the first time I had a train run on me. All six of them were friends of my father.

It wasn't the first time I got raped.

That *honor* was given to me at seven-years-old by dear old dad.

My mom had been passed out drunk in the other room. But even if she were sober -which she never was- she wouldn't have bothered to stop it.

So, when you start your story with those particular highlights, well, it went to follow that the rest wasn't white picket fences, hot cocoa, or Sunday cookouts.

I was a mistake, plain and simple.

I wasn't an *oopsie.*

I wasn't an *unplanned blessing.*

I was a fucking *mistake.*

I was never meant to come in this world.

My mother was thirty-four when I was conceived after a week-long bender in which she must have forgotten to take her Pill. I heard about the bender directly from her.

Damn tequila shots are the only reason your skinny, snot-filled ass exists.

I was five the first time I heard that, not quite understanding at that point of course.

The Pill part I speculated for myself, several years later when I understood such concepts.

But, yeah, I was an epic fuckup that she absolutely did not want. Why she didn't abort me was completely beyond my comprehension. When you were as against having kids as she was, being that her life was dedicated to chasing the promises found at the bottoms of bottles, I couldn't imagine what made her decide to have me.

To be perfectly honest, there was a chance she didn't know until it was too late.

It was a fucking miracle I wasn't born with fetal alcohol syndrome. Though, to be honest, there was an argument to be made for there being some of that damage leftover. Namely in my social skills - or lack thereof - my impulse control, and my somewhat strong tendency toward obsessive behaviors.

But, to be fair to a woman who didn't deserve any fairness whatsoever, all those things could have very much to do with my abuse later in life than the amount of booze she downed while pregnant.

My father, well, he was like every other scumbag I put in the ground as an adult. This meant that he was mainly, above all else, an incredible fucking actor. His whole life was a lie. His every smile, every word of encouragement, his every pat on the back, it was all a mask he wore so no one would ever look deeper and see the evil just beneath the surface.

Thankfully, I didn't see much of him when I looked in the mirror. If I did, well, I likely would have taken a blade to my face a long time ago.

I looked like my mother- tall and thin, all arms, legs, and torso. I had her dark hair, her dark eyes, her cheekbones. My jaw, well, who the fuck knew where that came from. Some grandfather five generations back or some shit.

But yeah, I'd rather look like my mother, the mess, the coward, the selfish bitch, than look like my father, the twisted, sick, perverse, child molesting freak.

There's no way to describe what it was like that first night, the night I came home from little league, beaming because, for the first time, I struck a kid out, face still sticky from the ice cream we got on the way home.

It was maybe the highest moment of my young life.

Followed by the lowest.

Because my father didn't fit the 'pattern.'

My father didn't slowly escalate.

It didn't start with inappropriate talk, then move on to touching, then masturbating, then oral sex, then the full act of penetration.

I learned later in life, during a brief stint in counseling with a therapist who didn't seem like a complete and utter quack for a change, that this was likely because I was not his first victim. Because almost all offenders escalated. They had to test the boundaries, make sure they didn't get caught.

Other little boys had suffered at his hand at some point.

And given that he was forty when I was born, that left several decades and an unknown amount of misery before he finally had me.

Little old defenseless me.

Right under his very own roof.

A convenient-to-grab sex toy anytime the mood struck.

And it struck often.

Almost nightly.

Starting that first night when I was held with my face in a pillow so no one could hear me scream.

And I did.

Scream, that is.

I screamed so hard that I felt like I had strep for a week after, that I bit my tongue so bad that it was flooded with blood and made speaking and eating impossible for days.

I screamed.

And cried.

And begged God to end it.

But he didn't.

I searched for meaning that Sunday in church, shifting in the pew because no matter what way I tried to sit, it hurt so bad that tears stung my eyes. I heard words of sin and punishment, my sad, confused, betrayed little mind trying to make sense of that, trying to see what I had done to warrant such punishment.

I tried after.

To be a better boy.

To keep my grades up.

To never get into scrapes with other boys.

To do my chores without being asked.

To keep quiet.

To never get in anyone's way.

It didn't do any good.

My sins, apparently, continued.

As did my punishments for them.

How did he keep me silent, that might be your next question. After all, in these times, how can a child not know their father isn't allowed to touch them that way?

The answer is both simple and complicated.

First, let's go with good old *he was my father*.

At seven, your brain doesn't think too far beyond that. Parents are, for all intents and purposes, like gods to their kids. They know all; they make the rules; they are who you go to with problems.

Likely because of my father's perverse tendencies and my mother's rampant alcoholism, I was very much raised with the idea of never 'airing your dirty laundry.' If there was a problem, it was handled in-house. We didn't drag strangers in to check out our soiled sheets.

So reaching out, at that time, never crossed my mind.

Second to that, I was taught nothing, not one single shred of sexual education. Not at home, nor at school. We didn't *have* cable. I didn't even know what sex *was*, let alone *rape,* until my teens.

Third, we didn't live anywhere near other houses. We backed up to the Adirondacks. We didn't have neighbors to talk to who might have noticed something was off about me.

And if you aren't taught that something is wrong, even if it *feels* wrong when it is happening, how the hell are you supposed to know it is abuse?

I did, however, have a pretty good idea of the fucked-upedness of that fateful night when I was twelve, when my father got all his pervert friends together, and they all took turns abusing me.

I had an idea a year later when he rented me out to one of those friends again, one-on-one because he needed to spend some time with me, because he wanted to 'bring me to heel,' because he was a sick fuck who loved knives and cigarette burns and whips.

I had an idea as I nursed wounds for weeks after one of his visits, having to wear hoodies in summer to cover them up.

His last visit was when I was fourteen, on the cusp of too old for all the old pricks to desire anymore. Maybe sensing the end of our time together, the knife seemed bigger, seemed sharper, and it meant to brand me forever, to make it impossible to forget him.

So my father held me down, cock hard at my screams, as another man carved the word 'slave' across my chest.

And I was.

A slave, that is.

I was a slave before then physically.

Afterward, I was a slave mentally for years.

But that night, that night when I was fourteen, bleeding openly from my chest, my whole body sore from other treatments I had already received, that was the night when grown men stopped putting their hands on my young body.

Because it was also the night I first learned how to take lives.

As my father exited the room to go get them a round of drinks to celebrate another night of successful rape, my 'master' moved to look out the window, chest puffed out in his satisfaction, the moon making him look even more sinister than he already did to my young eyes.

But he had left the knife on the bed, still slick and red with my blood.

I knew the knife.

Winchester clip point with a wooden handle.

I had been acquainted with it monthly for over a year.

I knew just how sharp he kept it - sharp enough to slice the skin from my body with the barest of brushes.

Sharp enough to do damage.

Permanent damage.

I don't know why that night was my breaking point.

Didn't matter how many times I sat in various therapists' offices and tried to pinpoint the breaking point. The best I could figure was, it was simply the last straw. And I somehow knew that it was the last time I would see my 'master.'

My father's other friends had lost interest in me over the past year, my budding manhood becoming less enticing for their particular proclivities.

And I knew this was the end for me and this particular sadistic bastard.

And I was sick and fucking tired of being helpless.

The second my hand closed around that handle, helpless was the last thing I felt.

I felt powerful.

For the first time in my life.

And that feeling was heady, overwhelming, to someone who had been nothing but a victim.

So when I rose from that bed, seven year's worth of pain, sadness, impotence, and rage rose up within me, a cocktail that had my blood screaming in my veins, my pulse pumping so hard in my ears that I literally couldn't even hear the scream when my knife slammed into his heart, sending a flood of warm, sticky, red blood down my hand and forearm before I could find the strength to pull it back out.

It was a done deal, of course. There was no way for him to survive it.

But I wasn't done.

I had years to make up for. I had scars covering my whole body from his knives, his cigarettes, his whips.

So I stabbed and carved that knife into his body until I was literally slick with blood, until his body was just a mess of open wounds.

Until I felt my father's hands close around my shoulders.

My hearing came back in a rush.

"What have you done!" he shrieked, sounding horrified.

As he should have been.

The image was straight out of a horror movie.

And I was no superhero. I was just a scared, traumatized kid.

So my immediate response was to freak out, to beg, to cry, to look for mercy.

I watched as he moved me away, kneeling down next to his friend, checking for vitals. It was ridiculous and ultimately fruitless being that the man was mincemeat, but he did it regardless.

And then he did the one thing he could have done to wipe away my own horror at the whole scene.

He turned over his shoulder with huge eyes, and he spoke.

"Why would you do this? He never did anything to you!"

It was right that second that I understood, not even having anything to truly understand, I did. There was no remorse in him for all the pain he had caused me. There was no regret. Because he genuinely did not think it was wrong.

There was no cure for his sickness.

Don't ask me why, but that was a blindingly clear revelation for me.

There was no fixing him.

And I remembered something in that moment.

I remembered when I was ten, and we walked into the yard to find a raccoon in the garden, hissing, snarling, wobbling around.

Rabies, he had said.

Incurable, he added.

You can't fix a rabid animal, son, he went on, *you just have to put them down.*

He grabbed gloves, picked the raccoon up by the tail, laid him on the block, and decapitated him.

A lesson was learned. And remembered, stored away for when I would need it again several years later.

My father was a rabid animal. There was no fixing him.

He needed to be put down.

Maybe it was instinct, pure memory of our hunting together out in the mountains, or maybe it was just what was easiest to do, but I gripped the knife with the blade out sideways, and I sliced it across his throat.

The blood spluttered out as he howled, hands going up to cup at it uselessly, like he could push it back in.

It wasn't clean.

It wasn't quick.

My experience with killing was with small animals only. I had no idea how much more pressure I needed to use to cut deeply enough for him to bleed out in less than a minute.

So he slowly drained of blood. I watched him go pale. I watched the life flicker in and out of his eyes. I watched as he became too weak to stay kneeling, and fell over.

I watched as he gasped out his last breath.

It took an eerily long time.

And it should have been sickening. I should have been vomiting all over myself and the floor, crying, something.

But I wasn't.

I was cold.

Detached.

Level-headed.

I walked out of the room and to the bathroom, diligently washing the blood off my body, off the knife, then carefully seeing to the cuts across my chest, my stomach lurching at seeing them reflected at me in the mirror.

I dressed carefully in jeans, long socks, hiking boots, a tee, and a black hoodie with white hood pulls. I stocked a backpack with money stolen from both men's wallets, a change of clothes, some food, a fire starter, a pot, and the knife. I rolled up a knapsack and tied it on top.

It was spring in the Adirondacks.

If there was ever a time a young boy could hope to survive there, that was when.

Sure there were no other options, sure the cops would be looking for me within hours, I also grabbed my father's machete out of the barn, and tore off into the mountains.

I spent enough time out in them to know it wasn't the best plan. First, because I was alone and could fall to my own death, or get caught in a damn bear trap and die of infection. Second, because my own stupidity and lack of training weren't the only things to contend with. For instance, not only were the Adirondacks home to cool things like beavers and marten, but one could also expect moose, black bears, coyotes, bobcats, and, as legend goes, cougars. Any one of them could put an end to a fourteen-year-old boy's life.

Spring would lead into summer where ticks came out by the billions, where mosquitos wouldn't give you a moment of peace. Summer would give way to fall where bears are looking to pack on the pounds for hibernation, making any meat source a good target. And winter, well, surviving on your own in the freezing depths of winter without losing limbs to blackness was big enough of a problem, doing so while not becoming prey to some desperate coyote or cougar was even more of a problem.

But there were cabins, I knew.

If you were strong enough to make it there, hunters had set up cabins. Survivalists as well. And, though you definitely didn't want to invade them, drug dealers who liked to grow their pot in the mountains, unseen, had cabins there as well.

By the time I found one such cabin, almost a month later, I was thin from hunger, thinner than usual which was saying something. I was skin and bones.

I could kill.

I was good at killing.

It was the tracking and trapping that I sucked at.

And those were kinda the more vital parts of acquiring protein.

I had been mostly surviving on wild blueberries, strawberries, Indian cucumber-root, and as disgusting as this was to admit, bugs, and small lizards.

I was getting weak.

And I was going to die if I didn't find shelter and a small supply of something protein-packed so I could refuel to seriously be able to hunt or fish again.

So when I came across the cabin, I didn't care to inspect what kind it was.

I didn't even notice the field out back.

All I saw was a small shanty that provided a place to rest that wasn't hard ground, that didn't expose me to the elements and predators.

Inside, I found a bed and a supply of canned beans.

It was stealing, technically.

But survival rules, my father taught me, allowed for such things.

I ate the beans straight from the can, leaving the cash that was useless to me in the place of said can as a thank-you to the owners for their hospitality.

And I went to sleep.

I woke up to a gun in my face.

"Ease up, G," the man behind the man with a gun said, looking down at me. "He's just a kid."

"Fuck off with that kid shit," G said, shaking his head. "I was running the street at his age."

I didn't really need more than that.

Drug dealers.

Most likely, pot farmers.

Of course.

I released the machete I had been gripping to hold my hands out, palms up. "I just needed food," I admitted, waving toward their pile of supplies. "I left money to replace it even."

There was a second of silent communication between the two hulking guys in their mid-twenties, indeterminate of heritage, but seeming mostly white. The one who wasn't G turned to me. "You lost up here?"

"I... ran away," I supplied.

"No *shit*," G said suddenly, pointing toward me, and doing so with the gun. "You don't recognize him? Man, he's that kid all over the news. They said you were abducted."

Well, that sure worked in my favor, didn't it?

No one was suspecting me of murder?

It felt like a weight was lifted.

"Wait," G said, head cocking to the side, eyes going a bit more wise than you would expect from a typical thug. "If you weren't kidnapped... and you ran away..." he trailed off, smile going a bit wicked. "You did it, huh? You sliced those guys up? Your pops and his friend? Damnnnnn, that's cold, kid." G was apparently loving this information. "So, what now, daddy-killer? You gonna just shack up in these mountains all your life? Become some backwards woodman?"

I slowly pushed up in bed, rolling a kink out of my neck. "I didn't think that far."

"No shit. You're like half fucking dead and this is the easy season."

G, you could tell from first meeting, was a filter-free kind of guy. He grew up on the streets of Baltimore, dodging bullets, and putting them in others. He was not one for mercy, not even to a fourteen-year-old kid. But he was one for mutual respect. And he, as rough around the edges as he seemed, was a businessman through and through.

His buddy, Mickey, came from the same neighborhood, but had a decent upbringing, had some love in his life that made him a bit softer to a trespasser in his cabin.

"So, you get that you just showed us your hand, right?" G asked.

"My hand?" I repeated, feeling my spine stiffen.

"Daddy killer," he repeated. "I mean, what? He whoop your ass a time too many?" I meant to show no reaction. I didn't want anyone to know. Because while I only barely grasped the fact that what he had done to me was genuinely wrong, I still felt some sort of shame surrounding the whole thing.

But sometimes you didn't need to say anything to give something away.

"Oh yeah?" he asked, mouth pressing into a firm line. "He was a fucking kiddie diddler? That was his thing?" he asked, tone angry. "I don't mess with that shit. Those fucks deserve to be put down. You did God's work there, kid. Though, it would have been just as poetic for him to end up in the penn with some burly ass biker with five kids at home he loves and hasn't been able to protect in a decade who doesn't take kindly to people on the streets who could prey on kids like his own. Ass full of countless dicks, that is the only fair payment for those shitheads. Aight. Aight. Well, your situation sucks. Know what else sucks? Dragging my ass out of the city where I got a fine piece just waiting to suck me dry every night."

"G... for fuck's sake," Mickey hissed, shaking his head apologetically.

"Oh fuck off. He's old enough. Yeah, so I don't like leaving a chick who could suck the paint off my truck, less she get any ideas of doing some shopping around in my absence. And I sure as fuck don't like ruining these kicks in that fucking wilderness," he said, waving a hand toward the door. "But we got product to protect up here."

I was fourteen. I barely had enough 'street knowledge' to understand what he meant by 'product,' but I was still somehow putting it together.

He didn't want to make the trek out of the city to come and check on his pot. But it needed to be watched. So people didn't come picking. So the weather or bugs didn't destroy it.

And I was in no position to turn them down.

First, because I was going to die in the wilderness without shelter and possible food coming to me.

Second, I couldn't go back out of the mountains because I was technically missing.

Third, as G said... I had shown them my hand.

He owned me.

"You want me to watch your pot," I guessed.

"In exchange, you can have all the food we can have one of the boys trek up here. And this shack. I mean... dunno what the fuck to do with you after summer, but that's not our problem. For now, you can keep a roof and a full stomach. It's more than you'd get out there. And if you come out of these mountains, begging for food or money, it's only a matter of time before you're found. Then they'll question you. You're weak still, kid, you'd crack and give it all up. You'd be put away. Maybe in juvie. Maybe in a nuthouse. But away. That what you want?"

"No." I wasn't trading one prison for another, not if I could help it anyway.

"Good. Then Mickey here will give you the lowdown on growing the product. And harvesting it and shit. You'll do it. And you won't smoke any of it," he added with a look. "And you can stay here and eat and get some meat on your bones again, think about your future. Hell, I'll even be nice and give you a little slice once we get the product on the street. Deal?"

Was there really any way I was going to turn that down?

In my situation?

There wasn't really even a choice.

"Deal."

So then I became a pot farmer.

I got my crash course from Mickey. I was told to help myself to the food around and that more provisions would come up with Mickey and some guy named Ace in a couple weeks.

"You know, we need to make sure you didn't croak on us or some shit," was his reasoning for the visit.

I took care of the plants.

I harvested and packaged it for distribution.

Then I pack-muled it back with Mickey and Ace early that fall to where G was waiting in some nearby town.

I pulled my hood up, and kept my head down, eating the McDonalds they bought me, pretending to not be listening.

"You can't send him back into the woods, G. I know you're a vicious fuck, but he's just a kid."

"He's a killer," G said nonchalantly. "He can handle himself."

"Being a killer won't help him not freeze to death in the fucking mountains, G. He dies, we have no one to help next season."

Appealing to G's business sense, Mickey knew, was always the best bet.

"Alright, fuck, yes," G said, sighing somewhat dramatically. "He can come crash. But he doesn't leave the fucking building, got it? He's the new house cat."

And I was. I was shuffled into the back of his SUV whose blackout windows made me relax slightly. Then we drove into New York City, a place even a child daddy-killer could disappear in. I was shuffled into what had to have been an abandoned office building in Washington Heights. I was given a room, a bed, some clothes - everything black like I preferred anyway- a laptop, a cell, and a - believe this shit or not - pile of dirty magazines.

"Know your old man fucked you up," G had said when I eyed them skeptically. "But therein lays your salvation. Tits, ass, and pussy. That's all you need in life man - a good bitch, and money to spend. So, ah, yeah... don't leave the fucking building."

That was about all the supervision I got.

I learned this wasn't odd about two days later when I finally ventured downstairs to the sound of the men in G's operation hanging out. Half of his dealers were my age. It was no wonder he didn't see me as a kid.

And that day, I stopped seeing myself as one too.

And if I wasn't a kid anymore, I was responsible for myself. That meant I needed to get my head right; I needed to learn about this world I was suddenly in.

So I read the manual, and got started on the laptop. I researched my father's murder. I researched a phrase I didn't understand about my father's friend whose name turned out to be Bill.

Allegations of child molestation.

Then I understood. I read article after article, website after website, about the topic.

Child abuse.

Molestation.

Rape.

I understood the concept that, while I had personally experienced them hands-on, I hadn't understood them intellectually.

I puked for twenty-four hours straight once it sank in. Once I realized how fucked up it truly was.

That December, just shy of Christmas, G came into my room, dropping a stack of money on my desk without a word.

The 'slice' he had promised me.

My 'slice' was five grand.

Five *thousand* dollars.

I may have just turned fifteen, but I wasn't stupid. That was a lot of fucking money.

And because I wasn't stupid, I knew better than to do what all the other dealers G had did - blow it. No. I stashed it. I carved up the floorboards under my bed, stashed it in a backpack, and piled all my shit under the bed to make sure no curious eyes and thieving fingers got ideas.

That winter, I studied the internet, the things I could find.

By spring, I was ready to head back into the Adirondacks. I stacked a backpack full of books. I brought as much food as the three of us could carry. Then I holed up for six months in the shack in the woods.

Then back to the city.

Where I learned about the dark web from some of G's men who bought their guns there, who found new buyers for product there.

Then back to the mountains.

Shower. Rinse. Repeat.

Until I was eighteen, fresh back from the mountains, excited to have my laptop back because I was eyeballs deep in my obsession with the dark web, with all the secrets that lay within it.

I found the men.

You know, the other men who had run a train on me six years before? Yeah, I fucking found them.

And I had an idea...

See, even though I spent half my year in a cabin in the mountains, the other half was inside the belly of a criminal enterprise. G was a ruthless leader. I had seen a lot of torture and dying in the years I spent with him.

Necessary evils, Mickey had defended with a shrug.

And those words, they buried deep. They rooted. Eventually, they stretched out and broke the surface again.

Necessary evil.

Yes, I believed that.

I believed that some evil was necessary in life.

Like taking out baby rapers.

So you might call it fate then.

Almost as soon as the thought first formed in my mind, there was a crash.

And all you heard was people yelling.

NYPD. Get down. Get your hands up, motherfucker. We got you now, G.

I heard them making their way around the lower floor, knew they would be coming up next.

I threw myself down, ripping the floorboards up, grabbing the backpack that had needed to be upgraded to a hiking one to hold all the cash, shoved the laptop inside, threw the straps on, grabbed my cell, tossed myself out onto the fire escape, and made my way up.

Because G was smart. The roof was only a three-foot jump from the one next door. That one was only four feet from the next. And once you were two buildings over, you could rush down the fire escape there, and disappear down a back alley.

I had no record.

I was the house cat.

No one knew who I was.

I barely ever went outside.

Once I was on the street, I was safe.

I was getting ready to make the jump to the second building when I caught sight of G on the street below, looking up at me, his hands cuffed behind his back. I froze, unsure, feeling like a traitor. G might not have been a father, or even a proper big brother figure, but he was someone who gave me a way out, who saved me. It felt disloyal to run.

But he looked at me for a long second before his face broke into a smile. He gave me a reassuring nod before he was led away.

It took away the guilt.

Six months later, after finding he had been sentenced and shipped to - gotta love the irony here - the Adirondack Correctional Facility, I took my new fake, top-of-the-line IDs, and I took my ass for a visit.

I owed him that at least.

"Got your balls finally, kid," he said as soon as he sat down, grinning.

G wasn't the kind of man who was miserable he got sent upstate. Because G had spent a lot of his young adulthood in and out of jail and prison. To him, it was almost like coming home.

But he got a dime this time, and his whole organization got rounded up with him, so I wasn't sure he would be taking it in stride.

"That shit was fucked," I said, it being my emotionally crippled way of expressing my sympathy and my sadness at losing my sort of makeshift family.

"Fucked, yeah. Inevitable, maybe," he said, shrugging. "I got my hustle going here already. Shit will be comfy cozy for the next ten years. What about you?"

"What about me?" I asked, confused. Was he... worried about me?

"Asking some odd questions lately," he said, giving me a look because we knew we could be overheard. I knew exactly what he was talking about. Because most normal eighteen-year-olds don't ask about where to buy lye in the neighborhood. And any hardened criminal would know what that was about.

"It's time for some people to... show their penitence."

He snorted at that. "Thought you handled that as a kid, yo."

"Two out of eight," I agreed, nodding.

"Shit," he hissed, looking disgusted. "Aight. Tell you what," he said, all business, making me stiffen a bit. "I got my hustle," he said, and I knew better than to ask what it was. "But I want my commissary filled every week," he said, and I had a feeling there was going to be something interesting to follow. G wasn't the type to ask for shit for free. He wasn't expecting me to take the money I earned over the years, and funnel it to him through his prison account. "Remember that place you vacationed every summer?" he asked, obviously meaning the shack.

"Hard to forget."

"Maybe I took a cue from you and your clever hiding technique." He knew about my stash under my bed. That didn't surprise me. You couldn't piss in his place without him knowing. And I was away for long stretches of time. So he was telling me that he had something - money or pot or both - stashed under the bed in the shack in the mountains. "Do the math. Cap on my commissary is one-fifty a week. Fifty-two weeks a year, ten years."

Almost eighty grand.

That number maybe should have been shocking. But one had to figure that each pot crop each year made G pure profit of over two million. And that was only part of his operation. He also bought from others and sold.

"The rest..." he said, waving a hand casually. "You did me good. You've been through shit. I support your life goals. Make it happen."

"What about when you get out?" I asked, not wanting him, the person who gave me a shot in life, to leave with nothing.

His smile, though, was wicked. "You aren't the only good saver, kid. I got me plenty to get back on my feet. Don't you worry. You do you. And don't forget my commissary. Oh, and kid," he said as he went to stand, turning back. "Eddy's on 23rd." At my quizzical look, he shrugged. "Answer to one of those strange questions you were asking." Where to get lye. I felt myself smile, unable to help it. "Cash is always smart." With that, he was led toward the door. "Don't forget my commissary."

I never did.

G got out for good behavior in eight years.

But every week, I was putting in the one-fifty. Fifty-two weeks a year, no excuses. A little over sixty-two grand, all said and done.

What was stashed under the shack in the woods, under the actual shack itself, it turned out, since there was nothing under the floorboards but dirt, was over two-hundred k.

It funded my mission as I tracked down and killed the men who hurt me and countless others.

Then, worried, I took off to China for a spell, studied some more, did some more research.

Then I came back.

I got good.

I got so good that I never needed to run anymore.

I got so good that I could lure them to Navesink Bank, bring them back to my place, one after another, and never even have one cop sniff around me.

I had the dark web to thank for that.

And I had G and Mickey to thank for the dark web.

They became my number one and number two contacts in my pager system. I didn't hear from them often, but every once in a while, they heard about, as G insisted on calling them, a 'kiddie diddler,' knowing those were my favorite bastards to take down.

G got free and started a new operation in the city. So far, never getting caught. I didn't know, and didn't need to, who he had farming the pot in the mountains where I had spent so much of my time. I wished him nothing but the best, as odd as maybe that was given he wasn't exactly a *good* man.

That being said, neither was I.

I was as bad as they came really.

But I *did* some good, just as G and Mickey had done.

Eventually, I did seek out counseling, when the dreams made me wake up retching, when I couldn't sleep for weeks on end. Most were quacks, complete and utter wastes of time and money. But there were two or three who gave some insight, who helped me get over some of the shame.

Some.

I was convinced there was no way to get rid of it all.

There was a part of me that would always be that little boy with his face in a pillow, the slightly older, but still small, boy with six men using him brutally, the young teen who had his body carved up by a man while he raped me.

I would always be that kid, somewhere underneath.

There would always be that ugliness, those wounds that could never truly heal.

And I had done a good job most of my life never letting anyone see that, never letting anyone see what I kept behind the vigilante persona. I never let many people see the damage, both physical in the form of the scars, or psychological in the form of the memories.

"Until you," I concluded, taking what felt like the first deep breath I had in over an hour. That was how long it took to give her all the dark, ugly details of my life. An hour. We were almost going to be late.

Evan pressed her lips together, taking several long, deep breaths. She had tried, I would give her all the credit in the world, not to show any emotion during my story. She had held her breath or slow-breathed. She had blinked frantically.

In the end, her emotions won out. The tears streamed as I spoke, ones she didn't even bother trying to swat away because just as soon as she would, new ones would replace them.

But she didn't sob.

She didn't ask me to stop.

She took it in.

Then she did the healthy thing, she purged it through her tears.

It was the only way a well-adjusted person could receive that information.

I didn't blame her.

In fact, I had reached out as I finished to swipe away the remaining streaks on her cheeks.

She moved inward, curling in against my chest, nuzzling her face into my neck, planting a sweet kiss to the side of the column of my throat.

"I meant what I said," she said, arm around my back squeezing me tight.

"What, doll?"

"I meant it when I said it doesn't matter," she said, making my stomach tighten. She couldn't have meant that, not really. Right? "I'm sorry that happened to you. That is wrong on levels I can't even express, Luce. But it is even more proof of what a good man you are. That you were able to survive that, to break the cycle. So many abused kids become abusers. But not you. You were stronger than that. And you didn't curl up in a ball either. You went out there and you systematically rid the world of all the others like your father and his friends."

"By killing them," I specified, not wanting to mince words.

"A fitting punishment," she insisted.

"Why?" I asked, the word choked-sounding.

"Why what?" she asked, kissing me under my ear.

"Why would you accept a guy like me, Ev?"

"I don't seem to have a choice."

"What the fuck is that supposed to mean?" I asked, stiffening. Did she think I would somehow... force her to stay with me? Christ, did she actually think I was someone who would...

"It means I'm in love with you, Luce," she said, shocking the shit out of me enough to completely shut up my swirling thoughts. "So of course I accept you. Sad, dark, twisted," she went on, shrugging. "Scars and all. I love it all, Luce."

I had led a colorful life.

I had seen things most would never see.

I had done unspeakable things, but had seen just as many wonderful ones.

I had had a family.

I had made friends.

Never before.

Never once before, not in my entire life.

No one had *ever* told me they loved me.

I mean, how could they?

I wasn't a lovable man.

I knew that. I accepted that about myself.

But here was this woman, this amazing, beautiful, confident, sweet, strong but vulnerable, skilled, worldly, woman in my arms, naked, fresh off of hearing about all the sordid shit I had done in my life... and she still said it. She still felt it.

She loved me.

Fuck.

What was I supposed to do about that?

As a knock sounded at our door, there was a strange, small voice that said maybe I was supposed to love her right back.

The problem was, I didn't know dick about love.

I didn't even fucking know what it felt like.

But maybe, possibly, it had something to do with the swelling feeling in my chest as her eyes went big when her mother's voice called hello through the door.

Yeah, it could possibly feel something like that.

FIFTEEN

Evan

My mother was at the door.

My mother was at the door where I was naked with a man who I had just declared my love to.

After hearing his whole awful story finally.

I felt like I was caught with my hand in the cookie jar. Even though the door was locked. Even though I was a grown ass woman. Even though I hadn't even known my mother until a day before.

It was ridiculous.

Yet I shot up in bed, frantically grabbing for the sheet to cover myself as though the woman had x-ray vision or something.

"Just a minute, Gabriela," Luce called, openly laughing at my strange behavior as he got up, and reached for clothes to cover up. "Ev, gotta get dressed, doll," he said, smiling as I sat frozen. He leaned down, reaching into my bag, and producing clothes. "And you need to prepare for questions." When I obviously didn't seem to grasp why, he shrugged. "Your face, Evan."

Christ.

I almost forgot.

So much had happened, it seemed.

I hadn't even felt the throbbing I had been so distracted.

But as I climbed off the bed and dressed, it started again - dull but insistent.

Fully dressed as I fumbled to slip my shoes on, Luce went to the door, giving me a small smile over his shoulder. "Ready or not," he warned, unlocking the door, and opening it.

"I thought I'd stop here. It's on the way," she explained as she walked in, all smiles, clearly delighted to spend more time with me, which made me feel rather guilty for wanting to get out of the country as soon as possible. "I'm so hap... no," she said, freezing halfway in the door, every inch of her body snapping straight. "You!" she accused, turning on Luce, hands curling into fists.

"No!" I snapped, leaping off the bed, throwing myself in front of Luce. "No. Luce didn't do this. He *didn't*," I insisted, eyes holding hers. "Someone came to the room last night while Luce was getting food at the market."

"Who?" she asked, teeth gritted. "Who here did this?"

"Someone who had a grudge against Alejandro," Luce supplied. "From the last visit he had to this area. He wanted vengeance."

"Tell me he didn't get it," she said, lip quivering in rage.

"He didn't," Luce assured her. "What you see is all that happened. And he won't be a problem again."

Gabriela looked at me with eyes so familiar for a long couple of minutes. Then she gave me a nod. "Well, let's get to town, spend a few more hours together. Then you need to be going. First plane out," she said, moving past me to, I kid you not, start packing us.

"Gab... Mom," I said, finding that it somehow didn't feel awkward to say, even so soon. "We can..."

"No," she said, shaking her head, shoving my discarded clothes into my bag. "You have to go. You need to get clear of here just in case."

"I want to spend time with..."

"Yes. Yes. And with a man such as this," she said, waving one of Luce's hoodies at him before shoving it into his bag, "I am sure you can find a way to get me there, no?"

Luce shot me a very 'told you so' kind of smile. "I can arrange that, Gabriela. As soon as you are ready."

"All will be worked out. With the internet, all things are possible these days," she said, reaching into her pocket, pulling out a phone, and handing it to Luce. "Your number, so I can be in touch. You will message me as soon as you land." She was saying all this as she *stripped the beds*. "Hold on," she said, going back outside. There were a long couple minutes of nothing before she came back, rolling in a freaking cleaning cart with her. "Come on, get to work," she said, waving at the cart.

So, well, then we got to work.

By the time we were done, I was pretty sure it was the cleanest motel room in any country in the world.

"Please say you pay in cash," she said as she rolled the cart outside.

"We did," I agreed. The only thing I paid for with a card was the reservations for the plane. But from there, no one knew where we went. We were, essentially, ghosts.

Sure, people had seen us, but that didn't mean much.

"I was careful, Gabriela," Luce promised as we made our way to the bus that would take us to town. "It's good to be overly cautious, but I was careful."

"Good," she said, touching his knee. "I can trust you with my Evangeline, yes?"

He looked at me for a second, eyes deep, then over at my mother. His voice when he answered was full of conviction. "Yes."

So then we went to town, our bags on our shoulders.

We had lunch.

We talked.

We bought trinkets.

Then my mother kissed my cheeks and hugged me like her life depended on it as she left us at the bus that went back in the direction of the airport.

We promised to call.

She promised to visit as soon as the paperwork was ready.

And with that, we were on our way back home.

It was eight hours until we were back in Jersey, lucking out with a nonstop. Then from there, it was an hour and a half until we were back in Navesink Bank.

Most of this time, all there was was silence.

There were so many things for both of us to mull over.

Me, his past, the visit with my mother, the man who hurt me.

Him, exposing his vulnerabilities to me, the murder, the cleanup, my declaration.

There wasn't distance per se. In fact, as soon as we dropped into our plane seats, his hand went to my thigh and stayed there the whole trip. While he watched a movie and I stared out the window, thinking.

It was nice, I felt, to be able to sit and think things through without having to worry that the other person was worrying about my silence.

It was just... easy.

"Alright," Luce said as we shuffled into my car that was still at the airport. "You want Diego, or do you want to head home?"

"Is it wrong that I would just like one more day? I know Barrett is doing well with Diego and..."

"Ev, you're going to have to share custody of that damn bird with him from now on. I'll text him and let him know we will be by tomorrow to pick him up."

I didn't miss that.

We. We will be by tomorrow to pick him up.

The way my heart squeezed let me know I hadn't just dipped my toe into love. Oh, no. I was swimming in it.

Maybe that was a little bit scary.

But I was okay with that.

"Evan," Luce said, the way he did so making me think he had maybe said it more than once.

"Yeah?"

"You dropping me, or am I coming with you?" When there was a split second silence, he rushed to add. "Just need to know if I should be mentally preparing myself for the climb."

"You've barely slept in days, Luce. Come home with me and sleep."

He turned away, but even with my eyes on the road, I could see the smile he tried to hide. "If I get you anywhere near a bed, Ev, the last thing I'd be doing is sleeping."

"Well, how about some *not* sleeping followed by some sleeping?" I offered as I turned into my driveway, my house almost seeming foreign even though it had only been a few days.

"I think I can make that work," he agreed as we climbed out of the car. "Any chance you can throw together some of those badass burritos at some point too?" he asked, grabbing our bags, and heading toward the door.

"I think I can manage that."

We walked in, me moving through the house to drop my mail on the dining table, turning back when I didn't hear his footsteps following.

"Trinkets," I supplied, shrugging when his eyes fell on me.

"Do you have any more trinkets?"

"Ah... yeah. All over, I guess."

"Anything you drink out of?"

"I, ah, have a coffee mug set, yeah."

Luce moved past me, going into my cabinets, one after another, until he found the ones in question.

"Ev, doll," he said, turning with two of them. "These aren't sealed."

"I know. I don't put them in the dishwasher or anything."

"Yeah, but... who the fuck knows what kind of shit they used to paint these."

"That shit," I said, taking them from his hands, "was natural berries. I watched them make them for me. They are sun dried. Why are you so obsessed with them?"

"It was an interesting vacation, Evan, but we're back to reality now. And in reality, you were being poisoned. No new lines meant that when you were away from it long enough, you were free of the shit. So it has to be something here. Did you have your water tested when you moved in?"

"No, I'm an idiot who doesn't get a proper inspection," I said, rolling my eyes. "Of course the water was tested."

"Alright, what else do you have around here that was not bought at a store somewhere? And I mean an actual store, doll," he said with a smile, "not some market in a third world country."

I snorted at that, figuring most of the stuff made in villages was a lot safer than the stuff made in major factories full of who-knew-what contaminates.

"Um... I have some jewelry in my room. There are some combs in the bathroom."

"What about this?" he asked, touching the huge, intricate, beautifully crafted cutting board that took up the majority of my counter space.

"That's from the US," I said, shrugging.

"From a store?"

"A gift from a friend of my fath... Alejandro's."

God, when would I stop almost calling him my father? Days? Weeks? Years?

Would I ever get there?

"He made it?"

"Yeah, he does really cool things with wood. He cuts down the trees on the farm himself."

"What's Alejandro's friend's name, doll?"

"Larry," I said with a shrug. "He's a farmer in the south. Has a huge garden and acres of animals. He doesn't trust the government to feed him or something. He was a bit of a loon. But nice. He kept all my trinkets in his barn for like twenty years."

"Larry, huh? What state?"

I felt my brows draw together.

"Mississippi. Why?"

"Do me a favor," he said oddly. "Don't use this anymore, okay?"

"You think this is the source?"

"Do you want to take that chance? You more than anyone knows the long-term effects of arsenic exposure."

I did.

Abdominal issues. Tachycardia. Pulmonary edema. Kidney issues. Pancreatitis. Seizures. Coma. Lesions. Aplastic anemia. Peripheral neuropathy. Hypertension. Diabetes. Lung, bladder, kidney, lymphoid, liver, or skin cancer.

Yeah.

Okay.

I wasn't going to use the cutting board again.

Or the cups, even though I knew they were safe.

"Okay. No more using things I didn't buy in stores."

"Just until we have answers," he offered, walking closer, wrapping his arms around my hips. "Deal?"

"Deal," I agreed, leaning into him.

"So, I heard something about a bed..." he said, eyes going heated.

Then he saw something about a bed.

Then there were burritos.

And sleep.

But apparently not too much sleep.

I woke up the next morning, groggy, disoriented, lip stinging because I had been sleeping on my face for some reason. Reality came back slowly.

Coming home.

Luce's freakout about my trinkets.

Fast, hot, hard, sweaty, delicious sex.

Food.

Then sleep.

But Luce must have been up for a while, because his side of the bed was cold.

I stumbled up, going to brush my teeth and get my hair in some semblance of order before I faced him.

But I felt it as soon as I walked into the living space.

Something was off.

When I started to look for what gave me that unease, I found my laptop sitting open on the table. Beside it was a note. And a couple strips of paper with orange coloring on them.

Gone hunting.

- Luce

Curious, I sat down, blinking the sleep out of my eyes for a long minute so I could focus on the screen.

The browser was something I had never seen before and definitely did not install on my computer myself. But there it was anyway. And I had a feeling it was that 'dark web' thing I heard him mention before. Where he found out dirt on people. Where he found out about Alejandro.

And he had a page open dedicated to Larry Manson.

From Mississippi.

Of course.

Of *course* my father wasn't friends with some nobody loony farmer who didn't trust the government with his food supply.

No.

Because my father was a poisons expert.

And he was a rapist across many continents.

He didn't have normal friends.

He had criminal friends.

He had *rapist* friends.

Larry Manson had been locked up for rape at the ripe old age of eighteen, having drugged and forced himself upon his next door neighbor's daughter, abusing her with foreign objects instead of his dick. He got ten years. He was let out when he was twenty-eight. He never went back in.

Not because he stopped raping, but because he stopped getting caught.

This was likely because of all the missing persons reports filed for eighteen-year-old women who all looked eerily like his first victim across the whole state of Mississippi.

A few bodies were eventually found, but too decomposed for anyone to ever know what happened to them.

The research went on from there, making me aware that Luce was either a freak who survived on next to no sleep, or was ridiculously good with his online investigative skills.

Maybe both.

But some things were clear.

He was on his way to Mississippi looking for Larry Manson.

He was going to kill again.

And while part of it was for the other female victims, I was sure a part of it was due to him wanting to hurt me as well.

I knew this because those slips of paper with orange coloring on the table by the laptop and note were *arsenic tests*.

Orange meant high level positive.

And my freaking cutting board was missing.

SIXTEEN

Luce

"What can I say, Larry?" I said, flipping the cutting board around in my hands. The thing truly was a work of art, a mix of different grains all expertly put together into a lovely pattern.

See, the only problem with it was it was so full of arsenic that the tests turned a brighter shade of orange than the chart of levels even showed.

"I don't like men who try to poison women." He was tied up in his barn. Normally, I didn't like to do off-site work. It was messy. It was harder to clean up evidence. But I wasn't too fond of carting people across state lines and breaking federal laws either. "I mean, I think that is just a general rule. No one likes men who hurt women. It's cheap. It's cowardly. It suggests your cock is about as impressive as a pencil. But anyway, I digress. I really, really don't fucking like men who try to poison *my* woman," I said, spinning around, swinging the giant piece of cutting board, slamming it into the side of the man's head.

I wasn't one for torture.

But what could I say?

The man wouldn't fess up.

I needed him to tell me he did it.

And I needed to know why.

Because no matter how much research I did the night before after Evan passed out and I got an hour or two, I could not figure out why. So he was friends with Alejandro. So she was his adoptive daughter. So... what?

Evan wasn't Larry's type.

He only liked short, plump, blonde-haired women.

He never deviated.

So he couldn't have been pissed that Alejandro never let him get on his daughter.

What the hell was the motive then?

"Men turning on other men because of some fucking split-tail," he cursed, spitting blood onto the hay on the ground.

Split-tail.

What the fuck?

Who still used phrases like that?

What a backward fuck.

"Christ," I growled, shaking my head. "Why poison the fucking cutting board? What did Evan ever do to you?"

"Made a bitch out of that man," he said, shaking his head.

"Out of Alejandro?" I asked, squinting at him. "He raped women in every country he visited even after raping Evan's mother and kidnapping her daughter."

"The things that man did before her..."

Ugh.

Shit.

I wanted to rip his heart out of his chest and squeeze the life out of it.

He wasn't exactly wrong.

While I couldn't find any actual evidence online, as it predated most of the dark web, there were stories attributed to a man who fit Alejandro's descriptions. Ritualistic, sadistic rapes. Long, drawn-out torture that left women half-dead and usually fully signed-out mentally.

"You know, he forced me to agree to take care of her if anything happened to him."

"Take care of her didn't mean fucking kill her, dipshit."

"Lots of interpretations of that phrase, asshole."

"Why arsenic? Why not just kill her when she came to pick up her shit? Oh," I said, curling my lip.

Yeah.

For most shitheads like Larry, the act of murder was sexual. The rape itself was power. The kill was what got their cocks hard. The one woman he was sent away for, he apparently sodomized with an unknown object. I bet my life on him jerking off on the corpses before he buried them. He didn't want to kill Evan with his hands because she wasn't his type.

Fucking blessing, I guess.

"The fuck could it matter? He's dead. She's moved on. Why kill her now? Why not ten years ago?" He looked away, refusing to answer.

I hated the fucks like him, the ones that made me play guessing games, read their body language, figure it all out myself.

"What? Because Alejandro would see the signs in her? Eventually trace it back to you?" I sighed out a breath. "Kinda a shame that he didn't get to do the honors. I hated that twisted fuck, but he would have made this truly excruciating for you."

"What? And you're not?"

"Normally, I am pretty cut and dry with the killing. A bag over the head. A knife across the throat. Simple, really. See, I'm not a sick fuck who gets off on hurting someone like *some people*. I just want to rid the world of sick fucks such as yourself. Usually, I even give you a choice. You can go to the cops or die."

"But I'm not getting that choice."

"Nah. I mean, what, so you can sit in protective custody until you die? Can't be that far off. You're what? A good one-fifty overweight. You gotta have high blood pressure, cholesterol, and I hate to think what your arteries look like. Your ankles and calves are the size of fucking watermelons with water retention. Renal failure. You don't have that long left anyway. And while it might be kinda poetic for you to be stuck in a cell breathing in air that smells like shit all the time and eating the government food you hate so much, I'm afraid you aren't going to get to choose that."

"Because that bitch belongs to you."

I sighed out a breath. "Hate to break it to you, but this is America. In the twenty-first century. No one *belongs* to anyone anymore. But as long as she doesn't get sick of me, yeah, I'm with her. And even if she does get sick of me, I still give a shit about her. See, that's how normal, healthy relationships work. I know the concept is foreign to you."

"Right, I'm supposed to take advice from some skinny little computer hacker."

Christ.

He was a dick.

His past of abuse, and wanting to kill Evan aside, I wanted to take him out. Just for being a miserable human being. Thank God he lived on his giant farm and didn't often bother people with his terrible personality.

"So now what, little shit?" he asked, completely unperturbed by the fact that he was tied up and I obviously had all the power.

I had a feeling it was a front, though.

He was a man used to having the power.

Having it taken away must have been eating him up inside.

"I should take this shit," I said, reaching for the bottle of herbicide so rank with arsenic that I was worried about even touching the container. He used that along with a discontinued (because of the arsenic level) wood preservative on Evan's cutting board. "And force it down your throat. Every last drop. Then you could slowly, and painfully, see what you would have eventually done to Evan. But, I don't want your ass taking up any more of this air. So... we'll do this the quick way."

Well, not totally quick.

Slitting his throat would have been the fastest route.

But it was also the messiest.

I was fully aware we were in a barn full of hay and equipment. The clean up would be labor intensive and frustrating, to say the least, if I got blood everywhere.

So the bag it was.

And it wasn't quick.

And it was pretty terrifying not to be able to breathe.

But I had a feeling this fuck suffocated the women he victimized, so hey, it was a fitting end. It was good for him to see the torment of not being able to breathe that they went through in their final moments before death.

Three of them.

That was how long it took someone to die.

Granted, they would pass out within twenty seconds. But twenty seconds of not being able to catch your breath was pretty fucking terrifying.

A fitting end, I felt.

I didn't like burying bodies.

I did it out of necessity back in Brazil, but it created a much higher likelihood of getting caught than, say, melting the body completely and leaving no trace it ever existed behind.

That being said, the man owned like thirty acres.

Ten of them were plots for gardening.

Mr. Manson would become, in the truest form of the word, fertilizer.

Several hours later, after washing the body thoroughly, I dragged him out to his garden bed, digging a hole deep enough to bury three bodies, dropping him in, covering him back up, then fucking planting some green beans on top of him. They would be flourishing in a few weeks. The ground wouldn't look overturned.

I took myself back to the barn, scooping up all the hay in the general area where I had been with Larry, and bringing it back into his house with me, washing both our sets of clothes with bleach, drying them, then burning them slowly, along with the hay, in his fireplace until there was nothing but ash left.

I redressed.

I made my way back to the old dirt road on the side of his property where I had some clunker of a car I bought on a song back in Jersey. I traded the real ones with fake plates to keep it from tracing back to me in any way shape or form.

I climbed in, and drove that fucker all the way back to Navesink Bank, stopping only twice for gas, one of those times calling Larry's local police department to anonymously say I was worried because I hadn't seen him in a while. Normally, I'd keep the cops as far away from a crime scene as possible, but he had animals. The ones grazing in the field with their own stream would be fine. The chickens and horses... not so much.

I might have done a lot of dark things in my life, but it took a real monster to kill animals for reasons other than food or mercy.

I stopped at a wash-your-own car place, spending over an hour making sure I got every speck of Mississippi off of it, then returned it to its hiding spot, and made my way back to Evan's on foot.

It was only four days.

But it felt like a lifetime.

And every single time I thought of her in the interim, there it was again - that warm, swelling sensation in the chest.

It only seemed to intensify as I walked up the path to her front door, raising my hand to knock, wondering if she would be pissed, or would understand.

What the hell was I even supposed to say when she...

"Barrett?" I asked, jolting straighter at seeing him inside her house. "The fuck are you doing here?"

"Diego," he said in a very 'duh, you idiot' kind of way as he moved to the side to let me pass.

"You don't call, you don't write, you could have been dead in a ditch somewhere..." Evan said casually as she noticed me step in, giving me a smile as she walked plates toward the dining table. "Did I miss any?"

"Maybe something about candy from strangers, kidnapping, and, oh, the state of my underwear."

"The... what?" she choked out on a laugh.

"Guess that's an American thing, huh?" I asked, looking over at Barrett.

When Evan's gaze went there, Barrett shrugged. "We were all raised to make sure we had on clean underwear in case we got into a car accident."

"Ah... why would that matter?" she asked, squinting.

"Because the doctor and nurses might see it," Barrett supplied as Diego let out an epic squawk that made me and even Evan wince, but Barrett was unmoved as he raised a hand for the bird to fly onto.

"That's idiotic," Ev concluded, shaking her head. "Alright, well, are you going to say hi or what?"

A smile tugged at my lips as I crossed the room to her, the warm and swelling thing so intense that it almost made it hard to breathe.

Her face looked better. The cut on the side of her head was mostly sealed, red and angry, surrounded by a smattering of blue and purple bruises still, but healing. The split on her lip was gone, probably already scabbed and impatiently pulled off by a self-conscious Evan. She didn't look quite so broken anymore.

"Hi," I said, hands sliding around her lower back, pulling her hips flush with mine, even with an audience, feeling my own desire start to course through me. "How was your hunting trip?"

"Successful."

"You don't have to talk in code," Barrett told us casually, walking Diego over to a tree stand and putting him down. "I swept the place."

"Ah, you did what now?" Ev asked, pulling back so she could look around me.

"I swept the place."

"For what?" Ev asked, clearly out of the loop.

"Bugs. What else?"

"Like termites or... oh," she mumbled a little self-consciously as I chuckled, pulling her in, and kissing her temple. "Like recording devices. Why would you sweep my house?"

"Because he's here," I supplied with a shrug. "Barrett likes to make sure nothing gets overheard."

It's one of the most appealing traits of his, his carefulness. Because, let's face it, private investigators didn't always work perfectly inside the law. Barrett especially, thanks to some pretty impressive hacking skills that aired on the side of *very illegal*, and setting up his operation literally across the street from the Navesink Bank Police Department, wanted to make sure none of his skills ever came back to bite him in the ass.

"Just make yourself at home, man," I said, lips tipped up, but brows furrowed as Barrett moved around the kitchen getting utensils and napkins and then going into the fridge for drinks.

Evan was trying to keep her lips from smiling, but losing the battle. "Excuse us for a minute, Barrett," she said, reaching down to grab my hand, and pull me down the hall into the bedroom.

"One hacker slides out, another slides right in," I teased, watching as she ran her hand through her hair, making the strands settle in a new configuration. It was a weird, small thing, but I had somehow missed it while I was gone.

"You were right," she declared, looking a mix of amused and dumbfounded.

"Well, I always like hearing that," I said with a chuckle as I reached down to pull off my hoodie. "But what was I right about this time?"

"He and Diego have like... bonded. And he drops by twice a day to see him."

I laughed at that, remembering saying they would likely have to share custody. Barrett never struck me as much of an animal person, but exceptions could apparently be made for one as smart as a parrot.

"Diego calls me właściciel now."

Polish.

I fucking knew it.

"The fuck does właściciel mean?"

"Owner," she supplied, shaking her head.

"What does he call Barrett then?" I asked, curious.

"Przyjaciel. Friend," she explained, still standing half a room away from me as I sat down on the edge of the bed.

"You mad at me?"

"What? No," she said, shaking her head. "I mean, a little heads-up would have been nice, but no."

"Then I can't figure out why you're still half a room away from me," I said carefully, not wanting to sound like I was demanding her to come over, wanting to know her genuine reaction.

"I just... I didn't know if maybe you needed a little... space. You know, like, after..."

"Doll, do *you* need space, you know, like, after?" I asked, trying to keep the mood light even though it was a somewhat heavy topic.

Because, while we hadn't done a whole helluva lot of talking about it, my so-called career was absolutely a factor. Her *reaction* to what I did was the biggest factor.

"Um... no. I don't think so."

"Alright. Well, I sure as fuck don't need space. In fact, I need as little space between us as is possible."

She ducked her head to the side, smiling coyly. "And by that you mean..."

"Take them off, or I rip them off," I agreed, already yanking my tee off my body.

She smiled then, seeming relieved, like she had maybe been as stressed as I was about how we would handle me coming in from a job, both of us knowing the shit I had just done.

But the fact of the matter was, Evan wasn't your typical woman. While she didn't know about the nasty shit Alejandro did to women, she was fully aware that he used his knowledge of poisons to main, torture, and kill men. She had always known that about him. But she had been able to compartmentalize that.

So maybe I had that sick fuck to thank for the fact that she could do the same with my work.

She reached for her shirt, dragging it up her body.

My cock was already hard and throbbing in my pants as I moved to stand and remove them, watching as her hands slid down to remove hers as well, leaving her in a simple black bra and pantie set, nothing overly sexy about it, but it was the hottest fucking thing I think I had ever seen.

"All of 'em, Ev," I demanded, reaching to drag my boxer briefs down, grabbing a condom out of my wallet in the process, then standing to watch as her hands slid behind her back to unclasp her bra, as the material loosened, then fell from her body, exposing the perfect swells of her breasts, her nipples already hardened points.

My hand moved down to close around my cock, stroking it a bit absentmindedly as she discarded the bra and moved her hands down her belly in a path to the waistband of her panties.

"Fucking killing me here," I growled as she teasingly ran her fingertips across the soft fabric, letting a finger peek inside, then back out. "Oh fuck it," I said, charging away from the bed, pressing her back against the wall, reaching between us to snag the material, then yanking hard.

Her eyes went wide, and her lips parted on a hiss as the tearing noise let her know I was making good on my promise.

I was too far gone too fast. My balls felt tight, and my cock was almost painful I was so turned on.

I didn't have time to waste.

My hand slid between her thighs, stroking up her slick pussy, and locating her clit, finding it swollen. "Fucking soaked."

She let out a shuddering breath, leaning forward into me, resting her forehead into my shoulder. "I missed you," she admitted, making more pre-cum bead on my cock.

I moved my hand, shifted my hips, and let my cock slide against her wet lips, feeling the tremble course through her, feeling a similar one seem to move through my insides. "Fucking missed you too, Ev."

I meant it in more ways than one.

I missed fucking her, being inside her, hearing her moans and whimpers, feeling her nails in my back, her breath on my skin. I fucking missed that, sure.

But I just plain missed her too.

It had almost felt wrong to be away after spending so much time with her.

Maybe that was irrational. I mean, I had only known her a couple of weeks. But that being said, we had spent days and nights together. We had stood in long lines at airports, watched movies on planes, rode in rickety buses, sweated like fucking animals on hikes, had meals, slept near each other, slept *with* each other. We shared every small detail about our lives with each other.

I had never been anywhere near as close to another person as I was to her.

So I missed that.

And I missed the way she slept like the dead, the way she smelled, the teasing or the genuine smiles, the sound of her laugh, the way she clung to me before sleep. I missed the stories she would tell about the places she had seen, so rich with intricate detail even after time would normally wash that away. I swear you could see the reds and purples and golds of the saris in India, smell the henna as they intricately temporarily tattooed her hands and feet. You could feel the unyielding sun on your back in the deserts of Africa. You could taste the ultra spicy foods she sampled in Mexico. You could hear the calls of the wild macaws in South America.

I fucking *missed her*.

And while I had no fucking idea how to feel about that fact, there was no changing it. It was just something to factor into daily life.

I wondered absently if maybe it would change my life, if maybe I wouldn't want to be away from her on the long stretches I sometimes needed for jobs.

But then she whimpered into my neck, and I snapped back to the present, feeling another rush of her wetness coating my cock.

I couldn't take anymore.

I needed to be inside her like I needed my next breath.

"Wait..." she said as I walked backward, pulling her with me toward the bed.

"What?" I asked, turning so she was the one with her back to the bed.

"Barrett is..."

"A grown ass man who knows that after I'm away for half a week, I am going to be fucking my woman as soon as I get back. But if you're worried, I guess you're gonna have to try to be quiet," I said with a wicked grin. "Key word there being *try*," I added as I grabbed her, turned her, and pushed her forward toward the bed, pressing her legs wide so I could move behind her, grabbing one side of her ass with my hand, and slapping the other hard. She let out a loud, throaty moan. "Yeah, guess that's gonna be a challenge for you, huh?" I asked as I slipped the condom on.

Before she could say anything else, I slammed my cock deep inside her, fighting the urge to come as she cried out loudly, trying to muffle the sound with her face in the sheets, but mostly failing.

There was no taking it slow, no making it last, no soft and sweet.

It had been too long for both of us.

We both needed release like we needed our next breath.

So we fucked.

Hard.

Fast.

Loud.

I think she completely forgot the existence of a man named Barrett Anderson, let alone that he was in the house.

Because by the time her pussy became a vice grip on my cock, telling me one more thrust would send her quivering around me, she was borderline screaming.

I reached between her thighs, pressing into her clit as I slammed home, knowing it was the thrust that would send us both spiraling into oblivion.

Even as I thought it, her voice caught, and her pussy started pulsating hard.

I pressed deeper still, coming with her name on my lips.

And as soon as she got her voice back, she called out mine too.

We both collapsed back onto the bed, struggling for breath. My arm reached out to drag her to me as her body shook gently with aftershocks.

"Yeah, definitely don't need any space," she said, snuggling in closer, sounding somehow both giddy and dreamy at the same time.

Thank fuck for that.

I didn't realize how much I needed to hear that until she said it. With certainty. And maybe with a little sex still in her voice.

"Glad to hear it," I said, giving her a squeeze, then rolling her off me, so I could stand.

"How are you walking right now?" she asked, making me turn back with a huge grin, my pride enjoying that little ego boost.

"Doll, I've been on the road all fucking day. I think you were putting food out when I got here."

"I see," she said, folding upward, and reaching for her clothes, smile wicked. "Fuck you and feed you. That's all you want from me, huh?"

"Not even fucking close," I said, giving her a hard look that made her eyes go a little dreamy before I grabbed my clothes and headed out to the bathroom.

"Where's Barrett?" Ev asked a minute later, meeting me in the hall, fully dressed except I could tell she forewent the bra. And, hey, anything that gave me easier access to her body was something I was all for. "And Diego?"

We moved out toward the dining room, finding Barrett's plate empty, but with a note sitting beside it.

For once, it was neither in Polish *nor* code.

Diego is positively traumatized by your 'reunion.'
We're at the office.

- B & D

"He keeps kidnapping my bird," she said, shaking her head as she went about loading up plates for the both of us.

"I think it's time to accept that Diego isn't yours anymore. You now share custody with Barrett."

"I would be annoyed, but he somehow taught him to only do his business on the tree stand. And that is a damn miracle. So he can steal him all he wants."

She moved to sit down next to me, reaching for her fork.

My hand caught hers, noticing she had finally taken off the chipped polish. My thumb ran over the bed of her nail, the lines still there from the mid-point and down, but the fresh growth was clear. "The rash was gone too," I added, meaning on her chest.

"I feel better too," she admitted, giving my hand a squeeze. "I don't think I even realized how poorly I was feeling until it stopped. I have you to thank for that," she said, eyes going soft. Then she did the damnedest fucking thing. She leaned over and rested against my arm, her head on my shoulder. "I have you to thank for a lot of things," she added.

"Ev..." I said, trying to shrug it off, trying to shake the weird discomfort I felt inside at receiving her gratitude.

"If it weren't for you, I'd still be following a serial rapist across the world. I wouldn't know he wasn't my father. I wouldn't have found my mother. I wouldn't know I was being poisoned."

"You would have figured that out eventually, Evan."

"What? When I had kidney failure or cancer? Geez, take a compliment."

I smiled at that, leaning the side of my head down on the top of hers.

"Alright, I'll take it," I agreed, feeling awkward.

"You know what?" she asked after a long silence.

"No, what?"

"I think I'll take *you*."

EPILOGUE

Evan - 10 days

Oh, good lord, the movies.

Okay. I mean, alright, movies were great and all.

But Luce was extremely adamant about fixing my deplorable 'cinematic education.'

Every conversation seemed to lead to another movie that I would simply *have* to see.

I had a feeling, and I felt it with a sinking sensation in my stomach, that maybe Luce liked movies so much because he could live through them in a way his real life wouldn't allow him to.

He lived his life in cages. At his father's beck and call, in the woods watching pot grow, locked up in some dealer compound in the city. Then, as he grew and moved on with his life, mostly in a house on a hill all by himself. He barely maintained acquaintances, let alone friends. He didn't have romances. He didn't explore. He didn't have adventures.

So he watched all of that in film.

He could see the world, fight wars, fall in love, have road trips with buddies, go to outer space.

It wasn't that I didn't *get* it; I did.

It was somewhat how I felt about a good book, how I liked getting lost in the worlds. Though, I admit, I was nowhere near as devoted to novels as he was to movies.

And I had to say, when he lit up talking about some amazing action scene or unexpected plot point and how I *had* to see it, I was charmed. I also felt like, in seeing the movies he was so passionate about, I got to see different parts of him as well.

That being said, I was not used to spending every night of my life curled up on a couch. Granted, being curled up there *with* Luce was maybe one of the best feelings in the world. Because we never just watched movies. His arm was always around my shoulders, and sometime in the middle of a movie, his fingers often found their way into my hair, sifting through the strands gently. Many times, my legs would wind up over his lap, and his free hand would stroke up and down them, driving me to distraction until the credits rolled, and I could straddle him and get relief from the need coursing through me.

So, after ten straight nights on my couch or in my bed with some gem of a movie - and a couple ones that had me raising a brow at him - I decided I had had enough.

I was fine with following his preferred interests, knowing that my own interests were, well, making poisons and traveling, neither of which I could do in Navesink Bank, but he was going to have to give in a little too.

"Fuck, doll," he hissed when I walked out of the bedroom. Since we had been hanging out in the house for over a week, I had maybe gotten a bit lazy with the dressing thing. In fact, if I managed to slip into panties and one of his tees, that was a lot. We ended up naked most of the time anyway.

So his reaction to my tight black dress and heels wasn't overly surprising. I had put some time and care into my hair and makeup as well.

I figured getting him out of his comfort zone might take a little persuasion of the sexy nature. Which was something I was completely fine with.

"What's this?" he asked when I handed him an envelope.

"Open it," I demanded as I moved to stand in front of him.

He looked up, brows furrowed slightly. "Movie tickets?"

"I like sharing your movie interest with you, Luce, but I am about to go out of my mind being locked in this house. Normally, I would want to drag you to some salsa club or play or something. So let's call this a fair compromise, yeah?"

He watched me for a long minute, head ducked to the side. "Yeah," he agreed, giving me a nod.

It didn't seem like a big deal to most, but getting Luce out of the house to do anything other than hit the coffeeshop, Barrett's, or the grocery store was a real feat.

This was a small victory for us, and, I thought, a step in the right direction.

Luce - 5 weeks

I knew this day would come eventually.

We knew it would come eventually.

Because, no matter how strong my feelings were becoming for Evan, I was still me. I still needed to do the things I did. I still had a mission in life that didn't involve movie marathons, late night drives with meaningful conversations, and enough sex to make me actually need to remember to hydrate it was so intense.

All those things were fucking amazing.

They were way more than I deserved.

But they weren't, and couldn't, be everything.

For either of us.

This meant that Evan was doing some looking around in Navesink Bank for possible job opportunities, or even educational opportunities. She was keeping an open mind, and trying to find something to do with her life that gave it meaning, that made her happy.

I already had that.

And that was why this day had to happen sooner or later.

I had been ignoring my pager for weeks.

It was time for me to get back to work.

We both knew the day would come, that I wasn't somehow a 'reformed man,' that my missions had to go on.

Could I say that Evan was exactly thrilled about it? No. Of course not. Not because she would see me any differently, not because she had an issue with my killing scumbags. No.

When we talked about it, she told me her only worry was my getting caught.

And there it was again, that tight, swelling, warm feeling in my chest. It was getting stronger as the time went on, insistent and distinct enough for me to no longer be able to do anything but call it what it was.

Love.

I fucking loved her.

I loved her in a way I didn't know was possible, with a depth I didn't think I possessed, with a heart I was sure had shriveled and died in my chest when I had a face buried in a pillow at seven years old.

I was sure any goodness, anything even capable of feeling something as selfless as love was gone.

Apparently, I was wrong.

Evan brought that out of me.

I was pretty sure that nothing I could do, not if I tried for decades, could ever show her exactly how much that meant to me. It was humbling to realize how wrong you were about yourself, that someone else could see things in you that you didn't know existed.

And she loved me back.

Which was an even bigger miracle.

She loved me back, despite my past, despite my darkness, despite what I did for a living.

But this was the first time where I would have to, in essence, test that theory. We had been living in a comfortable little insulated bubble. Sure, she was certainly dragging me out with her more and more, taking me to see movies, music, going out to dinner.

I had been out on the town more in the past five weeks than I had in the past fucking five years.

And I liked it.

But we couldn't live forever in her house.

I had to go back to work.

I ignored a bunch of lesser offenders that had been sent my way over the past month, no one being a big enough scumbag to drag me away from what I had only just found with Evan.

But then I got a page with a 111.

And a 111 was shit that needed to be looked into.

A 111 was a human trafficker. Of children. Into the sex trade.

It didn't matter how much I loved spending time watching movies and bullshitting with Evan about her travels and plans for the future. I couldn't just sit there and pretend I didn't know that information, that I wasn't the only one who could take care of it.

"Three days," I told her as she came out of the bedroom.

Three days was too fucking long, but it was what I needed. I would only be a few minutes away from her technically, but I might as well have been a world away.

"Okay," she said, nodding, sounding completely unaffected. Then she held up something in her hands, some leather satchel with a belt to wear it around the waist.

There was a strange tightening in my gut that I couldn't place. "Doll, what's that?" I asked, hearing the uncertainty in my own voice.

Then she flipped the flap open, and produced a small piece of what seemed like pointed wood, stuck inside some protective plastic cover.

"You said a child sex trafficker, right?" she asked, holding the little arrow thing up to the light, and squinting at it, then replacing it, picking up another.

"Yes," I agreed, glad to be able to talk openly. This was thanks to Barrett dropping by every other or third day to pick up or drop off Diego, depending on his schedule, always doing a sweep when he did. The careful fuck.

"Okay, this one then," she said, holding out the second needle/arrow thing.

"Ev, what is this?" I asked, having a feeling, which was why my lips were tipped up, but wanting confirmation.

"Something that will kill him. Quickly," she added, shrugging. "But painfully."

Did I mention I fucking loved her?

Because *I fucking loved her.*

And as I tucked the item in my pocket, and pulled her in for a kiss, I knew it. I knew it down to my marrow.

We were going to be just fine.

Evan - 3 months

Three months.

That was how long it took Luce's buddy Barney to make the necessary documents for my mother. Barney was eighty-years-old if he was a day, living in a building that was practically falling down, but with an apartment that had freaking *gold* fixtures.

The best forger on the east coast, as the rumors went.

Which was why it took so long.

Not because he had too many clients, but because he was an absolute perfectionist. Which was good. When it came to forged government documents, you wanted them as close to the real thing as possible.

But the papers were shipped to my mother the week before.

And the plane had landed five minutes ago.

Me?

I was a nervous wreck.

Why?

I wasn't entirely sure.

This had always been the plan. I wanted her in the States where we could truly reconnect, where we could tell stories, build bonds.

Sure, there was a part of me that had my stomach in knots because, as I had told Luce in bed the night before, I was terrified to share my stories.

All of them involved Alejandro.

I finally stopped thinking of him in familial terms: father, dad, papi.

He was Alejandro.

He was the man who took me around the world, showed me things I would never have seen without him, sure, but he wasn't my father.

In fact, my actual father was some nobody farmer from Brazil who died in a freak bus accident just two months before I was due to arrive.

This was why Gabriela had made the decision to come try to move to the States- for me, for our future. She knew that if she stayed there with me, I would likely end up married young, working as a cleaning lady or on a farm, have a bunch of kids, and continue a cycle of poverty that her own family had been in for generations.

It was enough to send her on a two-year-long mission across Brazil, Colombia, Panama, Costa Rica, Nicaragua, Honduras, Guatemala, and finally... Mexico.

All I could think as she told me this over the phone one night was, how cruel was it for her to travel safely with a baby through *eight* countries, getting nary a scratch, only to be brutalized as soon as she finally, *finally* reached her destination.

"She knows exactly who you traveled with, Ev," Luce had said, shrugging it off. "She has had months to wrap her head around the situation. She might hate him, she might never forgive him - and she fucking shouldn't - but she isn't going to expect you to alter your stories to make them more palatable for her."

I was trying to put my faith to rest in that.

Time would tell.

"Stop wringing your hands," Luce said, grabbing one of them, curling his fingers in, and giving them a squeeze. "There's nothing to be nervous about. She loves you. You love her. When that happens, everything shakes out how it is supposed to."

I knew he was right.

But my stomach didn't unknot until she walked up, got into the back of the car, and hugged me from behind, letting off a string of Portuguese so fast that none of it made sense.

"That's all you brought?" Luce asked as he pulled away from the curb, and pointed us in the direction of Navesink Bank.

My mother's luggage was all of one large rolling suitcase. Aside from her purse, that was it. Granted, she lived in a small home, and couldn't have had many possessions to begin with, but still.

"I want a fresh start," she said, shrugging it off. "I have one box shipping in with house wears. That's all I need. I will buy new once I start work."

She allowed Luce and me to get her an apartment, only conceding when we informed her that the money wasn't from our pockets (or Alejandro's stash), but from the dickhead child sex trafficker who had almost thirty-thousand in his Bitcoin wallet. It was more than enough to pay for her apartment for a whole year, as well as do a few alterations like painting the walls, updating the appliances, and getting her a bedroom and living room set.

It was humbling to me to be able to give my mother the head start in America that she had wanted for me as well as herself. Twenty-four years late, sure, and after much heartbreak as well, but it happened.

We were together.

We were building our lives.

And all of that, literally every last bit of that, was thanks entirely to Luce.

If he hadn't been looking for - and found - Alejandro, if he hadn't made him disappear, if he didn't make it clear online that he had, I never would have sought him out. Had that not happened, I wouldn't have learned the truth of who Alejandro truly was; I wouldn't have known about (or found) my mother. And, you know, I likely would have been really sick from arsenic poisoning.

The crazy thing to me was that Luce never seemed to grasp the enormity of his presence on the earth. He had spent so much time angry, shameful, vengeful, that he wasn't able to see that through his actions, he changed countless lives. Maybe the men he had killed had hurt their wives or children who would then be free of his torture. All the children who might have been molestation victims never had to have their childhoods taken away from them. Women who had been stalked, raped, beaten, could sleep easier knowing their abusers were long dead.

Sure, he was a vigilante.

He killed people.

But that wasn't all he was or all he did.

It was my mission in life to get him to see the length of his reach, the depth of meaning in his actions.

Maybe I shouldn't have been okay with having a killer for a boyfriend. Maybe that wasn't normal. Maybe it wasn't even sane.

But that being said, I had grown up with someone who took lives for a living; I had seen the aftermath of actions men like the ones Luce killed left in the world. I understood the need for lives to be cut short.

I didn't mind his job.

In fact, some nights while he researched, I was right beside him, reading over his shoulder all the horrible things people have done, and suggesting which poisons might be the best bet for taking them out.

Which, in a way, made me an accomplice to at least three murders so far.

A child sex trafficker, a serial rapist, and a pimp who beat one of his prostitutes so badly that she had to have her jaw wired shut to heal.

I was okay with being a part of ending that.

I knew, though, that someday, it would be over. Someday, Luce was going to need to retire, hand over the reins, find a different way to spend his time.

And that was okay.

We would figure that out together when it came to be.

Luce - 3 years

There was a long pause, Evan watching me with a face I suddenly couldn't read.

"What do you think?" I asked, shifting feet, feeling uncomfortable.

"More importantly," she said, still not giving anything away, "what do *you* think?"

"These are the kinds of decisions that I believe we are supposed to make together," I tried. "You know, or that's what I've seen in movies anyway."

That softened her face, making her lips tease up. "You know, I mean... it's not like you have to retire from your old job. This sounds more like a part-time gig."

This was true.

See, it started out innocently enough.

I had been at She's Bean Around, having coffee like I did all the time, teasing Jazzy when she was between customers. Then in walked her man- Detective Lloyd.

And Lloyd had been doing big things for himself over the past several years, making a name and reputation for himself.

There were rumors of captain being a title he might be sporting soon, being one of the few members on the force who wasn't in someone's pocket.

"Alright," he said, dropping down across from me at a table, holding a reusable cup between his hands because Jazzy refused to give him paper because 'he's got two hands, and can wash out a damn coffee cup' or something like that.

"Alright," I agreed, brows drawing together, my spine feeling a little stiffer.

"Let's not sit here and pretend we both don't know who you are, and what you do."

"Is this an official meeting, Detective? Shouldn't I have bracelets on?"

He exhaled a breath, leaning back in his chair for a second, looking over at Jazzy who sent him a saucy wink that managed to make his hard face seem just a sight softer. "About what you do, this is me *un*officially talking. About this next part, it is official."

"Alright," I said, even more confused. "What's up, Lloyd?"

"I work in a department full of fucking incompetents."

"Not one for mincing words, huh?" I asked with a chuckle, knowing just how right he was about the force.

"We've been known to hire consultants. Shrinks. Profilers. Artists. Fucking psychics..."

I knew where it was going.

And, oddly, my first reaction wasn't shock or fear.

No.

I felt... relief.

"And what would my actual title be there, Lloyd?" I asked with a smirk. "Resident Vigilante?"

He snorted at that, giving me the closest thing to a smile I had ever seen him give anyone other than Jazzy. "Cyber Crimes Expert Consultant should do." There was a short pause. "Consultants make fucking bank," he added, sweetening the pot.

So, that was what brought me to informing Evan of the possibility.

Sure, she was blissfully happy at the job she got at a local independent vitamin store, taking to supplements with the same enthusiasm she took to poisons. Except now, she had herself, her mother, Barrett, and me as her personal guinea pigs to try fixing whatever ailed us with her new vitamin regimens.

And, yes, I made money - sometimes very substantial amounts of money - out of the Bitcoin accounts of scumbags I took out.

It just wasn't steady enough.

I wanted to know there was always going to be something coming to me.

Even if it was on the other side of the law than I usually operated on.

"You think I should consider it," I guessed.

"I think that while it is nice that you came to me with this, that the decision is yours to make. It doesn't matter to me what you do for work. I just want you to be comfortable and happy with your choice."

So that was how I became a Cyber Crimes Expert Consultant.

Evan - 4 years

I turned off the timer on my phone, looking down at the stick in my hand with an odd, strobe-like feeling in my chest and belly. I wasn't sure if it was worry, anticipation, hope, unease, or a mix of all of them. All I knew was it was making me even more nauseated than I already was. Which was saying something.

I don't know what the hell happened.

I had been on the Pill since I was nineteen.

I never missed a day.

It was a freak thing.

But I was staring down at two pink lines.

Luce and I, well, we never really talked about kids. Not about having them anyway.

I was never one of those women with baby fever. I had never felt that "uterus crunch" I heard other women talk about when I saw a cute baby. That just wasn't how I was wired.

I liked babies. I had bathed, fed, rocked, and sang to countless babies all around the world. I had seen some take their first steps, say their first words.

I just never really thought about having one myself.

I guess this was nature's way of saying *ready or not, here it comes!*

There were three crisp knocks to the door, making me jump hard.

"So, what's it say?"

A snorting laugh escaped me as I looked up in the mirror to find myself smiling.

Because I hadn't told him.

I hadn't even whispered about thinking I might be pregnant.

He had no idea I bought a test.

I just... wanted to know before I got him worrying too.

But, I guess, this was Luce we were talking about.

He knew - and saw - all.

I reached for the door, unlocking it.

A second later, it pushed open, and in he walked.

Four years later, and he was still in a black hoodie with white hood pulls. True, he wasn't weird with me about his scars anymore, but I think it was just habit. In fact, for his last birthday, I had gotten him a gift certificate to a local tattoo parlor where some guy named Hunter, who specialized in covering scars with tattoos, drew me up this huge, intricate, black & gray biomechanical piece.

I wanted him to never see 'slave' when he looked at himself again.

I was nervous giving it to him, but he had actually freaking... lit up.

But he told me the piece needed an alteration.

He wouldn't tell me what it was.

Not until he came home with it on his skin.

He had Hunter add a bright, red, vivid anatomically correct heart in the center. And, if you looked closely enough, you could see "Ev" in one of the valves.

And me, well, I cried like a freaking baby.

But he still was a fan of his hoodies.

Quite frankly, so was I.

"Well?" he asked, looking a little smug, like he was proud of himself.

"How did you know?" I asked, turning the test away from his all-seeing eyes.

"You've been pushing around your food more than eating it. You're pale. Your tits are sore. And, you know, you missed your fucking period, Ev. Kinda hard to not put all that together."

"We never talked about kids," I said, tone careful.

"It was never a factor before," he said, shrugging, reaching for the stick, and turning it over.

"Luce..."

He didn't speak for a long moment.

Then his eyes raised, unreadable, as they often were.

"Maybe we should keep the cabin in the woods," he said, lips twitching slightly. "If this is a girl, and some shithead ever breaks her heart..."

"You can't *murder* and *melt* our daughter's boyfriends, Luce," I said with a genuine smile.

"Wanna bet?"

Luce - 22 years

"No."

"Dad..." Louana, who had been called Lou since pretty much day one said in that whining tone only teenaged daughters could truly pull off.

She was the spitting image of her mother and grandmother- long and lean with shiny dark brown hair, tan skin, and delicate bone structure. The only thing she got from me at all was her eyes which were a little darker, a little more deep-set than Ev's.

I can't read them, Evan had complained when Lou was seven and in a particularly bad phase of trying to pass off fibs as truths, *just like I can't read yours.*

"No," I repeated. "That is a word that works in all languages. Including Brazilian Portuguese. Which you do not need to know since you will not be going to Brazil."

"Everyone else is..."

"Don't. Don't make me do it, Lou," I implored. "I will fucking hate myself if I have to use that goddamn phrase." Her arms crossed over her chest; her eyes went challenging. I was always out of my depths with her, and she knew it. Fuck. "If all your friends jumped off... Jesus Christ. I can't do it. Ev, you're up," I said, raking a hand down my face.

"Lou, you know why we don't go to Brazil," Ev said, dropping down next to me, legs going up over mine.

"Alejandro has been dead for, what, over twenty years now. I don't think we have to worry about his enemies, Mom."

So, we had decided, when she was old enough, to be brutally honest with Lou. She had grown up to be mature, level-headed, rational, able to put things in boxes, and analyze them accordingly. She knew of Alejandro, what he had done to her grandmother, how he had taken Ev and raised her, what he had done to women all over the world, and what he did for work.

"No, neat," Gabriela said softly, but there was steel in her voice too. "Tell your friends that Turks and Caicos is lovely this time of year."

We didn't want to keep Lou locked up and away from the world. Evan wanted her to have the luxury of travel like she had growing up. As such, twice a year, every year since she was two, we had been choosing places to visit. This was done with extreme scrutiny of locations that might have any ties to the late Alejandro Cruz.

Lou had seen some of the most beautiful places of the world, had played with children of all different cultures, had - and this set my teeth on edge just thinking - as she was older, flirted with boys her age across several continents.

But Brazil, while Gabriela's and Evan's homeland, had always been strictly off-limits. Because of Alejandro, sure, but also what I had done while I was there.

Was that maybe fair to Lou?

No.

But it was just how it had to be.

Lou's brow rose, eyes - which I could read since they were just like mine - going curious. "You would pay for Turks and Caicos?" she asked in all her eighteen-year-old excitement.

Ev shot me a look, and I shrugged. "If it means you won't even *think* about visiting Brazil until you're, I don't know, thirty, then *yes*, we will happily pay for Turks and Caicos."

This declaration was followed by a squeal that made Diego squawk loudly. "Oh, hush," Lou said, shaking her head at him. "You're just jealous because you can't go. Okay. I'm going to call everyone."

She scrambled off, and Gabriela gave us a nod as she moved back into the kitchen where she was cooking a massive Sunday dinner.

"You know," Ev said, resting her head into my shoulder. "We did pretty well with her. You know, considering I was a poisons expert and you a vigilante killer."

"I'm almost offended she came out so normal," I agreed, making her laugh as my arms went around her.

"We're going to have to tell her about what we did in Brazil eventually," she said, being a voice of reason.

"Sure, but I just bought us another twelve years before we have to open up that can of worms."

"That's true," she agreed, kissing my neck. "You do know she is bringing her boyfriend on this trip, right?"

I didn't.

Because I generally chose not to think too hard about that guy, believing whole-heartedly that not a single guy on earth would ever be worthy of her.

Then again, lowly old me got Ev, so who was I to talk?

"Fuck... I do still have some lye laying around downstairs, right?"

XX

Keep turning for a sexy excerpt from Luce's Lovers fan fiction website.

BONUS MATERIAL

Luce'sLovers//writing//fanfic//erotica//pg.26

- Scene 18. @ Work -

He wasn't supposed to be here.

I told him the last time in the alley.

It was over.

We couldn't do this anymore.

It was wrong on every conceivable level.

But there he was regardless, in the doorway of the shop, the rain cascading down the back of his already drenched shirt, making it cling to the muscles beneath. My eye slipped down to his arm, seeing a bead of water sliding down the intricate red and black tattoo that covered almost every square inch of skin. I had to force my gaze back up, not let it wander downward toward the fly of his jeans, knowing I would find his cock straining against the thick material, begging me to go to him, drop to my knees, and suck him deep.

Yes.

Eyes up.

I needed safe places to look.

Like his jaw.

There was scruff there, a good three day's worth. It would scrape across my inner thighs, leaving beard burn on the silky skin for days after, as he moved inward to find my clit, sucking it hard like he knew I liked.

Crap.

Okay.

The jaw was most assuredly *not* a safe place.

Edge of the ear, then. Yeah, that was as tame as you could get.

Except I knew from experience that he hissed and sank his fingers into my ass when I traced that spot with my tongue, when I nipped it with my teeth.

Ear was out too then.

What was left?

His hair?

Yeah, no. I liked how that looked with his face buried between my thighs while he devoured me with his tongue, penetrated me with his fingers. And I liked how it felt between my fingers when he was buried deep inside me, riding me hard and fierce.

"Daya," he growled.

He always growled it.

He never said it in a normal tone; it was always in that deep, primal, sexy rumble that made my insides turn to mush, made all my defenses crumble.

"You shouldn't be here," I forced myself to say, knowing it was useless, but trying to put up some sort of defense.

I needed to stop being so weak.

I needed to stop giving into him.

There was nothing wrong with a nice fling with a man.

But Luce was not just any man.

Luce was a vigilante.

He was *the* vigilante.

He took out the scum of the earth.

And then he came to me, cock hard, body hungry, smelling of blood and death and primal need.

But I told him as I shimmied back into my panties in the alley beside my apartment building the last time that it was, in fact, the *last* time. I couldn't keep doing this. I couldn't keep coming (both literally and metaphorically) when he crooked his finger.

I needed to find some willpower.

I needed him to respect my - admittedly very wobbly, hardly standing - boundaries.

It was *wrong.*

Normal women weren't turned on by men who showed up with someone's blood still under their fingernails, smelling of the smoke from bonfires of charred bodies.

What was *wrong* with me?

But then he moved inward, reaching behind him to turn the lock on the door and flip the closed sign. There were three hours until closing. True, it was a Wednesday night in November, and that meant we would likely be dead until closing and that I was, essentially, just being paid to sit and write, but rules were rules.

The Creamery was supposed to be open until ten.

Though, if there was anything I had learned from my time with Luce, he always made me somehow think it was a good idea to throw the rules out the window.

Still, I moved behind the counter, wiping the surface with a rag I had dropped there, despite it being as clean as it had been when I wiped it five minutes before.

I had a feeling it wouldn't be quite so clean within another couple of minutes.

"Luce," I said, meaning for it to come out firm, but hearing only a breathless need in my own voice.

"Yeah, that's what you're going to be screaming in a minute. Bend over that counter," he demanded, stalking around the side where a small, hip-level 'employees only' door was situated, ignoring it, and coming in behind said counter with me.

All the air seemed to rush out of my lungs as he came up to me, making me angle my head up to keep eye-contact.

A drop of water slid down a strand of his dark hair and free fell until it found a home.

Under the collar of my shirt.

Down between my breasts.

A shiver coursed through my system, making his eyes heat all the more. I'd swear the ice cream in the freezers beside us started melting.

"I don't have patience for games, Daya," he ground out, hands going to my hips, sinking into the softness hard, turning me, then shoving me down over the counter, my ass up in the air.

I could feel his soaked body press in behind me, wetting the back of my thighs.

I shouldn't have liked it.

When he came in and demanded things, when he pushed me into the positions he wanted.

I barely knew him.

I didn't even know his full name.

I had never seen him in daylight.

He only ever spoke to me directly before and *while* fucking me.

Then he zipped and left.

I should have felt used, disgusted with myself, something.

But all I felt was turned on.

His hands left my hips, grabbing the waistband of my jeans and panties, and yanking down hard, the material scraping over my skin because, apparently, Luce didn't have time to mess with buttons or zippers.

Except his own.

As he freed his straining cock.

"Ass *up*!" he demanded when my hips dropped slightly. A slap landed hard on my right butt cheek, the sound bouncing off the walls in the small shop, the pain radiating through me, making another stab of desire pierce my core. I felt his cock swipe against the spot that was likely bright red from his hand, making a wet trail of pre-cum mark me. "You want my cock, Daya?" he asked as his fingers slid between my thighs to stroke up my wet pussy, to find my clit and pulse his fingers against it.

That was such a complicated, complicated question.

On a basic, animalistic, primal, womanly level did I want his cock? More than I wanted my next breath. My pussy was so tight it was painful, so wet that I felt it sliding down my thighs as his finger started to work me. Every inch of my skin felt poised for his touch. Every thought in my head was focused on all the previous times he had taken my wanton desire and given me world-shattering orgasms.

But on a rational, logical, smart level did I want his cock?

Christ.

Yes.

Yes, I did.

What was the point in fighting?

There was none.

I knew this as two of his fingers plundered me- fast, unrelenting. Strokes, circles, taps against the top wall to press into my G-spot. He knew exactly what I wanted, what I *needed.*

One of his fingers left my pussy, sliding into my ass as the strokes became harder, faster.

He knew exactly what he had to do to make me forget that I was at work, that there were cameras, that the windows to the street were glass and anyone could look in and see me naked from the waist down having my pussy and ass finger-fucked by a man wet with not only rain, but blood.

"Fucking say it, Daya," he demanded, his cock stabbing against my inner thigh, so so close to where I really needed him.

There was no way I wasn't going to say it.

"I want your cock, Luce," I whimpered.

That was what he needed.

He had to hear it.

His finger slid out of my pussy to join his other finger.

His cock shifted.

And he slammed inside me in one hard, deep, thick thrust, stretching my walls around him, making me almost painfully aware that no one else would ever fill me quite so fully.

His free hand trailed up my back, sifting into the hair at the base of my skull, sinking in, but trailing down the strands, knowing it hurt more further away from the root, knowing I got off on that pain. Then he curled. And yanked. Hard. Viciously. Making my upper body lift off the counter as he started fucking me.

There wasn't a delicate bone in his body.

He fucked like he lived.

Rough. Brutal. Dirty. Without any boundaries.

His cock slammed into my pussy as his fingers stilled in my ass, pressing downward against the wall of my pussy, making an almost intolerable pressure build, promising another orgasm that would, as he said, make me scream his name.

I always did.

"You can pretend you don't want this all you want," he growled, pace getting somehow even faster, though how it was even possible was beyond me. "But my cock is fucking swimming in your tight pussy right now, Daya. You always want my cock."

He was right; I did.

Why did I fight it?

"That's it," he growled as my walls tightened around him. His fingers started pulsing downward as his cock became even more ruthless, not giving the orgasm even a second to ebb, driving me upward harder, faster, until there was no stopping it.

It slammed through my system violently, making his name scream from between my lips as my pussy spasmed hard around him over and over.

"Fucking squeeze my cock," he growled, thrusting through it until the waves finally stopped, making my entire body seem to go fluid.

Then he buried deep and came with my name on his lips.

It didn't last.

There was no snuggling, no love words, no sweet nothings.

No *nothing.*

I came.

He came.

He pulled out, zipped, gave my ass a squeeze, and left out the back.

It took me an almost embarrassingly long time to remember where I was, that my ass was out, that the windows existed. I reached for my panties, dragging them up, struggling with my button and zip to my jeans before pulling them up, and securing them back into place.

As I leaned back against the wall, taking deep breaths, I remembered why I always tried to fight it.

Because this was always how it ended, leaving me feeling satisfied, but empty, swearing off my vigilante.

You know... until the next time.

DON'T FORGET

If you enjoyed this book, go ahead and hop onto Goodreads or Amazon and tell me your favorite parts. You can also spread the word by recommending the book to friends or sending digital copies that can be received via kindle or kindle app on any device.

ALSO BY JESSICA GADZIALA

The Henchmen MC

Reign

Cash

Wolf

Repo

Duke

Renny

Lazarus

Pagan

The Savages

Monster

Killer

Savior

Stars Landing

What The Heart Needs

What The Heart Wants

What The Heart Finds

What The Heart Knows

The Stars Landing Deviant

--

DEBT

For A Good Time, Call...

Shane

Ryan

Mark

The Sex Surrogate

Dr. Chase Hudson

Dissent

Into The Green

Dark Mysteries

367 Days

14 Weeks

Stuffed: A Thanksgiving Romance

Dark Secrets

Unwrapped

Peace, Love, & Macarons

ABOUT THE AUTHOR

Jessica Gadziala is a full-time writer, parrot enthusiast, and coffee drinker from New Jersey. She enjoys short rides to the book store, sad songs, and cold weather.

She is very active on Goodreads, Facebook, as well as her personal groups on those sites. Join in. She's friendly.

STALK HER!

Connect with Jessica:

Facebook: https://www.facebook.com/JessicaGadziala/
Facebook Group:
https://www.facebook.com/groups/314540025563403/

Goodreads:
https://www.goodreads.com/author/show/13800950.Jessica_Gadziala
Goodreads Group:
https://www.goodreads.com/group/show/177944-jessica-gadziala-books-and-bullsh

Twitter: @JessicaGadziala

JessicaGadziala.com

<3/ Jessica

<<<<>>>>

Made in the USA
Columbia, SC
15 February 2022

56250743R00143